OLLIE OLLIE OUTS IN FREE

A Novel

Albert O. Martin

Library of Congress Control Number 2008908959

ISBN: 978-0-615-21113-8

First Edition printed by Albert O. Martin.
Printed in the United States of America.

For Kathie

AUTHOR'S NOTE

Ollie Ollie Outs in Free was chosen for my book's title because as children, almost everyone has played some version of **Hide and Go Seek**. Sometime before and during, World War II, this activity was being carried on between the Nazis and Jews, but with considerably higher stakes.

If a "seeker" (Nazi) found a "hider" (Jew), he would utter "Alle Alle Auch Sind Frei" (German version of Ollie Ollie Outs in Free) to bring the other hiders into home base (Gestapo headquarters). The captured "hider" was then out of the game (to the gas chamber), and a new game was started.

I was surprised that of those queried, many had never heard of the expression. Those that were familiar had played the same game under a multiplicity of names.

Here are just a few:

Ollie Ollie Outs in Free

Ally Ally Um-Phum Free

Ollie Ollie Oceans Free

Ollie Ollie Oxen Free

Calling All The Outs In Free

Ally Ally Oats in Free

Ollie Ollie Income Free

Ollie Ollie Oxen Go Free

All Ye All Ye Outs In Free

Albert O. Martin

1934

Voice of God

February. Stuttgart, Germany. Karl Koenig sat bolt upright in his living room chair wondering if he had just experienced a dream or a premonition. Whichever it was, he had an uncontrollable urge to place pen and ink in hand and rush a letter to Walter Boenke, whom he hoped after some 25 years was still in Berlin. Walter was a fellow professor at Berlin University when Karl was head of the Sociology department there. His letter, sent to a mutual friend for hand-delivery to Walter, expressed fear that Boenke, also a Jew, might be brought into Gestapo headquarters.

"Walter, you must leave the country immediately. The Nazis want to bring you in for questioning. You may never see your wife again. Don't ask me how I know...I just know. Please destroy this letter!" Karl then wondered, how in blue blazes *did* I know?

Several days later Karl received a short call from Walter's wife, thanking him for the warning. He could almost hear the sigh of relief as she related the event. "Walter got away just hours before the Storm Troopers came banging at our door. Hopefully, we will reconnect later. I did destroy your letter."

What she and Karl did not know was that the Gestapo had caught him while he was en route south. Someone had seen him and informed the authorities. Flagging down his train, the Nazis unceremoniously jerked him out of his seat, clubbed him senseless, dumped him into the back of their Volkswagen, and took him to the local police lockup.

It had been a quarter of a century since Karl and Walter had shaken hands goodbye. It would be another decade before they would grip hands again! Karl would miss their reminiscing, mostly about the music of Wagner, Mendelssohn, Beethoven et al. When discussing Mendelssohn, however, they had to speak softly, as his music...even the mention of his name...was banned because of his Jewish heritage.

Karl's face was ashen when he telephoned his son-in-law, Albert. "Can you come over this evening?"

"Of course! This sounds urgent, yes?"

"Does a jackass bray when it has no grass? Yes! Could you get here by seven?"

"Certainly," as he smiled to himself. Get there by seven? We live only two blocks apart!

He wondered what could be bothering Karl, who was sometimes fairly excitable when rattled. Otherwise, he was your classic curmudgeon. Albert arrived at seven on the dot. As Karl opened the door, he thought, what a magnificent young man he is: Tall, blond, and handsome, without an ounce of fat.

"Herr Koenig," smiled Albert, towering over Karl's 5'5" frame.

"Herr Steller," replied Karl as they shook hands. This ceremony was a tradition with the two since their first meeting two years ago when Albert came to ask for the hand of his daughter, Kristine.

"I assume you've had dinner?" ashamed that he hadn't at least extended the invitation.

Yes," said Albert. "I thought we should get right down to the libations." Karl handed him a scotch rocks then a Dutch Master, which was instantly lit. Getting right to the point he asked, "Do you remember my suspicions of being 'Roh-Eh Hanoled,' you know, the ability to see future happenings?"

Karl having needed someone with whom to share his ability had casually mentioned his gift/curse to Albert when they were first getting acquainted. He had said no more of it until now. Sworn to secrecy years ago, Albert was also aware that Karl was Jewish.

"Yes I do," replied Albert, still smiling. "It would be a wonderful gift if really true."

"Well, I'm afraid it might be. And it wouldn't be a gift, it would be a curse," growled Karl, who went on to relate to the incident about Walter Boenke.

Albert reflected with a whisper of amazement in his thoughts, Mein Gott, could this be true?

"Any thoughts? Answers?" asked Karl.

"None that I could offer now, said Albert with a shrug.

Born Karl Theodor Cohen in Berlin, he changed his family name to Koenig in 1909 because of his anger with God following the death of his new wife, Amy. She died soon after giving birth to Kristine. He declared to himself that he was no longer a Jew, revoking Judaism. He quit his position as professor of Sociology at Berlin University, then drifted about for two years before starting a new life in Stuttgart, instructing at the local university.

Along with his name, his physical appearance also changed. At Berlin he was 40 pounds heavier with a rounded face and a full schnurbart (moustache) compared to his present wiry frame, horn-rimmed glasses and hawk-like facial features, reminiscent of someone in a perpetual state of anger. Karl exuded a somewhat angry disposition, and was capable of being explosive. Belying these characteristics was a very dry wit, able to find humor under the most dire circumstances.

Albert Otto Steller, born in 1905 the son of Hermann and Lisa, was a student at Stuttgart from 1923 through 1927. A sociology major under Koenig his first two years, he was a model student—brilliant and behaved. His appearance was that of a natural athlete, but somehow he didn't choose to specialize in any sport other than boxing.

Much like Karl, Albert showed a mild temperament and a developing sense of humor, due in part to his exposure to Karl's sporadic stream of jokes, practical and otherwise. His penchant for bringing home stray cats, and siding with the underdog, made him popular with his friends, classmates, and adults alike.

It disappointed Karl greatly when Albert changed his major and graduated in Engineering Sciences. But Karl knew it was the correct move, especially after Albert taught the subject for two years at the high school level, and then earned his Master's from Oxford in 1931. His parents died in an auto accident two days after his graduation. Still in England, they mistakenly were driving on the right-hand side of the road and hit an oncoming car.

He began his university teaching career at Stuttgart, two rooms down the hall from his former mentor, and (unique to a father/son-in-law relationship) present good friend.

"Why do you think you possess the ability to see the future, this 'Roh-Eh Hanoled'? Couldn't this Berlin letter just be coincidental?" mused Albert, still thinking Karl was setting him up for one of his famous jokes.

"It all started in the early 1920s," Karl recalled, "when I became a little dizzy, then began to see, from time to time, 'things.' I thought even then, could this be Roh-Eh Hanoled? Things were happening so fast on the political scene. I didn't know whether that which I was seeing was a peek at the future or reacting to the present. It was Hitler this, or Hitler that. When he became chairman of the National Socialist German Worker's Party, I thought, Mein Gott, the party name is longer than our national anthem. Then he becomes the party's Fuhrer. Almost funny was the time when he tried to overthrow the government of Bavaria. Can you imagine!

They called this the 'Beer-Hall Putsch'. However, he received his comeuppance when he tried to out shout another party's leader. Such a fracas! It took only a small group of German policemen to beat back some 3,000 of Hitler's 'Sturmabteilung,' sometimes called 'Brownshirts,' a.k.a., 'Storm Troops.' Hitler ran away when bullets began flying. He was arrested the next day, and tossed into jail. It was there he wrote *Mien Kampf*. I refuse to read it.

"Through all of this," explained Karl, "I felt like I was seeing a movie picture, while getting dizzy on a roller coaster. With the appointment of Hitler to Chancellor in January, my skin was again crawling. A month later, someone set the Reichstag building on fire. It was first called a Communist plot, but eventually some poor Jew got the blame. I can't recall his name. Anyway, I definitely got that old feeling two days before, but couldn't identify what evil was about to happen.

"A month later, same eerie feeling, like I was peeking into the future. I heard rumors that the Nazis were building a concentration camp at a small village called Dachau, a few miles from Munich. Himmel! That's only 195 kilometers from here!

"There's more: Two days after the Dachau rumor that sneaky Reichstag enacted a thinly veiled power grab, I think called the 'Enabling Act'. Like it or not Hitler's cabinet has complete control over the legislature for four years. He owns Germany! Nothing stands in his way to become a dictator.

"Another act of insanity just last month. Quotas were applied to the number of Jewish students allowed in higher education. And did you know that Jews are now prohibited from working in any government position? Just as sure as I'm sitting here, Hitler and his Nazi goons are going to make discrimination against the Jews a national policy."

"Karl, you're scaring the devil out of me," uttered Albert.

"You needn't be; you're not a Jew."

"But you are, and if what you say becomes reality, I'm fearful for you—and Kristine. Besides, if the Nazis discover your past, I could be in trouble for not turning you in."

"Don't worry, I've covered my tracks. I lost some ugly pounds, cut off my equally ugly schnurbart and voila! emerges the handsome devil standing in front of you. Moreover, Kristine is not aware of her heritage."

"What!" exclaimed Albert, "Are you serious? You haven't told Kristine? And you used to wear a moustache? I'm not sure which is the more amazing."

"I said earlier I'm not joking," Karl repeated.

"Is this why you were in such a snit to see me?"

"I wanted first to give you some history on my 'condition' before asking a large favor of you. I would like some verification."

"Verification?"

"Yes, on whether I have the ability to see, or perhaps feel, ahead. I'm not ready yet to call it a gift or a curse."

"So, what do you have in mind?" asked Albert.

"I'm getting a shivery feeling again. Let's keep our eyes and ears open the next few days."

"To see if something portending evil occurs?"

"Exactly! Mark your calendar. Today is February 7."

Albert then asked Karl, "I didn't pay much attention to political history when I was growing up. Can you tell me something of Germany during your younger years?"

Karl filled the two glasses, this time with brandy, and took a puff on his cigar as he leaned back in his overstuffed chair. Looking wistfully at the ceiling, he recalled: "Before   I begin I want to tell you something. Did you know that Jews have been living in Germany for 1,600 years? 1,600 years! You think we could make a few friends in all that time. Why are we so disliked? What is it we do?"

Karl was eight years old when he remembered his mama spit on the floor and muttered the words 'Anti-Semitism my tochis!' He didn't know what it meant then, only that it made his mama real angry. But he did know what a tochis was.

"That would have been Wilhelm Marr who coined the term 'Anti-Semitism,' " said Albert.

"The very same. Then," continued Karl, "I was heartbroken when Richard Wagner, my very favorite composer—I loved his music. It was so stirring," his mind drifted a few seconds.

"Richard Wagner, what?" said Albert impatiently.

"Richard Wagner you know what. When he wrote that little essay on Jews as the 'demon causing mankind's downfall', that's what!" groused Karl visibly peeved. "I was only 10 years old then. I was crushed, but I still love his music. That same year some German big shot smart guy argued that the Jewish type was a biological danger to the German people."

"Was that Karl Duehring," asked Albert.

"Yes, Karl Duehring. That swine, I knew him in Berlin. He wanted Jews exterminated to save the purity of the superior Aryan race. Well, you seem to know it all so why am I telling you? Let's get back to the business at hand."

"How do you want to handle this verification process?"

"Well, I suppose the next time, if there is one, that I get that 'dizzy view of something' feeling, I'll let you know immediately. If an event evil or ominous occurs within a reasonable period of time, that will be a start. But more verification will be needed."

May. Three months went by. Nothing.

Karl, feeling very antsy, phoned to ask Albert to be sure to call if he hears anything. With summer coming, he was feeling spry and almost hoping nothing would turn up.

"Nothing special has crossed my desk either, and yes Papa, I'll call," said a smiling Albert feigning childlike obedience.

The next week Albert called. "Karl, good news—or maybe bad news. A friend of mine in Berlin telephoned me to say that he is sending me a letter that is coded in Turkey German, a language that we used to keep out prying eyes and ears. It should be here by Friday. We were at Oxford together and agreed to stay in touch."

Karl came to Albert's earlier than usual Saturday morning. They decided it would be the civil thing to do by waiting until at least noon to break out the cigars and brandy. Albert handed the letter to Karl, "Here, read this."

"What is this gibberish?" protested Karl as he adjusted his glasses. I can't read a word."

"Oh," grinned Albert, "it is in code. We agreed if the news were even remotely incriminating that we would communicate in Turkey German. Try reading it again." Karl began to read, "Barpooks arpare barpearping barpurned parpublarpiclarpy arpin barperlarpin. Enough nonsense, tell me what the letter says."

"First I'll break the code," said Albert. "We'll want to use it someday. To begin, divide each word into syllables. Then put the word 'arp' immediately after the first letter of each syllable. One exception, if the word starts with a vowel, the 'arp' goes first. Let's try it."

Albert started, "Take the 'arp' out of barpooks and you have...?"

"Books."

"Now here's that exception. Next word, remove the beginning arp and you have...?"

"Are."

"Take away the arps in the next word."

"Being."

"Try and read the rest yourself," said Albert with encouragement.

"Burned...pub-lic-ly...in...Ber-lin." Karl smiled. "Nothing to it, but it does sound more complicated than it really is."

"So," continued Albert, "here's the letter, top to bottom":

"Books are being burned publicly in Berlin. Thousands of students are milling around and tossing what I would guess to be about 15,000 of them into the bonfire. Most of those incinerated were written by Jews: Einstein, Sigmund Freud, Andre Gide, Helen Keller, Jack London, H.G. Wells, Emile Zola, to name a few."

"*Idiocy*," uncharacteristically cried Kristine, who had come to the parlor door to see if the men wanted some lunch *"Do those stupid nitwits think they can halt the intellectual evolution of man by burning a few books written by a few Jews? They will do far more damage to mankind when they begin burning Jews instead."*

Silence! No one spoke. Karl was transfixed. Albert was trying to grasp whether or not he actually heard what he thought he had heard.

Then Kristine blurted out, "Papa, what are you saying?" her tone reflecting her disbelief. "Those poor people have had enough misery!"

Kristine heard a male voice. She thought it was her father, as did Albert, who saw Kristine's lips move but couldn't bring himself to believe Kristine spoke the words.

Karl mumbled in a very deliberate voice, "Kristine...did...not...speak...those...words." He breathed deeply and continued more normally, "I know those words came out of her mouth, but not out of her consciousness. She did not speak!"

"Then there's a ventriloquist in the house," mused Albert.

"Albert, how can you be joking at a time like this?" scolded Kristine, "and tell me what is going on?"

"In 25 words or less?"

"Albert, stop that!" demanded Kristine.

Karl's mind was racing, and did not hear Albert's inappropriate jokes. He was quietly mulling over this phenomenon as Albert gave Kristine a quick review of the past month's events. His out-of-taste jokes were intended to keep Kristine's thoughts otherwise occupied rather than somehow blaming herself for the voice's disturbing words. He, of course, did not reveal the term Roh-Eh Hanoled nor the fact that her father, ergo she, was a Jew. This was Karl's task.

Karl, silent during Albert's explanation began to speak very slowly and quietly, then with increasing speed and volume, "I know I did not utter those words. It couldn't have been Kristine; it was a man's voice. I'm sure it wasn't Albert, the voice was too deep."

More silence. One could almost see Karl deliberating, analyzing, considering. Then the inescapable, inevitable conclusion from one born to arguably the world's oldest religion. Could it have been the voice of God? By this time he was shaking his fist in the air while nearly shouting, "Whatever you are up to God, it won't work. I'm still angry with you! I am very very angry with you. And you leave Kristine alone!"

"I'll go fix some lunch," said Kristine nervously, leaving the men to ponder the meaning of this 'faceless voice.' She, too, thought a voice had spoken to her over the years, but was afraid to tell her father for fear of some type of retribution from its messenger.

Kristine Amy was born in 1909, the only child of Karl and Amy Koenig. Karl was like the song 'So in Love with Amy' that he never remarried, although only 38 when she died. Kristine was an image of her mother, somewhat plain looking, but possessing a striking demeanor set off with a hint of red hair. At age six she contracted scarlet fever. She dropped out of school for over six months, got behind in class work and became somewhat stunted. Thinking she was slow minded, her classmates teased unmercifully, giving her a marked inferiority complex.

One au pair after another cared for her until she was able to be on her own by her final year of high school. She chose not to attend college. Instead, she went one year to a nurse's training facility. Somehow, she couldn't generate enough interest to continue, even though her mother had been a nurse. Being a homebody, she was content to work around the house, yard, and cook for her father.

She met Albert through her father and married him directly after he obtained his Master's two years ago. As a couple, they fit perfectly: She a timid personality and he a prince in shining armor. They have, as yet, no children.

"All right, let's get serious," suggested Albert. "What was the voice trying to tell us? It wasn't spoken in Turkey German."

"I don't know," said Karl in an exasperated tone. "I've heard that God works in mysterious ways. What wonders are we going to behold? I just wish he would come right out and tell us what he wants in plain German."

"Let's forget whose voice it was and concentrate on the message," suggested Albert. "Wasn't it something like 'damage to mankind by burning a few Jews'?"

"Something like that. But I have an idea." said a now calmer Karl. "Let's enjoy what Kristine has fixed for us, top it off with some cigars and brandy, and then we go home. Let's sleep on all this. Right now my head is spinning, and I need to clean out some cobwebs. We meet at my house next time. I don't want Kristine to hear any more."

September. The two had no occasion to meet for several months. Finally, they took time to discuss Karl's condition. The university had sent Albert to Munich University to audit a portion of their Engineering Sciences class.

Albert took some extra time on the way over and back from Munich to see if he could get a look at that rumored concentration camp at Dachau. If some ragged looking shacks surrounded by a twenty-foot barbed wire fence makes for a concentration camp, then the rumor was probably true.

"And I have some happenings to report," added Karl solemnly. "Several Jewish organizations, including the 'Gemeinde' and the 'World Jewish Congress' are encouraging emigration from Germany. Did you know that over 37,000 Jews have already left, but still about 500,000 remain? Oddly enough, the Nazis, who are always on the opposite side of the fence from anything Jewish, are also promoting this. The icing on the cake: Jews are now actually forbidden to be employed by businesses having to do with theater, the press, literature, art, broadcasting, etc."

"How do you like those apple strudels?" asked Karl through pursed lips.

"I like Kristine's better," answered Albert, sucking in air between his teeth as if tasting the delicacy.

"Putting this aside, I believe that I'm closing in on some alternatives to the meaning of 'burn a few Jews'," stated Karl.

"I'm not there yet!"

"Then you may recall the saying 'getting burned', similar to doing something, then having things go awry. Or being 'burned up', i.e., being angry?"

"Possibly," answered Albert, "but damn it Karl, we're both dancing around the ugliest of alternatives, literally being burned with real flames. But, it's so hideous a possibility I doubt even Hitler could do it."

"Did we assume it was the voice of God uttering those words?"

"Not exactly, but would it make any difference?"

"Yes. If God can cause an earthquake to crack open the earth's surface and swallow up a whole family of Israelites, or drown Pharaoh's army, he can sure as hell put a bunch of Jews to the torch." said Karl with a steely glare.

"If there were good reasons?" asked Albert.

"God has his own reasons."

"Then let us assume that it was the voice of God," concluded Albert.

"Much as I find this possibility mind boggling, I'll have to agree until proven otherwise," sighed Karl, "meanwhile I haven't seen or felt anything. But that doesn't mean we can't continue to have our social time."

Albert emphatically agreed.

1935

The Sturmabteilunger

<u>January.</u> More delays. First, Albert was called to audit classes in Berlin, Hamburg, and Leipzig. Karl fought the flu. Christmas came and went. Finally, cigars and brandy!

"Well, how's your arthritis?" probed Albert.

"It's not arthritis," grumbled Karl, "You know very well what bothers me."

"But I thought you said you weren't experiencing any of those odd feelings."

"I haven't, but I have a feeling I'm going to get the feeling," sighed Karl.

"Oh, by the way, guess who came to visit last week for a few hours? Martin!"

"Martin Zoner? I haven't seen him since he was a teenager!"

"Yes, and when he stood in the doorway I didn't recognize him at first. I thought I was being arrested!"

"Arrested?"

"Yes," laughed Albert, "he had on his Brownshirt uniform. He is now a 'Sturmabteilunger' (Storm Trooper). He wears the uniform well."

"A Storm Trooper! That's terrible!" as Karl put on a sour face.

"Being a Storm Trooper is not my idea of a real job," admitted Albert, "in fact, it's not a real job in this instance. It's like a fraternal organization that wears a uniform while participating in various events, similar to being in a reserve unit. At least that's the way he explained it to me. He still works for the city auditor. Got a promotion to assistant director."

"I'm curious. How did you and Martin get to be such good friends?" Karl asked. "You're so different, and it seems you rarely see each other."

"It's a long story."

"Am I leaping out of my chair?"

"No, but you might get up and pour me another brandy," said Albert, holding out his glass.

Albert began the story: Martin was a year younger than he, but was two years behind in school without question due to a miserable childhood. He was motherless since age 9. Martin rarely saw his father, except to get a beating. His classmates constantly taunted him because he was small for his age, and that his father was the area garbage hauler and local drunk, spending most of his off-time at the Rathskeller. He later was killed when he fell off the garbage cart and broke his neck. Not a good childhood.

By this time Martin was age 16 and could take care of himself reasonably well, but was always on the edge of being afoul of the law. He finally grew some, topping out at 5'9". A towhead earlier, he now has jet-black hair.

Their friendship started back in grammar school. Albert was about 12 years old. Heading home from school, he saw this small boy, Martin, with his back to a brick wall, edging up to the corner of the building. He looked around, and then sped across the street to another building, again with his back to the wall. Suddenly, from around the corner where Martin was heading, a boy ran toward him yelling and screaming. Startled, Martin ran the other way, only to smack into the grasp of this giant of a boy, or so he seemed to Martin.

The big kid was only slightly taller than Albert, but was fat! He struck a very menacing pose. He immediately threw Martin to the ground, sat on him and began choking him. Meanwhile old fatso's instigating accomplice was hollering, 'hit him, his old man is dead drunk on the garbage cart.'

Albert thought, whomever this young kid was, he didn't deserve the treatment he was getting from someone twice his weight. So he ran over and grabbed the bully by the back of his shirt, pulled him off Martin, and threw him to the ground. His accomplice, the little weasel, ran away, and after sizing Albert up, so did the fat kid. Only later did Albert know who he was.

Albert asked him if he was all right and then helped him get to his feet. He said yeah he was all right and that this wasn't the first time he'd been punched out by ol' fat fart. Albert told Martin that maybe he could arrange an end to those harassments. Then Albert asked him if he wanted to stop off at the malt shop. His treat.

Martin was unaccustomed to this sort of friendliness and was at a loss for words. He at first refused, saying that he really needed to get home. Albert persisted, he agreed, and they went to the malt shop. Albert listened in awe to how the boy had survived up to this point.

For the next five years Martin virtually haunted Albert's home. But his parents enjoyed his coming over, especially Mama. They became very close. His brushes with the law became a thing of the past. And, with Albert's help, he became fairly proficient in the 'manly art of self-defense'; but Martin had to drop out of high school to look for more than part-time work. Albert's parents arranged for him to find a position in the mailroom of the City Auditor. A smart kid, he is doing well.

March. Karl and Albert usually lunched together at the university, but since January had had little to discuss regarding the Mystery Voice. Then the flighty Karl cornered Albert in his office, "I got a pretty good tingle last night. See you Sunday?"

As the appointed day finally rolled around, Albert was anxiously awaiting the news as they took their seats in the parlor. "Well?" he inquired impatiently.

"Well what?" responded Karl as he poured the drinks slowly to maximize the suspense.

"You know very well, well what," said Albert in pretended irritation.

"I felt, saw, I can't be sure, something more clear than before, not just the shivers," said Karl excitedly. "I could see the Swastika clearly, but a blurry image of Martin."

"What would he have to do with anything?"

"You're asking me?" Disappointed, Karl said, "I was hoping you would know. I produce the images. You're supposed to figure them out. This one was the biggest jolt I've had yet. It must mean something!"

"Give things time to develop."

It took six long months for the signal about Martin to manifest itself.

September. Albert motioned Karl to come into his empty classroom. "I received a call from Martin. Said he's now in Berlin, and doing well. He's wearing his Brownshirt fulltime, and getting a decent wage."

"So why shouldn't he be?"

"You tell me, it was your vision—and don't be so grumpy"? Albert chided. "Anyway, Martin will be back in Stuttgart in a week to tell us something. He can only stay overnight."

True to his word, Martin arrived by train exactly one week later, accompanied by First Lt. Piotr Siegel, on a courier service run to Stuttgart. He and Martin struck up a conversation about their respective youths while on the train from Berlin. They found much in common, so Martin was comfortable in inviting him to dinner. Kristine set an extra place at the table for the two, who, during the meal, complimented her cooking almost to the point of embarrassment.

Ignoring the usual preliminary pleasantries, Martin declared, "I'm strongly considering resigning from the Sturmabteilung. It must have been Hitler's orders. I see no other reason why Germans have been killing Germans. It happened two weeks ago." Martin spoke disjointedly.

"What!" exclaimed Karl.

"There's more. The Schutzstaffel, Heinrich Himmler's SS boys, virtually purged our leaders…just the leaders. They even killed Ernst Rohm, a long-time member of the Storm Troops and close friend of Hitler himself. I can't imagine what he could have done, or said, to get himself killed," said Martin shaking his head.

"And it looks as though Hitler is adding another layer of protection," continued Piotr. "He is now selecting from our Storm Troops his personal bodyguard, called the SS. All members are required to pledge loyalty to Hitler himself, not to Germany."

"The Storm Troops are still needed by Hitler as his personal army, so I guess we're in no immediate danger of losing our jobs," reasoned Martin. "Did you know they number over 400,000? An army for just one man! Our Fatherland's army numbers only 100,000."

"Limited by the Treaty of Versailles," added Albert.

"Yes," confirmed Martin angrily, "as if taking away some of our land wasn't bad enough; they make us pay reparations too."

"So, Hitler murders his friends. It doesn't seem significant enough to warrant my shivers," smiled Karl. "No love lost there."

"Maybe there's more to your shivers than what it may or not portend," offered Albert.

"Maybe these precursory shakes were for the benefit of Martin. After all, you saw, or felt, him."

"That could be," agreed Karl.

"Silence fell over them for an inordinately long time. Finally, Karl opined, "Somehow I feel that Martin should not resign from the Brownshirts. Could you hold off for awhile, Martin?"

"I could, if you'd give a good reason. And tell me what these nervous ticks are all about."

Albert took it from the beginning: the cigars and brandy get-togethers, the mystery voice, and Karl's shuddering premonitions. All. "As for you, Martin, just keep your eyes and ears open and maintain a high profile. I want the Nazis to look upon you favorably."

Martin agreed to stay put, for a while.

"What are your plans, Piotr?" asked Albert.

"I'm in this for the long haul and plan to make military service a career, I'm hoping, for the same country."

Dead silence! No one knew what to say, so Martin, seeing a few raised eyebrows, broke the ice with his understanding of Piotr's situation. He explained that Piotr's father was German, his mother French, but he was raised in Poland.

He exchanged his Polish officer's uniform for a German one several months ago because he felt his loyalties were with Germany, the Fatherland.

Piotr needed to speak. "The meal was wonderful, but I must say adieu and find lodging for the evening. My 'delivery' is ready, and I must take it on the morning train to Berlin. Will you be on the same schedule, Martin?

He nodded yes.

The next day he had no idea who the beaten up old man was, arms chained to the seat in front of him. For sure Karl would have recognized him.

Albert had taken an immediate dislike toward Piotr and felt that he had not told the truth. He had reason for his mistrust. Was it Piotr who turned Walter into the authorities and watched as he was severely beaten? Was it Walter who was the object of Piotr's 'delivery' to the Gestapo in Berlin?

Martin, also, was beginning to doubt his newly found friend.

December. Karl and Albert could see the noose around Judaism's neck tightening. First, the Nuremberg Laws were decreed, turning Jews into second-class citizens. Marriage and sexual relations between Jews and non-Jews was disallowed. Discrimination's door was wide open. By the end of 1935, Jews had been dismissed from civil service. Moreover, they could no longer call themselves German. Ironically, during World War I some 12,000 German Jews died in the trenches for the Fatherland. Many wore the Verwondetenabzeichen, the insignia for injury during the war.

1936

The Moses Connection

<u>April.</u> Karl was experiencing some dizziness late in the month, when a spell surfaced. It was the most vivid to date and a repeat of the Swastika with an image of Martin. Its origin was quick to become clear when the phone rang. It was Martin.

"Karl, I couldn't reach Albert so I called you," said Martin in a hushed but urgent tone.

"What is it?"

"I can't say, nor talk long. Won't be able to come up there for I don't know how long. Must get some information to you."

"Impossible," cried Karl, "there is no way I can come now."

"Albert?"

"It's possible. He could audit some classes there. How can he reach you?"

"I'm staying at the Volkshausen Hotel. Have him meet me there, in the bar. I'm usually in by six. Must hang up now."

Berlin. Albert had to pull some strings, but caught the Berlin express two days later. Confirming that his "cousin" Martin was staying there, he checked in at the Volkshausen around four. Martin arrived right on schedule, looked for messages, smiled broadly then turned immediately to head for the bar, where Albert was on his second Schnapps.

"I'm delighted you could make it," Martin exclaimed. Smiling, and in a low voice continued, "Say something pleasant, we may be being watched."

Albert spoke a bit louder, "Oh Yes, Cousin Martin, it's been a long time. Shall we go out for dinner?"

"Good idea, I know a good quiet place," said Martin.

After walking a few blocks Martin breathed easier, now that he knew no one was following. And he really <u>did</u> know of a good place to eat. They sidled into a corner table of the Bistro as Martin began to explain that he had been reassigned to a special unit commanded by an SS officer, Christian Wirth.

"Never heard of him."

"And rightly so. This whole operation keeps a very low profile. You've heard of euthanasia."

"Yes, doesn't it involve mercy killing?" asked Albert.

"In the Nazis' case the only mercy involved is that it's quick. Some of the patients are incurably ill. This I could maybe justify. But most are asocial, suspected enemies of the Fatherland and other types deemed 'life unworthy of living.'"

"Unbelievable," murmured Albert, "and you say it is quick?"

"Reasonably quick, although no one is around to say for sure."

"How can that be?"

Leaning forward, almost choking on his words, Martin whispered, "Gas chambers."

With a twisted look of disbelief, Albert just sat, groping for words.

Martin, shuddering, indicated that there was more. In most cases the dead are taken to a mass burial site miles out of town. But some are incinerated in ovens. Most believe it's on an experimental basis. Probably will get worse. There are estimates of some 30,000 who have died there already, only about one-third of what will eventually be the total."

"Judas priest," exclaimed Albert under his breath. "If they just burned a few Jews," repeating Karl's—or whoever's voice it was—prophetic words back in mid 1934.

"What will you do now?" asked Martin. "Actually, what can you do?"

Deep in thought, Albert sighed, "Or maybe, what *should* we do? I must leave soon, get back with Karl, and repair some fences at the university."

"I realize this information will leave you in a negative demeanor," lamented Martin. "Let me tell you something on the lighter side."

"I would welcome it," grinned Albert.

"Do you remember that big bully back in grammar school?" exclaimed Martin. Assuming a yes response he went on, "I met him, here in Berlin. We're old friends now," he smiled. "His name is Fredrik Marr. Then we called him 'Fat Freddie,' although he has lost quite a bit of weight since we were in school. His accomplice was his brother, Wilhelm, whom I think is still in Stuttgart.

"I've told Freddie very little about my work, but he jabbers like an open fire hose. He is a guard at some facility near Sachsenhausen, I think, another concentration camp.

"Freddie remembers you. How you rescued me more than just the time when he was about to throttle me. Your words of advice still ring in my ears:

"Martin, you've got to learn how to not just defend yourself, but to take the offensive.

"Don't attack the smallest guy in the crowd to get in a few licks before the big guy grabs you and knocks your lights out. Next time, stand there and let fatso come up.

"As he is about to grab you, hit him with all your might right in the nose, he won't be expecting it. Don't worry about anyone else bothering you; after the fat guy falls to his knees yelling in agony they'll scatter. And the big guy shouldn't bother you from that point on."

"Freddie said he remembered my punching him on the nose and that it hurt like hell. I had broken his nose."

"There's something I need to know," said Albert solemnly, "what is your job at the euthanasia factory?"

"Inventory."

"Inventory?"

"Yes, when a patient comes in I record him or her along with pertinent data on the person. Like, 'when admitted,' 'diagnosed illness,' 'recommended treatment,' that sort of thing," explained Martin.

"And their release," questioned Albert. "How is this recorded?"

"Most patients are recorded as being released but in truth never were. They just disappear. Some deaths are recorded as 'burial in institution cemetery' but there is no headstone and, of course, no one buried there. I feel fortunate to have had the experience that I did in the city auditor's office there in Stuttgart. Evidently the Nazis felt it qualified me for my current position."

Albert encouraged Martin to keep the faith, and stay in Berlin. We are going to develop a plan to aid the Jews; at least in Western regions No one was going to abandon him, although it may seem that way from time to time. We're going to do our best to keep in touch and inform you on our progress

Meanwhile, Kristine was anxious for Albert to return home. An ominous feeling had come over her and she didn't want to be alone. She could sense what lay ahead.

Stuttgart. May. Albert had been gone a week When he arrived home he immediately contacted Karl at the university to set the evening's agenda. After a quiet meal with Kristine, they met later to review Albert's report. As he talked, Karl sat silently just shaking his head.

"I know, as there is a God in heaven, that this is only the beginning," lamented Karl, "a prelude of what will assuredly come. We can hold meetings to discuss future annihilations until the cows come home. They will only confirm what we already know. I need time to think. Right now I'm tempted to leave Germany."

"Karl, don't get discouraged," counseled Albert. "Things can't be as bad as all that. Tell you what. Let's take a month away from this monster. We've gotten too close to it to be straight-thinking."

"Yes," said Karl with resignation. "Contact me when it's time."

Three weeks later Karl phoned Albert to say he had thought it over, and that he's going to Russia, Eastern Russia. He implored both to come with him.

Albert immediately hung up the phone and jogged over to Karl's house, away from cupped ears, to caution him. Albert suggested it could be best not to say anything remotely incriminating over the telephone! The party line was full of busybodies.

"Yes, of course you're right. It's just that I'm so blasted upset. The thought of leaving Germany makes me sick."

"Sick, or maybe dizzy as with your premonitions."

"Could very well be," answered Karl. "I can't help feeling that Hitler is going to take over all of Europe, and massacre as many Jews as possible in the process."

"So why go to Russia? You don't think that if Hitler owned Europe he wouldn't be coveting Russia too?"

"Absolutely," assured Karl, "but he would be Meshuga to try."

"Meshuga?" "Crazy. He would be crazy to try. It's a Jewish word."

"Oh really?"

"Oh really what!" said Karl, now irritated, "'Oh really' that it's a Jewish word, or 'Oh really' that Hitler would be crazy?"

"Both."

"Oh! Anyway, Hitler would be crazy to invade Russia because two of the most successful armies ever failed to conquer it," insisted Karl.

"The Tatars and Napoleon."

"Yes, the Tatars and Napoleon. But just in case, I'd go to Eastern Russia."

"Why so far?" puzzled Albert.

Karl's explanation was a musical metaphor; "Oh it's a long, long time from here to Kamchatka."

"Hang on for another few months," implored Albert, "I'm working on something that may change your mind."

"All right, I wait. But it better be good."

August. Karl wrestled with his conscience incessantly. He remembered vividly his bitterness when the love of his life died. He had gone to his Rabbi, prayed continuously, did all things his religion required. And when she died...seven days of Shiva...30 days of mourning. But he just couldn't move on.

Karl couldn't understand why he was being punished. She was a pure woman. He was a good man. The only course of action open to Karl, he felt, was to give up his religion—punish God!

All these years he had ignored the existence of God and now God was asking something of him, even though he couldn't hear His voice. Karl had been in denial for 26 years. It was time he gave up his anger. But, as Karl looked upward as if speaking to God, he thought, not now.

He called Albert to ask if they could meet this weekend. To stay out of Kristine's earshot, they met at Karl's, who jumped right on the agenda.

"Albert, we've both wondered to ourselves if what we heard was truly the voice of God, and what could he have been trying to say to me except 'free my people.' But, what can one person do?"

"Wait, a minute," Albert interrupted, "I thought I was part of this equation. Make that what can TWO people do?"

"One, two. What's the difference?" Suddenly, Karl cocked his head as if listening. He stood, eyes shut, breath held, unmoving, as if in a trance. Then he relaxed, opened his eyes, and said "I've lost him."

"Lost who?"

"God. He won't speak through me anymore. At least not as long as we spat. Go get Kristine. Unless I miss my guess, she may be our new conduit."

With downcast eyes Kristine came into the room. "Yes Papa, what is it?

"I'm sure you remember when the voice of God came out of your mouth last year. Do you think you can perform this service again, tonight? All you have to do is relax, clear your mind, and breathe deeply."

"I'll try Papa, but it was very frightening."

"That's because you didn't know what to expect."

It took only a few seconds for Kristine to experience the rapture. Then, from Kristine's mouth God spoke: **"Karl, you disbeliever, I know you can't do it all alone. You are only an instrument of my bidding. Just do as Kristine tells you. And remember, you have friends in high places."**

This was totally unexpected. God, through Kristine spoke the message. Although Albert heard it also, it was directed at Karl. In final analysis, Kristine was the key. She must perform the transmittal. He reminded Karl about Moses, who single handedly brought the whole nation of Israel out of Egypt. **"All right, so I helped a little."** said God. When He told Moses to go to Egypt and help free his people, Moses didn't think it could be done. He tried to beg off the responsibility and complained bitterly that he wasn't the right man for the job.

When Kristine awoke, she marveled at the feeling of bliss given by the voice.

Albert was getting nervous about the direction Karl seemed to be going.

"Here we were wondering what two people could do to help the plight of the Jews. We asked ourselves whose voice it was, and what was He trying to tell us. All along, subconsciously, we were trying to duck the responsibility. I think He thinks we're up to it!"

Albert stood up, "Amazing. These have also been my thoughts. September is coming up in two weeks and school will be starting soon. We need to take a break and get ready for the thundering herd, yet our project needs thought: Where to begin. How to proceed? Shall we shoot for harvest time?"

October. The men sat down to plan the Jewish evacuation, even though the Nazis were currently encouraging it. But Karl knew this would change. "First we have to decide to which country we take them, and the escape route. I still like the idea of going to Russia."

"I know how you feel about Russia," began Albert, "that Hitler would be 'Meshuga' to invade, and he will surely eye England instead. However, if Hitler is as successful in controlling Europe as we think he will be, he will be flush with victories and consider himself unstoppable. Even then, you may be safe in Eastern Russia, but how will your band of Jews get there? Further, there is no possibility, in my opinion, that the United States is going to remain neutral, no matter what Roosevelt promises. My money says the U.S. will side with England. Hitler may try an invasion, but it will not be successful."

"A very convincing argument," ceded Karl. "I need to think on this. You know, consult the Boss."

November. "I've thought it over, Albert, and I like your logic. I'll go along with England rather than Russia IF you can convince me that we can reach the shores of England. If our troop of refugees don't leave within the year, England will be very difficult to reach, unless they all swim like Johnny Weissmuller."

"The fellow who is the star of 'Tarzan and the Apes?'"

"Yes, I hear he's quite a swimmer."

"Well, I have news for you Karl. They won't have to swim, fly, or go by boat."

"Oh, so we put a tunnel under the English Channel," said Karl sarcastically. "And it will rest on the sea bottom, all the way."

"Karl, may I congratulate you on your perspicacity. How did you know?"

"Roh-Eh Hanoled!"

"Of course, I should have guessed."

"What material will you use in its construction?"

"I'm working on this, but probably something much less substantive than that used in submarines. Average depth of the channel is only around 120 meters. The route that looks the most promising is Dover to Calais, where the average depth is only about 45 meters."

"When have you had time to work on all this?"

"I've been doing calculations for many, many months—since before I told you I was working on something to change your mind about going to Russia. There are a few things I need to work out yet," admitted Albert. "I need to get back to my calculations. But, most important, we need a long term plan of action."

"I agree," Karl nodded. "It's late November already and 1937 is coming up fast. I'll need a little Roh-Eh Hanoled to get a feel for some specific events and when they may occur. But I can't give you a blow-by-blow account of the future," complained Karl. "Maybe just an overview."

"I'm certain you will be given a clear enough picture," assured Albert. "Oh, by the way, did you hear that our man Max Schmeling defeated the United States boxing champ, Joe Louis, a couple of months ago?"

"Yes," exclaimed Karl, "and I heard that Hitler was beside himself with glee. He couldn't stop bragging that our superior race would always beat the black race. Then, and this really tickles me, Schmeling turned down Hitler's offer to join the Nazi party. But the crowning embarrassment of Hitler was during our Berlin Olympics, when a black man won three gold medals. He said it was unfair for the U.S. to use 'subhuman brutes.'

"Who do you think will win the Schmeling-Louis rematch in '38?" grinned Albert.

"Louis, knockout in round one."

"Really?" questioned Albert, somewhat downcast.

"Yes," Karl felt confident. "So why the long face? You want Schmeling to win again?"

"No, that's not it," sighed Albert. "I just wonder how I would have done had I continued with boxing—I could have been a..."

"Yes, I know...a contender."

Back to reality, Albert proposed. "Now I suggest while you prepare your overview of events and time lines by early December. My efforts will be spent on devising a long-term plan of action.

December. "Cigars and brandy! This makes our concerns almost worth the effort," sighed Albert as he sipped his drink. So, what have you come up with?"

"Nothing a blind pig couldn't have rooted out," grumbled Karl. "It all seems so obvious."

"Sometimes the obvious isn't so obvious," assured Albert. "Don't belittle your calculations."

"As I see it," began Karl, "Hitler will take small bites to gain confidence. First, on small nearby countries, then on larger ones. All to the east, Austria, then Czech Republic. Lots of Germans live there. I'm not sure of his next move. It may be Hungary, then Romania. Or, it may be Poland, lots of Jews to kill there. If Poland, then France and most likely England will declare war on Germany."

Karl continued, "By now we'll be into a full scale world war. Hitler releases the hounds, first to Denmark then Netherlands and Belgium. The famed Maginot Line will be useless, so France will fall early. England? If your prediction proves good, the British may just cause Hitler to ponder. If so, they will be safe, but battered."

"What about Italy?" asked Albert.

"When Mussolini sees Germany's lopsided victories, he'll make a pact with the devil," Karl predicted.

"Russia?"

"Russia, Russia, Russia," lamented Karl. "What can I say? I was wrong. Hitler will invade, but as I predicted earlier, it will be a disaster for Germany!"

"The war, long term?"

"We have about one to two years before the fireworks begin. Early on, Germany will advance, almost without resistance," advised Karl. "Then the Nazis begin their long bloody retreat. The war could last five to seven years. The only good news is we'll have a year or so to plan and implement."

"It helps to know the Nazis will direct initial efforts eastward. This reinforces my guess that England is the place to take our lost sheep."

"I agree," admitted Karl, "but through an underwater, 34-kilometer (21-mile) tunnel, I'm not so certain."

"If not the tunnel, then something! Remember, you have friends in high places," mused Albert.

"This is no time to be flippant," scolded Karl. "I do see tragedy. We have to steel ourselves to the fact that we may save only a small fraction of Europe's Jews. Only about six percent are currently living in Germany and points west.

Most are eastward. The further from England the less chance they have."

"But there *will* be a remnant," stated Albert. "And just like Israel's exile in Babylon, some made it home just like I'm going to do now. You'll hear my plan after the first of the year. It still needs some work, and I have some special cards to send out."

The trio of Zoner, Siegel, and Marr was practically inseparable. A typical day when work was light, they would play chess, hearts, or some similar game, but no alcohol. Evenings were another matter. Lots of beer and cards.

It was a cool May evening, when an incident occurred that could some day threaten the viability of this exodus. As the three were leaving the Rathskeller, Freddie jokingly gave Piotr a playful shove out the front door. As bad luck would have it, he stumbled against a passerby. Piotr took this as an unforgivable insult, pulled out his luger, and brutally pistol-whipped the person into unconsciousness. He lay crumpled on the ground.

Freddie and Martin were in disbelief. A crowd began to gather. Piotr tried to make light of it as a mishap. All he could think to do was blame the passerby by saying "clumsy Jew, he had it coming," then hail down a cab to go elsewhere.

As good soldiers would never openly criticize an officer, Martin and Freddie stayed around until the authorities arrived. They wanted to make certain Piotr's actions weren't negatively exaggerated. They were shocked to discover later that the police, after questioning some of the remains of the crowd, proclaimed Piotr innocent. It was, after all, a Jew.

Martin and Freddie later that evening severely criticized Piotr for his insensitivity, and declared their friendship at an end. He just shrugged his shoulders and said, "It's your loss!"

It would be a year before they saw him again, advanced in rank to a Captain. Little did they know they would be serving in the same geographic area.

1937

The Bow is Drawn

January. Albert was excited when he and Karl met New Year's Day. "I think I have a great plan of action covering, hopefully, all the essentials."

"You have the floor, young man. May I interrupt if I need clarification?"

Albert's scowl at Karl was a tacit "if you must."

"First, we need financing; second, a team of experts, one for each facet of the operation; third, someone to coordinate and keep the operation up to speed, fourth, a name, someone respected who can pull a lot of strings."

"I think you just described God," suggested Karl. "So what is your plan to spirit our Jewish friends out of harm's way, and where do we find the above mentioned idiots who risk their lives for a pat on the head?"

"First the idiots." started Albert. "Remember my mentioning sending some special Christmas cards? God had spoken to Kristine, had given instructions on what message the card was to contain and the mailing addresses."

"She was also given an instant understanding of turkey German, so she could send the following note on the cards:

'Warpe narpeed yarpour harpelp. Interpret this. Then mailgram your answer to Karl Koenig, 135 Guten Strasse, Stuttgart, Germany.'

This message was sent to only three people: Wally Fournier, Lt. Vance Worthington, and Sol Rothsmann."

Karl wondered what good the letter was going to do. The odds of a reply were incalculable. The correct answer unfathomable. Dejected, Karl asked about the plan.

"The plan! Ah yes, the plan. Therein hangs a tale," sighed Albert. "Now keep an open mind, Karl, as I take you through the maze. All the pieces will fit, eventually. Remember, much of the plan's success will depend on how well your predictions come to pass."

"You're putting me in a pressure cooker!" snapped Karl angrily.

Albert began, "It looks like the Calais-Dover route is the shortest. Our tunnel will take this course. The Dover side is a simple arrangement. A small bay used by fishermen. A fairly large maintenance shed where all the machinery to build the tunnel units will be housed. From the air it will look like a haven for a few fishing vessels.

"The Calais side is more complicated," Albert went on. "We'll need to construct a fancy hotel and spa right on the waterline of the shore. The project will feature two towers to hold guest rooms. One tower will be completed. The other, intentionally, will not. The spa owners, in on our plan, will have run out of money and must abandon the project.

"We then acquire the property and remodel to fit our peculiar specifications, hopefully with the help of one of our new recruits. We will set aside the finished tower for the military—office space and housing. The sub-ground of the unfinished portion will be perfect for mock gas chambers and cremation ovens from which a hidden stairwell will lead to a holding area. From here the prisoners, supposedly exterminated by now, can enter the tunnel and walk 21 miles to safety in England.

"While all of this construction is going on, I will be selling the Nazis on the idea of a privately operated concentration camp for the sole purpose of killing and cremating Jews. Using professionals, our efficiency will save them money. Most important, we'll help keep the Nazis uniforms clean when the worldwide panel of war crimes comes calling."

"Any questions?"

Karl's mind was trying to gather in all the details of Albert's 'master plan.' "Yes, one or two. Smoke, as an example, what about smoke? Wouldn't a cremation oven put out smoke?"

"Yes," replied Albert," and we plan to cover this by burning logs and wood chips. They will be treated with oil and sulfur to give off a very offensive odor. No one will suspect it's not the real thing."

"Won't the Nazis see what is going on?"

"We should be able to convince them the prisoners can do the ugly task of carrying out the bodies from the gas chamber to cremation. This part of the job will, of course, have to be overseen by German soldiers, selected by the death squad leader, whatever title he will use."

"And they're all our men," realized Karl, slapping his knee with delight, "The whole operation is controlled by our men!"

"Yes, Karl, very perceptive, as usual." Hands with fingers interlocked behind his head, and leaning back, Albert had a big smile on his very satisfied face.

"Your death squad leader will have a very ticklish task trying to recruit German soldiers to betray the Hitler regime," noted a now somber Karl. "One misjudgment and it's the firing squad for him."

"A risk he'll be glad to assume."

"Any thoughts on who this wunderkind will be?" asked Karl.

"As a matter of fact, yes. Martin Zoner!"

Dumbfounded, Karl hesitated for a moment. "Have you talked to him about this?"

"No, not yet," answered Albert. "But if you think about it there are some things to his advantage. First, I can't imagine such an unpleasant position would be sought after. Martin will volunteer, 'for the glory of Mein Fuhrer.' Second, his experience at the euthanasia facility will help."

"Biggest question yet," continued Karl. "Why would the Nazis want to put such a facility right on the French coast, so close to England?"

"The resort itself is of no value as an impediment to an invasion from England, but a long, narrow concentration camp covering several miles of coastline might be at least an impediment for that particular geographic location."

"What makes it an impediment?"

"The bombardment prior to a shore landing, then the gunfire from both sides as the landing is attempted. Many prisoners in the area would be killed. The British wouldn't risk this," explained Albert.

"Then the Nazis would have a human shield!"

"Exactly."

"Ostensibly, then, the British would have to invade some other more hazardous location. Should please the Nazis," grinned Karl. "One more question: To what Nazi will this suggestion to build a concentration camp on the French coast be directed, and who will do the presentation?"

"That's two questions."

"So I fudged a little."

Albert continued, "I'm not sure yet to whom our story will ultimately be presented. It will be about two years before this will have to be done anyway. But I can tell you the technique we hope to use successfully. Ego will be our ally. Some underling on good terms with his immediate superior will comment something like this: 'I was thinking about what we discussed several weeks ago. Your idea about putting a concentration camp on the French coast really sounds good.' Then he reiterates the advantages. That officer didn't really think of the plan, but he's willing to take credit for it."

"And that underling is one of our men," interrupted Karl. "That superior officer in turn tells his superior until it gets up to, or maybe just close to, Hitler himself."

"All this time Martin is tracing the progress of the plan idea, keeping his foot in the door for a position as death-squad leader."

Kristine's first response from the "mystery letter" came from Sol Rothsmann. Not only was he intrigued by the perceived challenge, but also suspected it may be some sort of test sent by British Intelligence, an organization to which he had always wanted to belong.

It took him somewhat longer to "decode" than he had anticipated, then smacked his forehead with the palm of his hand once he discovered its simplicity. With a smile on his face he posted the mail gram, wondering what was next.

Wally Fournier was puzzled by the aura of mystery around the card. He had never been the recipient of such an unusual approach to gain his attention. Then, dipping into his memory, he tried, unsuccessfully, to connect the name "Koenig" with someone he may have known years earlier.

He almost tossed away the card, and then realized how dull his life had become since his divorce, plus years of being a professor of Engineering at Oxford, teaching the same subject year after year. It took him about a half hour to solve the key. He addressed the mail gram, and then put it in his outgoing box. It sat there for two weeks.

Vance Worthington, a Navy Lieutenant on loan from the U.S. to the British navy, was out to sea when his letter was delivered. Checking his mail when he came ashore three days later, there was nothing in his slot except Kristine's note.

Funny time to be getting a Christmas card, he thought, then smiled broadly when he looked over its contents. The words made no sense, but his curiosity was piqued. Curiously, Vance was the only one to receive the note who felt there was something genuine behind its author.

March. With the three mailgrams now in hand, Kristine put together another note in turkey German, for the three:

Tarpime tarpo rarpevarpeal arpour crarpy farpor harpelp. Plarpan farpor arpa thrarpee darpay starpay. Brarping farpisharping garpear. (Time to reveal our cry for help. Plan for a three-day stay. Bring fishing gear.)

More, in English. We will pick you up at airport. My husband claims to know one of you, so you shouldn't get stranded. Enclosed in the letter was a round-trip ticket from London to Frankfurt, back to London, with departure and arrival times arranged to fall on a weekend.

.

London. It was a half hour before boarding time. Worthington and Fournier were waiting at the airport, thinking essentially the same thing: I'm beginning to feel very foolish about now, and it could be very dangerous once I get to Stuttgart. Maybe I'm the only one signed up for this. Neither one knew the other was only three seats away.

When boarding time came, Sol still had not arrived. Vance and Wally had been assigned adjacent seats, still not knowing the other was a fellow traveler and could speak turkey German.

Sol made the plane just in time. The other two had not seen him race for the door. Even as he came down the aisle no one noticed him. Then, standing over his two seated partners he spoke Turkey German: Garpentarplmarpen, arpare yarpou garpoarping marpy warpay. (Gentlemen, are you going my way?)

Vance immediately stood up to greet Sol, whom he had met two years earlier. Recognizing the turkey German, Wally had a strong hunch that they were heading to the same place, so he threw out a line in turkey German: Yarpou tarpwo tarpurkarpeys. Garpet tarpakarpen arpin tarpoo. (You two turkeys get taken in too.) Sol and Vance burst out laughing as the stewardess signaled Sol to take his seat.

Fournier, who had no idea who their host was going to be, introduced himself. The trio engaged in small talk for about half the flying time. Then it became a guessing game as to what was in store for them when they got to Stuttgart.

Fournier was a hail-fellow-well-met sort of individual. Everyone liked him—mostly because he generally agreed with whomever was talking, didn't make waves, was easy to please, and never got in the way. He has no children.

Early in his professorship, Fournier was strict and thorough. He was short of stature, but cast a big shadow. As time went by, however, he became slipshod, drank somewhat to excess, and ultimately was divorced by his wife. Although his students loved him, subconsciously he knew he needed to reverse his present course. Maybe this would be an adventure, one he sorely needed.

Lt. Vance W. Worthington, a graduate of the academy, came from a long line of navy men, and always wanted a career in the military. Tall, with jet-black hair, and a slightly bent nose from playing football, Worthington looked like the typical naval officer. Although a by-the-book officer, he will use his good judgment to accomplish a borderline action.

He met his wife on an earlier tour in England, and then took her back to the states to get married. They have a three-year-old son.

A young army captain at the end of the big war, the title "captain" has always stuck with Solomon Rothsmann. Sol was born into money, but he never flaunted it. Au contraire, he went out of his way to almost deny it. Because of his wealth, most onlookers had him figured as a playboy; he wasn't married, nor had any children. The truth be known, he was a homebody. What he really wanted was to work in Army Intelligence, something his money couldn't buy. Rothsmanns banks are in London, Paris, and Vienna.

Frankfurt. Albert was waiting at the airport when the group's plane rolled in to Frankfurt. Fournier, Steller's professor at college, easily recognized Albert. It had been only six years since his graduation at Oxford. Still, Wally was totally shocked to see that someone he knew was behind this mystery scheme. Capt. Sol and Vance each breathed a silent sigh of relief, and introduced themselves to Karl. Albert and Wally's apparent friendship lent an aura of legitimacy to the venture.

"We could have taken the flight from here to Stuttgart, said Albert, "but I wanted to show off our new Autobahn. Besides, I don't think you would have enjoyed the flight this time of year. A bit bumpy going over the mountains. I can get my car up to 160 kilometers if you like. You'll hardly notice it."

"No thanks," Fournier was quick to respond. "One hundred and twenty will do quite nicely thank you."

Sol objected. As most of the roads in England are curvy and narrow, he had little opportunity to do much speed driving. He wanted to go fast.

After all the bags were put into the trunk and strapped to the car top, Albert spoke up to ask if the group would like, on the way to the house, to hear a briefing on the purpose of the meeting. A resounding "yes" from each member gave Albert the stage.

He went back to the beginning—Karl's early suspicions of his possessing Roh-Eh Hanoled; his ability to see into the future along with some examples to verify it; Martin Zoner's witnessing euthanasia; and suspicions of gas chambers and cremation; Anti-Semitism on the increase and becoming more brutal; the voice of God heard through the mouth of Kristine; and, that Karl and Albert were going to come to the aid of the Jews. God had promised to help.

"Pheew," Fournier whistled, "pretty heavy stuff!"

As Albert pulled his Opel onto the driveway, Fournier looked at his watch and commented, "I thought you said it was about 195 Kilometers to Stuttgart?"

"It is," assured Albert.

"But my watch..."

"I was going a bit over 165 kilometers most of the way. Rides nice, eh!"

Just shaking their heads, the group unpacked the car and followed Albert into the house. "I could do with a spot of brandy," said Wally, "haven't motored quite that fast before."

Kristine and Karl came into the parlor as Albert was pouring a stiff one for Fournier. Karl then performed introductions. Kristine's handshake was that of a child greeting a grandparent. She hadn't forgotten Wally's prior seniority on Albert. Karl shook hands warmly, knowing that these men may well become important links in the project.

Kristine had made some treats, in case the men were hungry. They were starved but passed on the brandy.

"So, you're the man with the shivers?" Fournier said to Karl tactlessly.

Albert, about that time having his own case of the shivers, chimed in before Karl had a chance to speak, averting a rare view of Karl's temper. "Yes, he's our man."

Fournier, realizing his faux pas, immediately apologized for being so crude.

"Quite all right," assured Karl. "The situation is a bit unbelievable. What I have always believed is that a few hours pursuing the wily German Brown clears the mind and strengthens a friendship. Anyone here want to beg off tomorrow morning's action?"

Sol raised a feeble hand. "I've never been fishing, but I'd like to tag along to get better acquainted with the boys."

Kristine was up at 5 a.m., fixing breakfast for the men. It was still dark as they left the house. The sun was still at the top of the pines when their car pulled into an area next to the stream, but it was light enough to begin walking the banks.

Karl wasn't much of an outdoorsman either, so he and Sol were content to just make idle conversation, but stay away from the fishing lines and flies whistling overhead. Karl was a bit disappointed. He had expected Sol to ask at least a couple of questions.

Around noon Karl told the sportsmen it was time to pull in their lines. Not much good fishing for the rest of the day, but plenty of time for a good lunch. Good thing, Albert was going to reveal his plan. Right after lunch Albert began:

"Gentlemen, here are our needs: First, financing, second, a team of experts, one for each facet of the operation; third, someone to coordinate and ramrod the operation; fourth, a name, someone respected who can pull a lot of strings; then, most important, a plan of action."

Albert asked the men to keep an open mind. All the pieces will fit, but not necessarily in chronological order. He took the group through the exact plan that he had earlier revealed to Karl: The underwater tunnel from Calais to Dover; the partially finished resort buildings; the owners in on the scheme, forced to sell to us; a mock gassing and cremation area hidden below the eating hall; then the holding area from which prisoners escape to England.

"While all the construction is going on," revealed Albert, "I will be selling the Nazis on the idea of a privately operated concentration camp for the sole purpose of killing and cremating Jews. And the coupe de grace: We hand pick all personnel. The whole operation is controlled by us."

There was another big side benefit. Because the resort was to be built right on the beach, occupying about 20 miles of beach front, the Allies wouldn't dare invade there for fear of killing innocent prisoners. This could be of immeasurable benefit to the Germans, as could the seaplane base it could provide them.

Not one question was asked from start to finish, so intent was the group on hearing a plan so audacious. This is precisely why some secretly felt it might work, except for the tunnel part and, if things fail to develop as anticipated, one could just walk away. No one gets hurt, including the bank.

"Do you really think this plan will work?" asked Sol. "I like the idea that the participants are all our own men, that we control our own destiny, and that there is a 'human shield factor' the Germans would buy."

Personal thoughts were rudely jolted when a deep voice sounded.

"Kristine!...Kristine!" The room went silent!

"Here I am, Lord!"

"You did well. These are the men I wanted! You acted wisely in your method of gathering them."

All was silent, just as it was when God's voice was heard earlier. Sol looked questioningly at Karl.

"That was for real, Sol. No gimmicks. Did you notice Kristine's lips? In perfect sync with the words uttered by God.

"He speaks to us through Kristine. I didn't think we would witness this phenomenon while we had visitors."

Wally and Vance were still awestruck. They didn't know what questions to ask, except to each other: Did you see that? Did you hear that? There was no question what had occurred.

Albert interrupted the trance, "We really do need your help, and I'll be honest, my biggest problem is with the tunnel, and I believe if Vance, Wally, and I could get our heads together we could solve the problems.

"In time we could contract out most of the work, but this would take time. How many would die in the interim? "Anyway your plane will be leaving at 4 p.m. tomorrow, and I don't want to push your decision. So, let's just get to know each other better and put off any decisions for at least a month. We'll be in touch, for certain. But please feel free to contact us if you need answers."

"Nice try," said Karl as he was scanning next day's newspaper and slurping his morning cup of coffee. He is especially fond of rubbing Albert the wrong way when things aren't going particularly well.

"Is this why you invited me over for coffee this morning? To insult me!"

"Insult you? I am giving you a pat on the back when I say, 'Nice try,' really! Besides, I wanted to point out a small article in today's paper about a Norwegian scientist by the name of Oskar Dvergsdahl who has invented something called 'plastics.' Some sort of building material. It might replace some metals. It is supposed to be very strong, yet light in weight for its specific gravity."

Not really paying attention, Albert mumbled something unintelligible, thanked Karl for the coffee, and went home to do his weekend chores. An hour later he ran back to Karl's kitchen to ask if he could read that article on plastics.

"This could be the answer to my biggest problem in tunnel construction," Albert panted. "I need more information. Actually I'll need samples of the plastic. I'll write a letter asking for some samples, and enclose 50 Deutsche Marks for mailing and handling."

His mailing address was unknown, so the letter was sent to the newspaper, and asked that it be forwarded to Dvergsdahl. It read as follows:

Oskar Dvergsdahl:

I am a representative of an anonymous group of investors wishing to investigate a substance, which would compete with steel as a building material.

The name of Oskar Dvergsdahl, along with a few others, came up as a potential supplier. We will need the material within 24 months, so your research and development time is limited. We will require a substantial amount, in the neighborhood of 5300 tons. I plan to vacation most of this summer, visiting some of your competitors in the interim. I would like to visit your plant, say mid-June, test the material, and consider your proposal, cost wise.

Respectfully requested, etc. etc., Albert Steller, using his home address.

May. Oskar was so delighted to get a response from the newspaper article that he express mailed some samples of articles made from his plastic.

Karl was even more delighted to get the samples so quickly. Albert was ecstatic because the material may prove to be just what he needed. He began immediately testing the items.

One sample resembled a discus. Albert took a hammer and struck it—first lightly, then harder and harder. The dents were barely noticeable. The baton, about three inches in diameter, was laid over a six-inch gap in a brick pile. Albert repeated the ever-increasing series of blows. No bend in the baton. He put both articles into a bucket of seawater he had been using for another experiment and left them for a week with no signs of damage.

He could hardly contain his excitement as he waited for the week to pass. He could wait no longer, so he sent a wire to Wally saying he was taking the noon flight to London this Saturday and pleaded with him meet the plane and keep the day open. He had just found the solution to his problem with the tarpunnarpel (tunnel), hoping to not reveal anything to snooping eyes. It would be great if Vance could be there also.

Wally thought, with the tone of the wire gram, Albert's discovery must be more than just ho hum. Wally would have picked him up even if it were just for a game of golf or for friendship's sake.

Vance was hesitant to spend the day away from his family, but agreed with Wally that with the effort Karl and Albert have put into this project, it must be of some importance and have some legitimacy. Wally gave Vance the directions to his office laboratory, and implored him to come by if he at all could, anytime after 2:00 p.m.

Albert had put the plastic samples in his carry-on bag, which he kept on his lap, clutching it as if he were carrying the formula for gold. He kept taking out the baton, scrutinizing it, then putting it back in the bag. His actions were so obvious even Dr. Watson would conclude that Albert was nursing something of value.

Vance was at the front door of the lab by 1:45, when Albert and Wally arrived. Jokingly he looked at his watch, frowning, and asked what kept them so long. That said, the group had a good chuckle, sat around the lab table, and urged Albert to "show the goods."

"Before I do," he explained, "I need to review the tunnel's components, so that you can understand why I am so excited about plastic. Please be patient, the facts are a bit boring at first, but they need some explanation.

"We're looking at 34 kilometers of walking under water without getting drowned. We need a canopy to walk under. Made of what? Wood, iron, rubber? I finally decided on tin, specifically a Quonset hut. Just like you see on every army base.

"Cover it inside, outside, and underneath with this plastic material, and we have one unit of our tunnel.

"How many do we need? If we limit the length of each to 50 feet, then we need 2218 units. I think 50 feet is about as long a unit as a crew of workmen can efficiently handle, because they are going to have to slide the end of one slightly undersized unit about three feet into a regular sized one, then slide the end of a standard size unit over the other end of that same smaller unit. We should now have three attached and bolted units in a row. Keep repeating this for another 2,215 times, and we've reached Calais, assuming, of course, we started in Dover and took a straight line."

Albert could see the two were getting restless, so decided to let them examine the plastic discus and baton while he continued to renew the details.

Before the units were shoved into the water, the front end of the leading unit would be enclosed all the way to Calais. The trailing units would be on land. If they continued to "launch" three units per day, always keeping the trailing units ashore, it would take two years to reach the French shoreline. The workers would be sheltered inside the tunnel all the way.

Figuring a "net after alterations" 8x8x50 unit, we would need to bend inward the bottom four feet of each unit's side so that the ends would meet and be welded together. A wooden floor would then be slid inside each unit to provide the escapees a firm, solid surface to walk on.

Launching the units would involve something pulling the lead unit, at selected intervals, along the route to Calais. Its construction would need to be extra strong. A 34-kilometer wench would not be impossible. But, hopefully we could enlist the aid of one of our subs for a tug most of the way.

"Now for the plastic." Albert finally opened some eyes. "The earlier used tin would rust before we got the tunnel complete. I've obviously been aware of this all along, and have been looking for something like plastic. Now we can cover each unit, top to bottom, inside and out, with a tough waterproofing that not only keeps the water out, but can take some punishment too."

They now have much information to gather, like how thick does the plastic need to be? Does seawater affect it? How is the material applied?

Too many questions, but not enough answers. There didn't seem to be any choice but see Oskar and get the grand tour. Wally asked to be counted in on the trip, and then indicated his willingness to lend any available time he had to working on Albert and Karl's project...i.e., to join up.

Vance wasn't ready to commit as fully as Wally had, but wanted to make that trip to Oslo as long as it was for no more than a week.

Albert sent a wire gram to Oskar stating their desire to visit his facility. Within two hours his answer came, encouraging them to come right away, as another party wanted to see it also in about two weeks. Albert grinned at Oskar's response. Both of us knew he hadn't had a nibble.

June. Oslo. Because of a storm over Oslo in mid flight, the trio's plane was diverted to Bergen, on Norway's west coast. Albert phoned Oskar on the delay, and that they would overnight there. They arrived in Oslo late the next afternoon.

A giant of a man, about six foot six, with stooped shoulders ambled toward them, arms swinging loosely at his side, and slightly in back of him. His stature was reminiscent of Bigfoot. He had a touch of gray hair and looked to be in his mid-fifties, and straight off the farm.

"How did you boys like Bergen?" asked Dvergsdahl?" Without waiting for a response, he picked up all three of their bags as if they were feather pillows "I was born and grew up there. A very friendly town. Great fishing and the weather, surprisingly calm."

Egad! Who wound up this chap? thought Wally. Then answering his host, "Didn't have an awfully long time to tour the town, but what we saw to and from the airport looked charming. By the by, what do your friends call you?"

"Oskar. Please call me Oskar. Everyone calls me Oskar. It's so much simpler to say, and spell, than Dvergsdahl."

"Alright, Oskar it is," agreed Wally, already taking charge of the conversation. "I'm Wally, these are Vance and Albert."

Oskar shuffled the bags around to free up his right hand, then, shaking each hand, gave Wally cause to quietly mouth "ouch!" It was five in the afternoon, ample time to take at least a cursory look at Oskar's facility. There wasn't much to view: A large vat sitting on a cradle, with pouring spout and handle; four steel dies from about six to fifteen feet long; a railway spur; wooden platform, and some dark gray objects

"Very interesting," said Vance with a questioning look on his face. "We'll be seeing the rest tomorrow?"

"This *is* the rest!" Oskar stammered. "This *is* tomorrow!"

"Well," said Albert, undaunted. There is still much to do tomorrow. May we go to our lodging?"

"Of course," said Oskar eagerly. "I've arranged for you to stay at the Scandia Lodge, about five miles from here. I'll come by for you at sunup. That would be around four a.m. I've a lot to show you."

"Gentlemen," announced Wally after the boys checked into their rooms. "We may have stepped into the proverbial pile of dog doo. How could anyone have referred to our provincial host as a 'scientist in the forefront of plastics research?' "

"Hold on," cautioned Albert, "Where there's smoke there's fire. Let's withhold judgment until we see what Oskar has to show us." Vance agreed. "If we've come this far, we should finish the research."

At four o'clock the next morning Oskar was banging on the boys' doors. One of them complained that he's already gone through boot camp. Finally after a quick breakfast, and a chilly ride, it was 5:30 a.m. when Oskar's truck pulled into his plant.

He lit a fire under the vat, and began tossing in what appeared to be large gray bricks until it was about half full "We add about a gallon each of three other ingredients then we should be ready to pour the mix into a die, "It takes about 30 minutes to liquefy," explained Oskar.

"This may surprise you, Oskar, but we won't be pouring your mix into a die," stated Vance." Do you have anything that resembles a paint spray gun?"

"Oh yes," replied Oskar, "I bought one not two weeks ago. Great invention. But if you're thinking of using my mix with a spray gun, it may not be able to handle the viscosity of the plastic. Promise you'll pay for my spray gun, and you can experiment with it on my back wall all you wish."

The mix finally liquefied. Vance was nervously shaking the gun to keep the mix as liquid as possible. He finally aimed at the wall, and pulled the trigger. Nothing came out. Oskar was mortified.

"Don't feel bad, Oskar. Evidently this gun wasn't built to accommodate your liquid plastic," consoled Albert. "We came ready to run some tests."

They cut the mix to one-half water, with only a thin spray dribbling out. Then, two-thirds water. Too thin!

Oskar suggested that the group go for lunch. "They ate at what appeared to be Oskar's favorite watering hole. As they sat down, Oskar asked if any of the three spoke Norwegian.

"Oh, a couple of words," said Albert.

"Well, speak up," Wally challenged.

"Skagerrak and Kattegat. A couple of words in Norwegian," said Albert, smiling. "They are the names of sea channels in the North Sea."

Then it was back to the plant. With little success the group stayed at Oskar's plant until darkness had nearly crept in. Disappointed, the trio had Oskar take them to their lodge.

They plotted and "what iffed" for three hours, then decided to sleep on it. Oskar came by at the usual time, and seemed somewhat closed-mouthed about the prior day's work. When they got to the plant, Oskar reached into the back of his truck and said, "Here, try this."

The spray gun was three times the size of the other. One end of a garden hose was screwed into the top back-end of the gun, and the other end dipped inside a 55-gallon drum full of his plastic, liquefied.

"Now try it," said Oskar, proudly. "It adjusts to a width of from two to six inches, depending on how wide you want to lay it on." Wally grabbed the device and began spraying Oskar's back wall. It worked perfectly and, as promised, to a width of from two to six inches."

Vance would never again see Albert's mouth as wide open. "How?" And before Albert could finish his question, Oskar explained, "I took my store-bought paint sprayer apart to see how it worked, and then just duplicated it to a larger size with bits of this, pieces of that, and an old five-gallon milk can. I did have to cut the mix about 10 percent. But I don't think it will appreciably change the integrity of the formula. By golly, I think it'll work."

The trio tried various thicknesses, waited for the plastic to dry, and applied a high-pressure hose to the whole wall. Not one whisper of plastic would wash off. Next they tried hammer and chisel. A direct cut did little damage, except for the two-inch thickness. Chipping at an angle did some damage, but not at the thicker applications.

"Can you boys tell me what you plan to paint with my plastic?" The three glanced at each other. Finally Vance explained, "It's hush-hush, Oskar. A small group of entrepreneurs have a specific project in mind and have combined efforts to manufacture certain," he paused, "things."

"Oh," replied Oskar, a bit disappointed. "I thought it might be something like that, what with an American, an Englishman, and a German in cahoots."

One thing puzzled Albert. The same mix used that morning was again used in the afternoon. How is the pot cleaned out before the substance hardens? The answer he discovered was too simple. It isn't—with heat it re-liquefies. So why does an object made of plastic not re-liquefy, when reheated? Again, he found the answer, which was not so simple. Some kind of chemical change occurs when it is iced down. After icing, it won't melt.

"I suppose Oskar just stumbled across these phenomena?" posed Wally.

"Guess I'm just clumsy," grinned Oskar. "I grew up in an area surrounded by seven mountains. In a valley between one of these I ran across some gray, gooey seepage covering about fifty square yards of earth. When I got home Mama about skinned me alive. It was near impossible to wash off— more like peel off. I began experimenting, adding this and that until, voila, plastic!

"Would you like to get the most disagreeable part of negotiations over with now and discuss product price?" asked Oskar. "And no sense including a volume discount, I can crank it out only so fast. How about two cents per pound, we deliver."

"We'll have to consider that a fair price," declared Vance, "we've nothing to compare it to." And speaking of money, how many Krona do we owe you for your 'store-bought' sprayer"?

With no idea where or when money to fund this "pie in the sky" venture was to come, Vance was enthused, convinced there was a more than even chance that they could get the job done, *if* they progressed one step at a time. He pledged to be partner number four.

Next step: Enlist the aid of Capt. Sol Rothsmann.

After receiving a short mail gram from Oslo stating just "Harpoorarpy, harpome arpin tarpwo darpays (Hooray! home in two days), Karl knew exactly what to do. He had had a vision yesterday. Nothing earth shattering, but enough to impress Sol: Another concentration camp is being built in Buchenwald. No one knows about it...yet.

Karl sent a wiregram to Sol, who had already been clued in on Turkey German: Narpew Carponcarpentrarpatarpion carpamp, arpat Barpucharpenwarpald (New concentration camp at Buchenwald). Plan on a visit from me three days hence at 2:00 p.m.

Sol wasn't sure what to make of the message, and the reason for his prediction, so he sent a reply: Okay.

With Karl due in London the next day, Albert's plane from Oslo rolled in around noon. Both started chattering at once, Albert all excited and Karl very serious. He won the battle and immediately informed Albert of his message to Sol, wondering if he had slipped up, or was the hero.

"Karl, you old seer! You did exactly the right thing. We need some immediate funding to put a down payment on the beachfront property in Calais so we can begin construction on the resort. Hopefully, before the note is called we can obtain long term money."

Albert briefed Karl on the Oslo trip on the way back home. He could see why Albert was so energized. Kristine was waiting for him in the kitchen. She didn't want to begin complaining about his constant absence the very minute he arrived home. Her subtle comment, "Mein Liebe, sind sie heute abend frei?"

"Well, of course I'm free this evening," Albert answered. I've been on the go so much these past two years, and I look forward to staying at home and spending some close moments with my wife. I did miss you, you know!"

Next day as Karl's plane was flying over the channel, he looked down at the large expanse of water. Mein Gott! he thought. Our people will be traveling under all this for miles, in a confined space. Himmel, what am I doing promoting this meshuga venture?

"Waitress," Karl said loudly.

Yes sir, what would you like? I'm your stewardess."

"I'd like a beer."

"Any preference?"

"Yes, a beer, I prefer a beer," snapped Karl.

"Yes sir, excuse my misunderstanding. I meant to say what brand of beer would you like?"

"German. Any brand that is German, thank you."

Karl chugged about half his beer, put his head back on the rest, and began reminiscing. How many years has it been since he flew over the channel, only towards Germany? How excited he was. He was going to be a papa! He had a very good paying position, the most beautiful alpine lady in all

Berlin, and he loved his work. Karl was nearly asleep. A voice came, "Honigkuch" (Honey Biscuit). Still in a quiescent state, he answered "Lecker" (Gingersnap); endearing names he and Amy had called each other. His eyes popped open.

"Please fasten your seat belts," the rasping static awakened him rudely. "We'll be landing in London in 15 minutes."

Karl took another gulp of his beer, smiled, and with eyes moistening, thought: It was a good dream.

London. It was about 4 p.m. when Vance arrived at his home. The first thing he did (after greeting his wife with a kiss) was to phone Sol to set up an appointment. Sol realized that his two messages had not been coordinated and thought that as long as Karl was coming at 2 p.m. the next day, Vance may as well be there too.

It was difficult to tell who was most surprised when Karl's taxi and Vance's car showed up at almost the same time. Sol, knowing the two had not had a chance to discuss the Oslo trip, was standing on the front steps with a wide grin on his face. He posed the inevitable question, "How was the flight?" Vance was so pumped up he would have said "great," even if the plane had flown upside down all the way. Grumpy Karl just said, "Don't ask!" He was still dreaming of his Amy.

As they walked into Sol's home, Karl noticed a screen with a newsreel-type movie playing. "Oh, it's a W.C. Fields movie, and my favorite line is coming up. May I watch for a minute?" Without a yes/no given, all three turned their attention to the screen. Enter Fields:

Bartender, bartender, did I drink a $50 bill in booze here last night? The bartender replied, you sure did! Fields is relieved. Thank God, I thought I'd lost it.

It was a good ice breaker. Vance gave Sol a thorough report and answered Sol's even-sometimes-trivial questions. Vance indicated that, even so, he would like to purchase about 2,000 gallons of his mix, along with a specially designed Quonset hut and construct a sample unit.

The 2,000-gallon figure caused Sol to blink, until Vance explained that at two cents per pound the 2,000 gallons would run only $400, and about the same for the Quonset hut. Then, there would be some lumber and miscellaneous materials.

"Do it. I'll pay for it," volunteered Sol. "But don't pick it up. It will be less expensive to have it delivered c.o.d."

"And I know just the place to ship it" said Vance eagerly, "an old closed sailboat repair shop right on the shore, where our tunnel will poke through. If the owner thought there was a chance that we would rent or buy the property, he would allow its use for pennies."

Then Sol asked Karl what he would like to add. "Having not been on the Oslo trip," he explained, "I have heard only sketchy details. I couldn't add anything to what Vance has told you. What I have to offer this august group would be in the area of foreknowledge. My mail gram to you regarding the new concentration camp at Buchenwald is of no immediate use. But when you begin to see foreknowledge save the lives of our Jewish comrades, this kind of information is going to prove to be extremely useful."

Karl then added, "I am very sorry, but I am very tired. May I call my cab?"

"Absolutely not," Sol said emphatically. "You are going to stay in my home this evening. It is the least I can do to reward your devotion."

"I thank you for your hospitality, and ask for one thing— that you check with your associates at British Intelligence tomorrow and ask them why they have not yet discovered what is going on at Buchenwald! Maybe we can chat a bit in the morning. He was then shown to his room. It was enormous, and the furnishings beyond luxurious—velvet curtains around the bed, and gold-plated fixtures in the private bathroom.

After Karl went to bed, Vance and Sol discussed how weary Karl was looking these days. According to Albert, Karl was having more and more "shivers."

"Normally Karl would have talked much more about his vision of Buchenwald," explained Vance. "But I suspect he wanted to 'save it' for you. You know, as 'leverage' to use when he wants to ask you a favor."

"Which is?"

"I'm guessing, mind you, but he would like you to introduce 'the boys' to someone to financially back our project. He is hesitant to come right out and ask, because he doesn't want to take advantage of what he feels is a growing friendship. I suppose we all feel that way. None of us is experienced in obtaining a loan with nothing down, although we could use our pension funds as earnest money and hope to find that 'angel' in the interim. Incidentally, before I forget. I decided to toss my hat in with the boys. Believe me, if I didn't believe our project was doable, I'd be running the other way as fast as possible."

"Damn," Sol said under his breath. "I didn't realize you lads were as serious about this project as it now appears you are. And I can see you are also anxious to get home to your family. I appreciate your coming by. I'll talk more to Karl in the morning."

Breakfast, prepared by Sol's "man's man," was fit for royalty. There were so many items Karl couldn't sample even half of them. He had to finally say, "I give up."

Sol smiled and suggested they retire to the smoking room. It was spotless and had a roaring fire in a castle-sized fireplace. All that was missing was a Great Dane lying on the hearth.

Rothsmann began the conversation abruptly, "May I be Frank?"

"Yes if I can be Karl." He answered instantly, and then paused. "Sorry, conditioned response."

"Quite all right, my man. Your penchant for humor has preceded you. But for now let me be the devil's advocate." Carrying on, he argued. "I'm not in agreement about Hitler conquering Europe. I can see where he may annex Austria.

Possible also would be freeing German citizens living in the Czech Republic."

"I agree," interrupted Karl. "This will happen within the next 12 months. A few months later your Prime Minister will cave in to Hitler, who will promise no more invasions."

"Wait," insisted Sol. "How can you be so sure?"

"I can't be 'so sure,' but I have a pretty strong feeling."

"All your activity and planning, based on feelings?" questioned Sol, shaking his head. It's hard to believe Vance has just joined you chaps."

"I think Vance's motivation is occupational as well as benevolent. He has witnessed what this plastic can do. He may just be looking at his position in it after the war. His foresight is of a different ilk than mine, but foresight nevertheless."

"All right, Laddie Bucko, I'll tell you what I would like to do. I don't feel the need to jump aboard your project, but I'll keep an eye on you fellows. If I can be of any assistance, including an introduction to whomever I know, by all means give me a ring."

Vance was waiting in the circular driveway in his car as Karl and Rothsmann came out the front door. He gestured for Karl to get into the car. Shaking hands with Sol first, Karl nodded, and then sat in the front passenger seat. He knew navy protocol had the highest-ranking officer in the rear/right seat, and was respecting the tradition.

They didn't speak for several blocks. Finally Vance mentioned the humorous W.C. Fields film clip they saw the evening before.

Karl added, with a trace of mist in his eyes, "He always gives me a lift.

"Have a rough ride over the channel?"

"Something like that!"

For some reason, crossing the channel would bring Karl's memories of Amy back to plague him. He was still on the outs with God. Looking upward, he pleaded that he could use a little help right now.

As Vance watched Karl's plane disappear, he was beginning to wish this whole project were a figment of Karl's imagination. 'A piece of undigested meat,' as Scrooge put it. He was becoming fearful of the impact upon his life that this attempted underwater rescue would have.

Karl, watching London fade into the darkness, almost wished his efforts were only a figment of his imagination, 'a piece of undigested porridge.'

Late the next day a wire came from Captain Sol in Turkey German:

Barpucharpenwarpald arpit arpis. Plarpease tarpake marpy carpongrarpatyarpularpatarpiarpons (Buchenwald it is. Please take my congratulations).

It took British intelligence eleven days to discover what Karl "felt" in two. Vance will be pleased, as it will give him bragging rights over Sol. All Karl had to say was, "he'll learn."

A week later, to everyone's surprise, Sol called Vance to set up a meeting that included Wally. He felt it was just a matter of time before "the four musketeers" were going to seek help from Sol in getting an introduction to the chief loan officer at Rothsmann's. Before this comes to pass, however, Sol indicated he would like to spend a few days with Wally and Albert at Stuttgart. He felt comfortable that he knew Karl and Vance well enough to recommend them. It took awhile to arrange schedules.

September. Stuttgart. Albert drove to the Frankfurt airport to pick up Wally and Sol. He wanted again to show off Germany's autobahn. "Very impressive highway," Sol remarked, "but how do you keep from running into each other, driving on the wrong side of the road as you do?"

Albert was up to the "quick comeback" challenge. "Nothing to worry about, just so long as we're all going the wrong way at the same time." Karl was waiting at the end of the driveway when Albert's car pulled in. He and Sol shook hands firmly.

Kristine, as always, was a bit shy when greeting a stranger. Again came the voice inside her head, "Chin up Zucker. Be Proud!"

Sensing this, Sol said, "The fame of your strudels has preceded you. I won't leave for home until I've tried some."

Kristine smiled. This time her head more erect. Wally also smiled and thought to himself, this Rothsmann chap, not a bad sort.

After dinner, which included strudels, the men retired to the parlor for cigars and brandy. Sol had something to say, that he holds the greatest of respect and admiration for what the group has undertaken. He would be honored to be included in such an august group, but on a more limited basis. He used an analogy of the four musketeers taking the initiative in engaging the enemy, while he would be on call when needed.

Much was discussed and decided upon in a short two days. Of primary importance was to raise money for the venture. This meant, ultimately, a session with Rothsmann's Empire and a meeting with Winston Churchill. Rothsmann's help was absolutely critical. Churchill's was extremely desirable. Sol agreed to be in on both meetings, but primarily to establish conference dates and provide introductions.

The group decided to approach Churchill first. Their goal was to get Winnie to give his secret blessing to the venture and some manpower when available.

Although Churchill himself had gone to Rothsmann's of London for small loans from time to time, and Sol had a nodding acquaintance with him, he proved to be difficult to pin down. Finally, Sol was able to reach him. Winnie was amiable and agreed to give Sol "and friends" a tentative audience in January.

Sol decided to use the waiting time as profitably as possible and do some sleuthing in preparation for the hoped-for meeting with his relatives. To his shock he discovered that one of the oldest Rothsmann's branches, Vienna, was going to close in 1938, next year! A wise move, as a takeover by Hitler was inevitable.

As a potential source for funding, the group's most promising just dried up. Then, hearing an offhand comment by a cousin, he went to Paris to scope out Claude Rothsmann.

Paris. An evening on the town with Claude provided much useful information. He wasn't bank president, yet, but his predecessor was failing rapidly. Claude also expressed many times his affection for his people. He should be most receptive to the group's mission.

A letter from Oskar came to Karl inquiring about the group's decision to use, or not use, his plastic material. Karl, via letter, reviewed with him the status of the agreed upon agenda, and indicated that funding of the project was imminent. Please start stockpiling. He concluded with the classic, "We'll be in touch."

1938

The Arrow Let Fly

The year 1937 had been fairly uneventful insofar as Nazi infringement on Jewish citizens' rights was concerned. Hitler's fist-in-the-air pronouncements about Lebensraum (living space, land in Poland and Russia that he thought belonged to the German people by right of their supremacy), fell silent. The bow had been drawn. In 1938 the arrow will be let fly!

As expected, Churchill contacted Sol to defer the tentative January meeting. It was rescheduled for early March.

Stuttgart. When Karl got wind of the delay, his comment was not a surprise to Albert. "That's one you owe us, Winnie! And speaking of Churchill, I heard a supposedly true story about him. He was having a drink at some mucky-muck party, when a woman came up to him and said, 'Mr. Churchill, you are drunk!' To which he responded, 'Yes, I am, and you madam, are ugly. However, when I awake in the morning I will be sober, and you Madam, will still be ugly.' "

Karl continued, "Last year I rarely shivered. This year already I'm tingling. Something is coming up. I've taken a two-year sabbatical and so far I've hardly gotten out of the house. When is all my 'coordination of activities' going to begin?"

"From your present tingling feelings, it would appear you'll be having some activity, including your meeting with Churchill," observed Albert. "Somehow I believe your March meeting will take place."

London. March. The Churchill meeting started with introductions. Karl had been voted beginning speaker. Others came in as the situation seemed right. They had 30 minutes to state their case. The boys stated it in an orderly and aggressive manner. Churchill was on the edge of his chair, dumbfounded by their daring plan. The meeting lasted three hours, unprecedented in light of Winnie's customary toddy about this time of day.

But, Winnie turned them down. "It seems that your successes are part and parcel of Karl's unusual abilities. I know others in your group are convinced of Mr. Koenig's remarkable ability, but I will need proof for myself.

Karl responded by asking Churchill to give him one day to see more clearly what was behind a growing feeling he has. It's like a cold coming on.

"By all means, give it a go," Churchill said with enthusiasm. "Despite an appearance of skepticism, I'm extremely interested in your abilities. But, you must understand my position. Please telephone me at my office anytime tomorrow. I can break away long enough to take your call."

Muttering under his breath, Karl took a quick look at the ceiling and said: "All right, God, you got me into this mess. Now get me out of it. P.S. I *might* consider coming back to the flock."

That evening Karl was struggling to come up with specifics. All he could muster was a tingling spine. He thought back to late 1936 to remember his long-term predictions: Hitler will take small bites to gain confidence, first on small nearby countries, then on larger ones, and all to the East. Then, the dam broke.

"That's it!" yelled Karl. Waking up Sol, and Albert, "Hitler is soon going to annex Austria. Shortly after, Austria will be ordered by Hitler to expropriate all Jewish property." A flood of other visions whisked through Karl's head, but they were of little consequence, and soon forgotten.

By this time Sol and Albert were knocking on Karl's door, checking to see if he was all right. Karl cleared up their concerns, then went on to describe what he felt was coming up in a bit over a week. Eleven days later word came out: In the Anschluss, Germany annexes Austria."

April. Karl would not be in London to "remind" Winnie of the event, so Wally was chosen to call and leave the message with Churchill's secretary. She confirmed that he had heard the news.

As they spoke, Churchill was in the Lord of the Admiralty room, trying to determine how they suggest the Prime Minister respond. Hitler has thus far achieved his goals by using his main weapon, the threat of force. They resolved to keep this fact in mind when giving their recommendations.

Karl's predictions were becoming mundane: Anti-Jewish laws about to be proclaimed in Hungary; German-Jewish physicians are permitted to treat Jewish patients only, but very little of significance other than potential inmates at the new "spa." He couldn't seem to turn off the switch.

Churchill was scheduled to attend a conference, called by Franklin Roosevelt at Evian-les-Bains for two hard weeks. Representatives from 32 nations will discuss to which of these countries the mass outflow of Jews could be dispersed.

By the time group members exchanged wires and letters, the conference was over, a miserable failure. Discussions not only failed to increase options for fleeing Jews, these countries began to add even more restrictions. Who wanted a host of penniless people storming their gates?

Winnie had no more than gotten home when he dictated a letter to the "Musketeers," via Wally: "Gentlemen: You may be our only hope to find an answer to the plight of the Hebrews. It seems that forced deportation has become Germany's new program of solving the Jewish problem. Wealthy Jews are being stripped of all assets In order to pay for deportation costs of the poor Jews. All are leaving Germany penniless, and Nazi coffers are bulging. For my permanent records, send me a letter and review again how you feel I may be of assistance."

Karl quickly contacted the others with the request that he be allowed to reply, by courier, to Winnie's letter. They approved. He wrote:

"Prime Minister Churchill: I'm two years ahead of my salutation to you. And yes, it will come to pass. I was told several years ago that I have friends in high places. Time will surely tell, but even now, you are in a position to pull the kind of strings necessary for our group to skirt a few roadblocks.

"Mainly we need manpower and some equipment. It would be understood that your name could never be used. We will contact you or your agent through some prearranged basis and explain what it is. If you can help, excellent. If not, we would understand. If your answer is yes, then don't scratch your nose."

Winnie could hardly stop laughing as he continued to read the letter. Karl would get approval by default whether or not Winnie did or didn't scratch.

"When we meet with Rothsmann, hopefully Claude, to seek financing, we would like to tell him that the Prime Minister of England has given us his support. And, of course, we would like his assurance of secrecy on this information. Inasmuch as you are not yet Prime Minister, he will think we refer to Neville Chamberlain, who, if questioned, will deny any knowledge of the matter. You remain clean.

Incidentally, regarding the upcoming meeting between the Nazis, England, France and a few smaller countries I can't give you many specifics, but this I can tell you that Hitler will out-and-out lie when he promises to cease invading these smaller countries. He already has plans to occupy Czechoslovakia.

Your Prime Minister will believe Hitler because he wants to believe, and will make some kind of pronouncement that 'we will now have peace.' The fact that Chamberlain was so taken in will bode well for your replacing him. Congratulations!"

Sol was delighted with the results of Karl's exchange of letters with Churchill. He immediately sent the following wire to Claude Rothsmann at the Paris office: Those to which I referred in our last meeting (night out on the town) would now like an audience. Would prefer three alternative dates so the entire group could be in attendance.

Getting their heads together, the group decided on the October 20 alternate. Karl had been having some very strong shivers and felt that Claude, like all others, would want to see proof of his prognostications. Karl felt that the event would be coming up a month or so before the end of 1938. Time was getting short.

October. Stuttgart. Sol, Vance, and Wally, who was able to wrangle two days from school, flew to Germany for a rehearsal of the Claude Rothsmann session. Sol, as instructor, took the lead.

"Remember, gentlemen, since 1743 when my great grandfather founded Rothsmann's Empire, it was built and continues to grow on unbending principal: Conservative lending and an abundance of collateral. Even though our request will run counter to what I've just told you, always keep it in mind. Our approach should be threefold:

"First, Claude expressed on numerous occasions his affection for his people. Exploit this. We are doing what no other group is doing...saving as many of his people as possible.

"Second, the fact that England's Prime Minister has given us his support may cause Claude to feel that England may be willing to co-sponsor the event. Try not to be pinned down on the matter.

"Third, this may be one of the few times in history Rothsmann's Empire has engaged in wholesale speculation. Have you chaps ever considered the residual value of your tunnel? After the war is over? My cousin may well want to pay for your whole venture in order to own the tunnel, personally."

Vance chimed in, "I have a difficult time swallowing the idea of a Rothsmann willing to gamble so much money to own a tunnel that may not do the job, may be discovered by the Nazis, or not even be completed."

"A bit of English history," began Sol. "Rothsmann's Empire staked a fortune in loans on the outcome of Britain's war with Napoleon. They did have a bit of an edge when the Empire received news of Wellington's victory at Waterloo before the general public did. We sold. Others followed suit, selling heavily. We bought at the bottom and made over a million pounds profit when the price rebounded."

Karl received another letter from Oskar. Same old inquiry, but a slightly different reply: We are very optimistic we will receive funding by December. Keep stockpiling. We'll pay for what you've done, even if we do it out of pocket.

The trip to Paris was fast approaching. Karl, getting antsy, felt the need to send Claude the following letter:

"My dear Mr. Rothsmann: I am looking forward to our meeting October 20, which your cousin Solomon so kindly arranged. Enclosed is information on some events, which have yet to take place. You may think this strange, but we hope you might feel more inclined to provide funds for a group possessing the advantage of foresight.

"Poland will soon be limiting German Jews from entering their country. The Nazis, in order to beat the deadline will brutally round up thousands of Jews and force them into Poland. Many will not meet the deadline and will simply wander about in no man's land, seeking shelter.

"A young Jew somehow will make his way to Paris and upon learning about the border dispute, shoots a ranking German official. The Nazis will welcome this event as an excuse to reveal some concocted Jewish conspiracy.

"What follows will be bedlam: The worst ever and most blatant attack on Jews.

.   "Goebbels will go on such an anti-Semitic campaign that the resulting public outcry against the Jews will see store windows smashed, shops looted, synagogues burned, Jewish people mugged, plundered and otherwise mistreated. The vandalism will be a prelude to many thousands of Jewish men, mostly mid-upper and upper class, arrested throughout the German Reich and sent to concentration camps. Adding insult to injury, Jews will be forced to pay an unrealistic amount for damages done to them by these vandals."

Paris. Wally was unable to take the needed travel time to make the Paris meeting. Sol chose not to attend, feeling his cousin might sense pressure. Albert, Karl, and Vance had readied themselves to meet Claude.

Albert rented an apartment nearby for Kristine so she would feel safer, would not be alone, and could cook for the men.

Apprehension hung like fog in the reception area as the three waited. This was it! All the hours and efforts spent were now on the line.

Rothsmann began, "I received the thorough review of your predicted upcoming events, Mr. Koenig. If the picture you painted unfolds as was previewed by me, I will indeed be influenced regarding the amount and terms of your loan.

The trio looked at each other but said nothing. Who had said anything about a loan? Without blinking an eye, Karl jumped in, "The subject of my glances into the future is the present and worsening plight of Jews presently in Germany. Our mission is to save as many Jews as possible by providing an escape to England."

"Yes, so I have been informed," said Rothsmann dryly. Then, without the hint of a smile added, "A very altruistic effort. And just how do you plan to affect this exodus?"

With lessons in the backstroke, you doofus! thought Karl. "By an undersea tunnel. We cannot tell you more nor emphasize too heavily that what we discuss here must remain in the strictest of confidence. The safety of your people hangs in the balance."

Rothsmann, silently, sat slowly swinging his chair side to side, and assured the group, "I understand completely. Confidentiality has always been thoroughly practiced here. Any additional information?"

"Yes," as Albert took his turn. "We have recently had lengthy discussions with a person of considerable importance in England. He has solidly endorsed our cause, promising assistance where it is in his power to render. I cannot reveal his name, but I can say that somewhere in the conversation the title: 'Prime Minister' did come up," explained Albert with a straight face.

"Very impressive! Can you tell me more about this person?"

"We prefer not."

"I understand. Anything else?"

"Yes," said Vance. "The tunnel we will be constructing has an immeasurable residual benefit, particularly, but not necessarily, if Germany loses the war."

Before Vance could continue, Claude, with incredulity said, "Excuse me, but did you say war?"

"Yes sir, and within one year. You can, pardon the pun, put it in the bank!" Then, before Claude could interject another question, challenged him with a question, "Can you imagine the income stream generated by a toll tunnel connecting England with France?"

Rothsmann raised his eyebrows, the first sign of any kind of emotion, followed by a minute of agonizing silence. He finally spoke, "Can you give me your projected costs and the type of collateral you have?"

Again the trio exchanged glances and again Karl took charge. He explained the cost for the tunnel and attendant facilities on the English side of the channel to be about one and a quarter million U.S. dollars. He hesitated a moment to see Rothsmann's reaction. Stoic! At the same time he had to silently come up with some figure for costs on the French side.

He thought to himself: Unfinished resort, fake gas chambers and cremation ovens, etc., then came up with a figure of $200,000 at Calais. For the third time three pair of eyes, trying not to show emotion searched each other.

"Then, rounding up, could we say $1,500,000 U.S. is sufficient for your project?" asked Claude.

The three looked around, shook their heads affirmatively, and, almost in unison said, "Yes. Sounds all right. I agree!" Karl then winced, knowing Rothsmann's next question. "And your collateral?" he asked nonchalantly.

"We are four working men, long on dreams but short on collateral. We are hoping Rothsmann's Empire will fund the venture in return for ownership to the tunnel and accompanying buildings on the English side and facilities on the French side."

No one uttered a sound. You could almost hear the dead breathing in the tomb that enveloped them.

Karl cleared his throat. Then he reviewed the loan advantages to Rothsmann's, emphasizing ownership of the tunnel, which could exceed the money made by his patriarch during the coup at Waterloo.

"Those were the venturesome years," said Claude, nostalgically, and now beginning to think of the respect he would garner with his extended family if this project were a success.

"There's more," said Karl, handing Claude a section of Oskar's plastic, and a hammer. "Try to break this material. We will use it in the building of the tunnel. Just about as hard as Iron, but much, much lighter. There will be many uses for this material someday. Would you like first chance at buying the formula?"

Claude hit the plastic several times, and answered Karl, "Well, I'd have to …" he got no further as Karl lit the fuse.

"And if I can add weight to better ties to England, this office will someday merge with Rothsmann's London, just before Hitler nationalizes it, along with your industrial holdings."

Karl you old devil, Albert thought to himself. You've got more nerve than a knife-thrower's assistant. Vance was smiling noticeably. Claude's mind was racing.

Karl was silently saying: God, I wish you would give advance warning when you are going to put these thoughts in my head. I thought we agreed that I would do only forecasts. Kristine would be the conduit for your voice.

Claude had been temporarily mesmerized by Karl's prescient words. Regaining his senses, Claude didn't know whether to be angry or docile. "I'll say this, Herr Koenig; you aren't inclined to mince words. But they ring of the truth, as unpleasant as it has been portrayed. What can I say?"

"A simple 'yes' will do very nicely, Herr Rothsmann."

"I suppose it would, Karl, if I may now call you familiarly. My heart tends to agree, but my head says wait!" He went on, "But I will make you this promise; you will have an answer before year end."

All but Wally decided to stay in Paris to sweat out Claude's decision.

Within a month all three of Karl's prophecies had taken place. All the ruckus caused by the shooting of a German officer now had a name: "Kristallnacht" (Night of Broken Crystal). Gotten Himmel, Claude thought to himself, his predictions came true.

December. Claude Rothsmann again met with the group in his office. Going beyond their best hopes, he consented to a no recourse loan, with the pledging of all things constructed by them as collateral. Funds would be provided on a "no accountability, when needed" basis. A progress report must be provided every six months, and fund disbursement by the bank may be discontinued at any time. Further, the group must arrange, on a best efforts basis, assistance from England whenever possible.

Vance had little time to develop his model unit, even though the materials had been on hand for a month.

He did complete the 8'x50' wooden tunnel floor, then sprayed on the plastic, top, bottom and sides to about a three inch thickness. After the plastic had dried, he took a hammer and chisel to check its durability. A 90 degree strike did little to dent the material, but when hit at an angle it did slice off the top inch of the plastic. He made a mental note to try another inch of plastic—four inches total.

Time ran out before he could attempt to ready the Quonset hut by bending the sides inward until they touched. His swabbies' instructions: Bend the bottom four feet of the Quonset hut inward. A simple enough task for the two weeks Vance was to be in Paris.

After the funding problem was solved, Vance rushed home from Paris, spent two days with his family, then went to the old boathouse and began investigating what his three "borrowed" sailors had gotten done in his absence.

The Quonset hut was a disaster. Where the lower four feet was to be bent inward, it was bent outward. And it wasn't even straight, zigzagging up and down where the bend was supposed to be.

Vance, openly irritated, said "Don't you swabbies know that you have to score metal before bending it?"

"Score?"

"Score! First mark the line where the bend is going to be, then take a sharp metal instrument, like maybe a chisel, and strike fairly hard where the line is. This makes a dent, commonly called a 'score,' and makes it easy to bend the tin. But, I've learned something from all this. Have the Quonset hut manufacturer do the bending. They have the machinery. Meanwhile go home for Christmas."

Then, Vance received a disappointing mail gram from Sol: Arpenjaproy Yarpour varpisarpit Harpome. Narpeed yarpou barpack harpere darpay arpaftarper charpismarpas (Enjoy your visit home. Need you back here day after Christmas).

The first thing Karl did after the meeting with Claude was to call Oskar, hang the French party-line snoops, and told him to ship whatever gray bricks they had stockpiled, then start cranking out more.

Sol also had been busy prior to the Paris meeting. With two-day long negotiations, unbeknownst to the group, he was about to purchase that beachfront property near Calais. It took nearly a day to research exactly who the land belonged to: The French Department of Natural Resources, six hours to locate their office and another hour trying to find out who ran the place.

There was no reception room, so Sol calmly walked into his office and asked what it would cost to get a 99-year lease on the beachfront property (giving him a reasonably close estimate of the exact location).

"Before you quote a price," warned Sol. "I have it on good sources that this area is where the Allied Forces will invade."

"But monsieur, there is no war."

"There will be, and soon!"

"In that case, 100 Franks."

The deal was finalized fifteen minutes later.

Sol had met the trio right after their final meeting with Claude and offered his congratulations, after which he treated the group to dinner and drinks. Now that the search for manpower and money was over, the inevitable thought surfaced: Can we really get an undetermined number of Jews from point A, Germany, to point B, Calais?

Time was of the essence with a new year just three weeks away. The group decided there was no choice but to spend the week between Christmas and New Year in planning, and there in Paris was the logical central location for the meeting. Meanwhile, all but Wally went home for a quick Christmas celebration.

Things were worsening for German Jews. The Nazis had just passed the "Verordnung Zur Ausschaltung der Juden aus dem Deutschen Wirtschaftsleben" (Decree Expelling Jews from the German Financial Sector). Jews were stripped of all commercial assets, forbidden to offer any commercial services, and forced to sell anything of value: Antiques, jewelry, stocks, and bonds at a fraction of their value. Then came "Zwangsarisiert." All Jewish real estate title was to be passed to non-Jews.

December 26 arrived, and with it a six-day grind. Sol, as usual picked up the tab for meals and lodging. "Happy Holidays all you gentiles...and Karl. Anyone want to get the ball rolling?"

Karl stepped in, "Sol, I'm beginning to like you, and not just because you keep paying the bills, but it helps. Your interest seems to lie in the area of intelligence work. For this reason I would vote for you to take charge of and coordinate the planning.

The others all agreed, to which Sol gave his thanks and the reminder that he must stay out of public view. He took it by the numbers first suggesting that the group assign areas of primary responsibility, both geographic and experience-wise. Geographic is simpler: Karl and Albert in Europe, Vance and Wally in England and Sol as the rover. Applicable skills are a bit short. Vance in the construction area of underwater devices, Sol a novice intelligence agent. Wally could be of great assistance to Vance, particularly as procurer.

"Procurer?" asked Wally with apprehension. "Yes," answered Sol. "When manpower and/or equipment is needed, contact Winnie and see what he may have available."

"Any possibility of having a title?" mused Wally.

"Albert and Karl's efforts will probably wind up in the undercover area. Develop as many contacts as possible with military people, particularly Nazis as distasteful as this may seem. I understand Albert has a good friend in the

Sturmabteilung. He could be invaluable to our efforts. Plan on hearing more from me than Wally or Vance."

Sol continued. "First, we should devise a production schedule, a bench mark. The elemental time frame to establish first is not how soon can we begin production, but when do we want the tunnel completed. This is our starting point! Karl, when do you expect the war to begin?"

"Late 1939, in about 9-10 months."

"I know where you're going with this, Sol," said Vance. The number of units, at 50 feet each, needed to stretch from Dover to Calais is 2,218. To complete the tunnel by, say, next November, would call for 7.4 units per day. Highly unlikely, if for no other reason than Oskar couldn't provide that much raw plastics production per day."

What if we set an arbitrary completion date of January l, 1941, two years out?" asked Sol.

Vance did a quick calculation in his head. "Two years time would bring production and Installation down to three units per day. Assuming Oskar would consent to moving the production site to Dover, it's doable."

"Well, it appears you chaps have your work cut out for you," stated Sol, "particularly in procurement."

Wally winced, "Looks as though Winnie and I are going to become great mates. Right away I have to bang on him for some manpower."

The conversation was moving too fast for Karl, "Wait, wait, two years is too long. What, do you expect to talk nice to the Nazis and say 'pardon us while we build a tunnel right under your noses?' "

Vance fielded the objection. "All efforts will be concentrated first on the Calais end, which could be completed in six to eight months. This would include the partially completed and abandoned resort, under which the bogus gas chambers and cremation ovens will be located, and the finished building where the Nazis will no doubt put offices and boarding. Work on the tunnel will all be underwater, and out of sight."

Sol posed another problem: Herding an undetermined number of Jews from Germany, and, hopefully even further away, to Calais. He opened up a map, which gave the group some idea of a big problem: transportation! The map showed there were only about 1,200,000 Jews in Western Europe, 200,000 of which were in Germany. These would be much closer to England, and easier of vacate, than the some 6,000,000 additional Jews in the Slavic countries. Then there's Russia, with 1.1 million.

Within this problem is the fact that it will be difficult to steer Jews westward as Germany builds more and more concentration camps where the biggest Jewish populations are, eastward.

Albert chose to say what needed to be said. "Karl, we can't save them all. From the way Martin explained it to me, the maximum number of people that were processed through the euthanasia facility on any given day was around 1,000. The average was closer to 600. If we could somehow be fortunate enough to save all 1,200,000 in Western Europe at that 600 per day rate, it would take five and a half years.

"Another problem: Processing, and how blatantly it can be done. Personnel on the inside will supposedly be performing the processing of gassing, carrying dead bodies to the cremation area, then putting them in the ovens. Of course, they will all be hand chosen 'good guys.' Equally important, no viewing areas for anyone to see what is really occurring. The prisoners are being led to the tunnel and ultimate freedom. Perimeter guards, outside the compound, will likely have to be whomever the camp commandant chooses. They will see nothing; but, from time to time, there may be a guard from the outside stroll through the compound.

"There's another man I want to bring into the group: Martin Zoner. You may recall my speaking of him earlier. My hope is for him to become perimeter head guard, but it involves the greatest groundwork, planning, precision timing, and luck. I'll be heading for Berlin shortly to meet with him."

"First of all," continued Albert. "Martin Zoner will somehow have to get himself transferred to the Schutzstaffel, otherwise known as the 'SS.' It is Himmler's pet that, among other things, provides staff for camp guards."

"Good show!" shouted Wally.

"There's more," Albert declared. "During those six to eight months that we need to work on the Calais side, Martin is going to groom himself for that head man position, and, here's where the luck part comes in, maybe, just maybe, get to choose the perimeter guards."

"How does Martin feel about this risky situation he's getting into?" asked Vance.

"Honestly?"

"Honestly," Albert replied somewhat sheepishly. "I haven't told him yet."

"Hate to say this, old boy," remarked Wally, "but won't your friend resent your putting him in harm's way while you lounge on the sofa having cigars and brandy?"

"Fellows, fellows," as Albert tried to explain. "As my father-in-law would say, 'now, you're getting your daily exercise, jumping to conclusions.' Let me go back to the beginning. The Nazis have been very secretive about the euthanasia facility. Martin says he saw nothing in writing about it. The Nazis are thrashing at the bit to begin a holocaust of the Jews, but are moving very slowly, at least for now. These are truly evil men who don't want to get their uniforms soiled."

"How much longer? Make your point," Karl pleaded.

"Let me represent a group of investors," he explained, "who want to take advantage of what they see as an opportunity of a lifetime to make a killing, pardon the pun, in the business of eliminating Jews. 'Let us do it' is our slogan, which should be very appealing to the Nazis. Think about it."

"I don't know about you fellows, but I'm dog tired," yawned Sol. "It's two in the morning and another shocker like Albert tossed us might bring me back to life. I need the sleep."

No one slept well. Albert had second thoughts about what he had said, in what could be called "teller's remorse." Sol was quietly admiring what Albert had come up with and slept the night fitfully. Vance planned the next step, a trip to Oslo. Wally worried the night practicing how he was going to ask Winnie for some men. Karl slept soundly. All of his recent forecasting continued to tire him.

After enjoying a no-business breakfast, it was back to Sol's suite.

Sol told Albert the group was more than anxious to hear the details of his plan. Because it smacked of the type of British Intelligence activity he was trying to break into, he was envious.

Albert's plan was to spend several months in Berlin, trying to get acquainted with as many ranking German officers as possible. With Martin's knowledge of many of these officers, it would be easier to drop a few Deutsche Marks, courtesy of Claude Rothsmann to get an audience with one of these newly found Nazi friends. He would be flattered for being so perceptive in seeing the advantage of the establishment of such a strategically placed concentration camp operated by civilians.

Wally was confused, "I think I'm getting the gist of your plan, but somewhere along the path I missed the part about why the Nazis would buy the idea of a concentration camp right on the French coast."

"Let me put it this way," explained Albert, "if you were the commander of invasion forces, by this time probably American as well as British, would you choose a beachhead where thousands of innocent people were housed? Stray gunfire from both sides would kill hundreds. Pre-landing bombardment would kill thousands."

"A human shield!"

"The exact words of Karl when I first reviewed my plan back in 1936."

"Forcing the invasion away from the safest and most obvious place, Calais, to a more dangerous location!" Sol beamed. "By Jove! I believe the Nazis will buy it."

"But won't the English be miffed?" asked Wally, "taking away such a choice invasion spot?"

"Not likely," replied Karl. "The invasion will occur at Normandy Beach. Plus, access to the tunnel will give the Brits the ability for a few commando raids."

Vance then suggested, "We've all got our assignments for the near term. My wife and son want me home. Let's bag it, each go home, and shoot for a February session."

1939

The Ground Breaking

January. London. Wally was on his break when Vance called. "Wally, it's very difficult to be on loan to British Naval Operations and work on our project too. As long as you'll be calling Winnie for manpower, ask if I can be put on TAD also. Tell him to call it Operation Oslo.

"And 'TAD' is?"

"Temporary Additional Duty, to a project called Operation Oslo."

"So named because you are head honcho tunnel builder, and you'll be flying to and from Oslo to see Oskar."

"Righto, old chap," beamed Vance, trying his best to sound British. "And I would like 50 men that I can hand-pick from my unit. About 20 of these men will have to be billeted in Oslo, unless I can convince Oskar to move production here."

Sol wired Albert, sans Turkey German, and said simply, "Sol here. Need plans for your resort, A.S.A.P." Meanwhile Vance had contacted Wally to arrange for a quick toddy after work. He needed Wally's input before he contacted Churchill.

His manpower list was re-read, and a list of equipment added: One crane, one dredging back hoe, two bulldozers, four dump trucks, the biggest wench with the longest cable line possible, and various hand tools.

Vance had chosen his best engineer to ramrod the Dover operation. After scrutinizing its overall purpose, he recommended that the main floor of the old boat building be used for storage and processing the raw plastic.

The sand-filled bottom floor would be laid out with concrete the size of a basketball court to use for assemblage of the tunnel units. Sloping away from here would be a "slide" leading into the channel. A simple frame covered with canvas would be sufficient to hide the units from the view of any enemy airplanes flying over.

Wally was nervous as he walked into Churchill's office. A chill went up his back as he asked to speak to the Lord of the Admiralty Churchill.

"Whom may I say is calling?"

"Wallace Fournier."

"Oh, yes," a well dressed, neat-as-a-pin receptionist said, "Winnie said you would be coming by soon."

Winnie? Wally thought to himself. Even secretaries call him Winnie.

"He isn't in right now, but said to give you this when you did drop by," she instructed, and handed him an envelope.

Wally had no idea what the envelope contained, didn't want to appear rude by opening it then and there. He didn't know whether to ask when Winnie would be returning, or to simply keep waiting.

"Open it now if you wish," offered the receptionist. "Make certain it's what you're looking for."

Wally opened the envelope, took a hurried look, couldn't believe what he saw, and told her it would do very nicely, thank you. There, inside, was a blank voucher, just fill it in. Outside Winnie's office was a red telephone booth. He immediately phoned Vance and invited him for a toddy, on Wally.

Vance was glad Wally's ordeal came off smoothly. Now it was Vance's turn to sweat it out. He needed to get up to Oslo and haggle with Oskar. By next weekend, the men and equipment should be unloading at Calais. Sol would be like a fish out of water.

Calais. Sol was getting nervous. He hadn't gotten Albert's plans, and had to leave for Calais in two days. The doorbell rang. It was a message from Albert. It read: I have your plans. See you at resort, via Pelican Inn.

Sol took a seaplane to Calais a day early and found the Pelican Inn, a nice enough hotel. Wally and Albert, not knowing the other was coming, went to the bar to await Sol and greeted each other warmly.

"I wanted to be here when we break ground," declared Albert as Sol joined him for a drink.

The group reviewed Albert's plans: Twin buildings, each three stories in height. The resort will go unfinished because the developer, as planned, will go bankrupt. One building will be completed, affording a lobby and two stories of rooms. The other building will stop at one story and will be used as a food dispenser. It will have a two-level hidden basement; top level built as a gas chamber, the bottom level as a crematorium with five ovens. Other than one true gas "shower" and one functional oven, all the other like devices will be bogus.

"Because Rothsmann supposedly will be loaning the money for this resort," explained Albert, "he will repossess and I, as representative of the group of investors wishing to establish a concentration camp in this vicinity, will purchase the note, and obtain ownership of the property."

Oslo. Sol decided to stay another week at Calais to look over the shoulder of Vance's contractor. Albert headed for Berlin, and Wally arrived back in London just about the time Vance was en route to Oslo. The weather was fair, so Oskar was able to pick up Vance there rather than at Bergen.

He wasted no time getting to the point. "Oskar, we have a problem. Let me frame it so it will be easier to understand. First off, how many pounds of your 'ready to liquefy' material can you deliver here in Oslo per day?"

Oskar beamed, "about 6,000 pounds," he said proudly.

"At that rate, Oskar, it would take about nine years to complete our project," explained Vance.

Oskar was devastated, all the air let out of his balloon. "There is no possibility of producing my mixture that fast."

"There would be," assured Vance, "if we moved production to England, leaving your full-time efforts to extracting and mixing, assuming you're using your same hired hands. And to add some incentive, we would give you a bonus of $50,000, payable over a 10 month period.

Oskar was stunned. "You would pay me $5,000 per month for 10 months just so you can produce it there?"

"But we would ask one thing more, to ship us the raw material from Bergen."

Oskar was flustered. "Why would you ask that?"

"Because that's where your gray, gooey seepage is located, you know, between one of those seven mountains surrounding Bergen. You as much as told us the first day we got here. We just put the pieces together. It's worth the $50,000 to speed up delivery. Why take a day to haul your raw material to Oslo, then another day to return to Bergen?"

With contract in hand to produce components in England, Vance returned home with amended plans for the Dover facility, essentially eliminating the need to billet 30 men in Oslo, thus enhancing available hours to assemble the units.

Stuttgart. Karl was restless but couldn't understand why. It wasn't any kind of vision. He wasn't coming down with anything. He decided to go for a walk through a residential area he rarely frequented, but before he walked out the door, a thought flashed into his mind. He turned back to ask Kristine if she would like to take a walk with him.

Her father had never invited her to walk with him before. "Go to your father, he needs you," a voice said. "Why yes, Papa, sounds delightful."

As they strolled further down the walkway there appeared tiny green buds fairly popping out of the elms and a pleasant aroma wafting in the air. Karl was reminded of similar wanderings many, many years ago. Suddenly he stopped. Not noticing, Kristine took a few additional steps before looking back.

"What is it Papa?"

Karl stammered for a moment. "I'm not certain that I've noticed this building before." He didn't know what else to say.

A voice, just over a whisper, said, "You know it's a Synagogue. Why don't you go in?" Both heard it, but didn't realize the other had also heard.

Mama? Kristine thought. Amy? Karl wondered.

Karl slept fitfully that night. Next morning at breakfast he said in a matter-of-fact tone, "I think I'll walk over to the Synagogue."

It was the beginning of "Parsha Truma," observed each year in mid-February for a week-long reading of the Torah. Karl had never attended this ritual and, for that matter, rarely went to the "A Parsha," held each Saturday when a portion of the Torah is read.

Karl returned home shortly after sundown. "Feeling better, Papa?" asked Kristine.

"Yes child, I am." But his thoughts were mixed. He felt guilt in the fact that he still bore a grudge against God, but angered by the thought that he would have to inevitably come to love Him again.

March. Berlin. After leaving Calais, Albert went directly to Berlin. He felt ashamed that over a year had passed since he had given Martin a progress report, much less reveal to him the group's current plans. He hoped Martin could still be found at his last known address: The Volkshausen Hotel.

Albert strolled into the hotel lobby trying his best to look ordinary. He thought it best if he didn't ask whether or not Martin was living there. This could elicit questions like, "who wants to know," or "I'll give him your message." Instead he gave the clerk instructions: "Martin Zoner usually comes in around 6:00 p.m. Would you tell him his cousin is waiting in the bar?"

Within 20 minutes Martin was given the message. His eyes scanned the bar for his "cousin," spotting him in the same corner booth as their last meeting.

Albert spied him with the words, "You haven't changed a bit, Cousin Martin."

"Took the words right out of my mouth, Cousin Albert. Shall we go out for dinner? I know of a good place."

"Must be an echo in here. Seems I've heard that before." They wound up at the same restaurant and the same corner booth as before.

Martin spoke first, "As you may remember, I got assigned to Reinhard Heydrich's staff but I'm so far down the line hardly anyone knew I existed, even after my assisting at the euthanasia project. Now Heydrich is dead. No one knows how he died. The whole Gestapo, SS, and affiliates are being restructured. I've been told I am soon to be a sergeant, and in Heinrich Himmler's unit, assignment unknown."

"Which one of these killers will, or does, have the most to say about Jewish affairs?"

"Not certain, but it used to be Adolph Eichman. He was accountable to Heydrich, but now I can only guess."

Albert gave Martin a comprehensive progress report: Members of the group; the loan from Rothsmann; Churchill's pledge of some men and machinery; a reliable source of plastic for the tunnel and ground broken on both sides of the channel.

"But the coup d'état will be convincing my group of "investors" to operate the facility. Otherwise we fail. Your role is equally as critical."

Albert explained his plan for inner and outer personnel at the bogus death camp. Inner workers should be about four of our boys, trained to fake the operation of gassing, and cremation. We'll need to keep a few Jews on hand to assist in carrying bodies from gassing to cremation in the unlikely event some outsider wandered in by mistake. You, of course, will prevent this from happening. Mostly the inner workers will aid in processing new incoming prisoners, keep them fed, and guide other prisoners through the hallways and hidden ramp to the escape tunnel.

"So, I'm supposed to get myself placed as head guard of the perimeter men so that I can hand-pick them. I got lucky, unknowingly, when Himmler put me into his unit. Maybe my luck will hold when the manpower puzzle is finally put together."

Albert then explained his idea of planting, in mid-level officers, a very "hush-hush" seed on the advantages of a concentration camp near the Calais beach. Martin is to water and fertilize the idea until it sprouts somewhere near the top of Himmler's chain of command. Then contact Albert.

"That," exclaimed Martin, is going to be tricky! Then you'll be in Berlin for awhile?"

"As long as necessary," vowed Albert, "and I believe it would be fruitful if it were known that we were childhood friends. This way I could do some watering of my own by spreading fertilizer about what a good fellow you are."

"It's getting late and the restaurant is closing," said Martin. "Let me give thought to some names for you to begin with. Let's meet at a different place tomorrow night, about two blocks west of here, called the Rathskeller. Same time. Stay at Pension/Fremdenhelm (boarding house). Officers are sometimes housed there, and there's one right across the strasse from the Rathskeller."

A sign in the boarding house front window said, "Zimmer Frei" (room to let). Albert rose early and was first at the breakfast table. Kaffee, Eier, Brotchen Tomaten und

Wurstchen (coffee, eggs, rolls, tomatoes, and sausage). Not what he had in mind. As each guest sat down he gave a less formal greeting, "Wie Geht's?" (How are you?).

The last man to come down for breakfast was a Captain. He had a familiar face, but Albert couldn't place it. He greeted him more formally, "Guten Morgen" (Good Morning), but received no response. During his entire stay at Berlin, Albert greeted the captain each morning and received the same response...nothing!

Albert spent the day in one coffee shop or restaurant after another. His attempts to strike up a conversation flopped. People were very disinclined to speak to a stranger He met with Martin at the Rathskeller that evening, anxious to see what names and ranks of officers he had come up with.

Martin first wanted to tell about the news. "Hitler now occupies all of Czechoslovakia. The troops just marched across the borders of Bohemia and Moravia just like they owned the place, which, I guess, they now do. That evening Hitler himself rode into Prague in his big Benz convertible."

"There are 120,000 Jews in Czechoslovakia," said Albert. "Adolph Eichman was the architect of the Austrian Jew deportation, so he must be drooling at the mouth right about now. What especially hurts is that the refugees will have no place to go but east, away from Calais."

Martin said he was on good terms with the lieutenants, the lower ranking officers. There was, however, a captain in the SS by the name of Erik Kreuger, who seemed to have taken a liking to him. Martin said he could probably arrange for a meeting, but it should take place in his office.

"I'm not fussy, his office, the men's room, wherever," said Albert impatiently.

"Very well, my friend," said Martin with a knowing grin, "I'll do my best, but I should warn you that he is partial to handsome men."

"Oh," Albert thought for a minute. "Then just tell him I've got a horrible disease, ought to slow him down some."

Martin rapped lightly on Capt. Kreuger's door early the next afternoon. The morning had been taken up with Martin's promotion to Sergeant, and transfer to the SS. He was surprised when he heard Kreuger's voice ring out.

"Come in Sgt. Zoner, I've been expecting you."

Martin was puzzled and thought to himself as he opened the door, how did he know I was standing outside?

Kreuger, seated at his desk, stood up with hand extended and said, smiling, "I knew you would be first to congratulate me, Martin. At the same time I congratulate you!"

Martin had to react quickly as they shook hands, "Ya, mein Kapitan, your promotion was well deserved. Where will you be going?"

"Sachsenhausen," answered Kreuger, "just a few miles north of here. My new rank will be Major. Perhaps you will be assigned there someday."

"I could only hope to follow in your footsteps," said Martin thinking to himself that he may as well stay friendly with this fellow. He may be useful someday. "I do have a friend at Sachsenhausen, Fredrik Marr."

"I will give him your regards."

Martin and Albert met that evening at the Rathskeller and agreed that, while Kreuger's transfer was a set back, his replacement may be approachable. Further, Sachsenhausen is only a few miles away, and Kreuger may yet be of some help. Also, Marr may be a candidate for Martin's perimeter guards.

I'll be staying here for a bit longer to make as many useful acquaintances as possible," Albert explained, "and then head back to Stuttgart. With the Calais facility not complete until around August, I don't want to be all dressed up and no place to go. Next trip I can begin in earnest to sell our 'merchandise.' "

It was getting dark as the two were about to part ways. Albert began staring at a captain walking their way. "That's him, the stuck up officer that not once returned my morning greeting."

"Mien Gott," exclaimed Martin. "You don't recognize Piotr Siegel? He's the fellow that I brought with me to dinner at Karl's home a couple of years ago. Must be the new uniform."

"Ah, yes. Now I remember. Hey, Piotr!" Albert yelled before Martin could stop him.

"Careful, he's looking for trouble!" said Martin, as Siegel was walking/weaving rapidly toward them.

"I heard that, pond scum!" slurred Piotr. "You're going to regret it," as he began poking his finger on Martin's chest. Martin didn't dare to do the same to Siegel, an officer, so he put up the palms of his hands as a gesture to back off.

Piotr suddenly gave Martin a hard push backward. Albert reacted, without thought, to separate the two. But equally reactive was Piotr, knocking Albert to the ground with an across-the-face sucker punch. As Albert was trying to get up, he was hit with a downward punch in the face. He was out cold.

Piotr just walked away.

Martin was torn. Go after Piotr or help Albert to his feet. Martin took him to his nearby room, and patched him up as best he could. The next day, Martin put him on the train to Stuttgart. Albert's plans to do some scouting would have to wait.

May. Stuttgart. "What have you been doing, swimming the channel?" Karl asked caustically. "No word for six weeks, and we didn't know where to reach you." He had not yet noticed Albert's banged-up face.

"Ah, home sweet home," exclaimed Albert. "I had forgotten how cheery your voice could be," then quickly added an apology for not keeping in touch. "I'll do better next time."

"Next time?" whined Kristine, "You'll be going back…, eek…, your face! What happened?"

Albert dreaded what he had to say, and explain. "Yes, Kristine, I'll be going back to Berlin, but just two times more and for only a few weeks at a time. As for my face, I had a tangle with Piotr Siegel. Subject closed!"

"On a more pleasant subject, the fishing village, our cover for making tunnel units and launching them into the sea, is nearly complete. We should be able to work undetected then break the champagne bottle on the lead unit by August of '41.

"So, it appears I won't have to put on my Kommandant suit for another year yet, unless more groundwork is needed to gain the Nazi's confidence. I've made some inroads in this area with the aid of Martin Zoner, whose recent promotion and transfer to the SS will be a sizeable help."

"As you may have guessed, I had a little jolt just before Hitler's ride into Prague," informed Karl. "And another is forming in my head. It puzzles me, though, why England is one of the few countries not allowing Jews to enter, unless they're just passing through. And yet the British Government is about to severely restrict Jewish immigration to Palestine, the mother country of Judaism."

"There's more," complained Karl, straight-faced, "Hitler is about to sign a non-aggression pact with Stalin. Accordingly, no one is supposed to invade the other's country. The door will then be wide open for the Nazis to invade Poland."

"I see this but can do nothing about it. Ach, your group has it easy. I've got to deal with the big dictator in the sky, who is always telling me what I need to do and say. All you have to do is sit around on your heinies and supervise. You remind me of donkeys who live in the grasslands of Argentina. We call them 'Pampas Asses!' "

Albert didn't react to Karl's objections. He was puzzled. "Why would the Nazis feel free to invade Poland?" If I were Stalin I would be very nervous. Maybe that's what Piotr foresaw when he changed sides."

Several hundred miles away, at Dover, the same conversation was occurring between Sol and Vance, who was puzzled. "Why would the Nazis feel free to invade Poland? Wouldn't that make Stalin nervous?"

"Not at all," Sol explained, "as long as the Soviets got part of the spoils."

"The rest of the world won't allow it," protested Vance.

"No, they won't," agreed Sol. "That's why there will soon be World War II!"

A reflective hush fell over the room, each forming an opinion of how it will begin, how nations will choose sides, and the ultimate winning amalgamation of nations.

This time Sol broke the silence. "Poland has yet to grasp what is about to happen to her. Most believe that all Hitler wants is only parts of Poland, like Bielskol, which used to belong to Germany before the 'Great War.' The poor Poles will wake up the day after that pact is signed by starting to draft male citizens, but too little too late. Germany will invade Poland within a week.

"Germany will be partitioned between Germany and the USSR. Germany's portion will be halved between the Western, 'Warthegau' part and the Eastern, German controlled Protectorate. The Warthegau will probably be totally cleared of Jews and resettled by Germans. The General Government area will be a dumping ground for the some 2.5 million remaining Jews."

Vance noticeably raised his eyebrows in amazement, and wondered how Sol came by this kind of information. Sol issued a request that what he had revealed was strictly hush hush. But Sol wasn't worried because he had just been inducted into MI-5, British Intelligence. Further, they have given Sol his first assignment: "Camp Calais."

Vance immediately sent the others a mail gram, in Turkey German:"Sarpol harpas narpow arpobtarpained harpis drarpeam jarpob. Arpalsarpo barpeen arpassarpigned farpull tarpime tarpo arpus. Carpongrarpatarpularpatioarpnce (Sol has now obtained his dream job. Also been assigned full time to us. Congratulations).

Sol has been making weekly two-day visits to the Calais facility. Dredging for the escape area is now complete, and foundations have been poured. The uncompleted resort should be ready for bankruptcy by the first of the year. Then Albert can purchase the note from Claude Rothsmann anytime thereafter.

Wally had little to do until the project was further along. He expressed surprise about how easy it was to get Winnie's cooperation in the needed men and equipment for Dover. But he was worried about the next request: "How the deuce do you ask the soon-to-be Prime Minister for the loan of a submarine?"

"To pull those tunnel units three by three early on will be easy. It's the final 3-5 miles that is going to be sticky!"

Vance tried to give Wally some comfort. "British navy is always on patrol. Destroyers are looking for subs and subs are looking for destroyers. When war comes, the number of patrols will quadruple. Taking an hour out of a sub's assigned waters won't be that big of a problem."

Everyone had agreed that the commencement of war would not affect their project completion timetables. By the time Hitler reached the French coast tunnel work will be unseen. Albert, however, was having second thoughts about his schedule. He wondered if it may take longer than he had calculated to sell his idea to the Nazis.

"Wait for the war to break out," suggested Karl. "See first which way the wind blows." But he was in no position to render much advice. His mind had become muddled with the quick passage of events and, for the present, seemed unable to be specific in seeing future happenings. His walks past the Synagogue had become more frequent, but he did not go in. Karl was feeling an aura of fear.

Both he and Albert were "on hold," teaching part time on a substitute basis only.

It was no surprise to the group that the German-Soviet Pact was signed on August 23, only six weeks after their meeting. Germany invaded Poland on September 3, 1939, when France and Great Britain declared war on Germany.

September. London. Wally was kicking himself for not getting in touch with Churchill regarding the occasional loan to the group of a submarine. Had he contacted Winnie before the outbreak of war it might have been a simpler task. Now, Wally felt, just getting his attention was going to be near impossible.

He pondered—Wally, old bean, it's time to screw up your courage. May as well, I've already screwed up this job. Go see Winnie.

The same receptionist looked up as Wally stood at the door of Churchill's office. "Mr. Fournier, do come in. I've been expecting you. Winnie left this envelope for you. Would you please read it now?"

Wally smiled as he sat in one of the comfortable reception chairs. He was beyond being surprised at Winnie's forethought, and began reading the note. "Wally, Sol filled me in on your group's need for an occasional submarine and said you would be contacting me. I have given this request to a sub commander, who will remain nameless. Enclosed are sealed instructions for Lt. Vance Worthington on advising the sub how to proceed. This is secret material, Wally. Try not to lose it. Also, would you initial the letter and give it to Sally?"

Wally initialed the letter and handed it to the receptionist. "I trust you are Sally? If not I may be in considerable trouble. By the way, are you married?"

"Question one, yes. Question two, no."

It didn't take long for Vance's foreman to get construction of the tunnel units onto an assembly-line basis: Build, then spray, top and bottom, the wooden unit floors with plastic. Buckle the Quonset hut "legs" inward. Solder them together. Apply plastic inside and out of Quonset hut. Slip the end of unit one, already attached to the unit ahead, over unit two, which slips into unit three. Bolt unit overlaps together, then, cover bolt heads and where units come together with more of the plastic goo.

But, Vance was becoming worried. His Dover crew was producing the units at slightly over two per day average. His goal was three, if completion date was to be September of '41, as hoped. Unit assembly time was ahead of schedule, but shipment of raw material from Norway lagged, and what Oskar had stockpiled earlier was used up.

Bergen. Vance decided to make an unscheduled, emergency trip to see Oskar. He found him as calm and unflappable as always "Vance, you worry too much. It will take awhile for your British crew to learn the ways of the Norseman in extracting our sticky mud from the ground."

"I'll grant you that," ceded Vance, "but can the crew improve to a doubling of results?"

"I'd have to think about that."

"Then think about this: For every day our project goes uncompleted, hundreds of our Jewish friends could be dying!"

"Oyve!" exclaimed Oskar. "Your project is that important?

"More than you realize. But what frightens me, and it should petrify you, is what happens when, not if, the Nazis invade Norway!"

"You can't be serious. Why would Hitler want to invade us?"

"For your natural resources, like, as example, your plastics' main ingredient." By this time Vance's stare was piercing Oskar's eyes. "And don't think they won't find out. They have a nasty way of making people talk."

"And one more peril we already face is the German U-Boat patrolling these waters as we speak. Can we have your permission to send over another 50 men? I realize this goes against your wishes for your extraction site to remain a secret, but it will in all probability fall into German hands anyway."

The thought of his life-long effort going to so evil a purpose left Oskar sullen. The look on his face was something Vance had never before seen. "I would be more than willing to comply, my friend, but 50 more workers would just get into each other's way. Send 20, and even then it may be too many."

"Is there nothing we can do to speed up extraction," said Vance in near desperation.

"There may be if a different extraction method were employed," was the encouraging response from Oskar. "I've toyed with an idea to do this, but there didn't seem to be a good reason to do so, until now."

The two reviewed Oskar's idea. It did involve a fair amount of expense, but mostly in labor costs, and the extra men he was to receive, would cover this. Vance didn't immediately grasp the concept, involving a monstrous tripod equipped with pulleys and an air born backhoe, but he did know whatever Oskar concocted generally worked.

"How soon before your contraption is functional?" was Vance's obvious question.

"Please," winked Oskar with a wry smile. "It's not a contraption, it's 'Oskar's Derrick.' With luck we'll be using it by March."

"March?" complained Vance. I'll double your cost on it if you can have it done earlier!"

Non-war events happened in rapid concession over the next three months: A curfew which forbad Jews throughout Germany from being out of doors after 8 p.m.; the Main Office of the Reich Security Bureau was established; the partitioning of Poland began; Polish Government-in-exile was formed in France; Nazis established the first ghetto in Piotrkow Trybunalski; Krakow became the capital of the General-Government; Lodz was annexed to the German Reich; Deportation of Jews from Lodz to other parts of Poland began; Jews and the General-Government were required to wear the yellow Star of David badge.

Wally doesn't appear too disturbed by all this. His thoughts are of Sally.

1940

The Immaculate Deception

London. A setback to the group's long-term plans came while Vance was in Norway. Franklin Roosevelt signed a Neutrality Act. Not only did he feel this would imperil Britain's chances of repelling a German attack rendering the tunnel useless, but placed a large question mark on the U.S. as an eventual home for several thousands of Jews.

Winnie, consummate politician that he was, didn't believe for a moment that the U.S. wouldn't eventually enter the war. He knew FDR, tossing a bone to his political opponents, had to go through the motions of neutrality, for now. So Churchill took the initiative even before he became Prime Minister, which, according to Karl, would be in the spring of '40. He sailed to the U.S. and conducted several meetings with FDR. Chief topics of discussion were the concepts of "Bundles for Britain" and a lend-lease program, not to be considered until Churchill became Prime Minister.

Churchill didn't forget his friends at Calais/Dover. He suggested to FDR that inasmuch as U.S. ships delivering goods to England would be dead heading (returning empty), why not fill them with escaping Jews. Then, not to leave any stone unturned, Winnie held a "midnight meeting" with Canada's Prime Minister encouraging his country to let Jews immigrate there. After all, wasn't Canada offering free land to homesteaders?

Word got back to the group of Winnie's efforts, via Sol, who put icing on the cake with assurance that the Calais resort would be completed by the end of January. This good news, and that of a likely increase in extraction of plastics raw material at Bergen, made for a more enjoyable Christmas, particularly for Sally and Wally.

March. The affects of the war hit civilians early in 1940 as food rationing began in Britain. They were fortunate. It was difficult to find any kind of food in France. What there was went to defending forces. It was during this time snails became a food source, and later on a delicacy.

The united armies of England and France, which included a few Polish fighters, were faring badly. Hitler's juggernaut was unstoppable. Once Poland was conquered, a matter of two weeks, the German Blitzkrieg turned westward toward the English Channel. No need to worry about the East. After all, hadn't the Nazis and the USSR signed a non-aggression pact?

As predicted by Karl, France's vaunted Maginot Line did little to stop the advancing Germans, who either flew over it in their dive-bombing Stukas or simply skirted its flanks at the Netherlands and Belgium. The allied forces were undermanned, outgunned, and outmaneuvered.

May. Winston Churchill did, in fact become Prime Minister on May 10th, just in time to oversee the June 4 evacuation of Dunkirk. While one of the most disheartening days of the war, it was, at the same time, one of the most encouraging. In an act of spontaneous national unity every available privately owned fishing boat, dory, motorboat, freighter, whatever could be mustered, joined the British fleet to evacuate some 300,000 British and French troops

High atop Dover's chalky cliffs, Vance peered intently at the scene developing in the waters below him. A lump grew in his throat and tears flowed freely down his face as he watched this mass display of heroism. His crew had no boat of any kind to join in the rescue and was angry about the helplessness of their circumstances.

Calais. The spa was only 15 miles south of Dunkirk. It was virtually unharmed, mostly because it already appeared badly damaged, plus, there was little return heavy arms fire from the British.

Vance knew what his crew must have been thinking. "No boys, we couldn't have rescued a one. We surely would have been discovered had we tried. We will, in due time, save many more than were kept free today."

Ten days later the Nazis, with no one to stop them, stormed into Paris. The next day Hitler, arm raised and standing on the floorboard in the back seat of his massive Benz convertible, led an army of goose-stepping German soldiers down the Champs-Elysees and through the Arc de Triomphe. No flags waved, only grim faces and tears.

On the 22nd day of June the French surrendered. It was an empty gesture, administered by French General Petain, considered by many to be a turncoat. Hitler then declared, "The war in the West is won." The world waited while Hitler ignored his generals' pleas to invade England. When he decided against it, the Battle of Britain began.

Warsaw, Poland. When Germany invaded, the persecution of Jews was immediate and humiliating. Even non-Jew citizens joined in the harassment, especially the youth. When the rounding up of Jews commenced, those in Schtetls (small towns) were first, followed by the city dwellers. The main objective was to consolidate all Jews into a very concentrated area. This action was called aussiedlung (resettlement), initially to city ghettos. Later would come the Evakuierung (Evacuation to concentration Camps.)

The Gesetz uber Mietverhaltnisse mit Juden (Law Concerning Rental Relations with Jews) had already come to Germany. This, in essence, meant cramming as many Jews as possible under one roof, making them easier to watch, deport and later murder.

Warsaw was home to some 350,000 Jews. Only in New York City did more Jews live. Within one year, over 400,000 Polish Jews were herded into a confined area within the

Ghetto, called a Zwangsgemeinschaft (Enforced Community), headed by a Judenaltester (Jewish Leader). The leader was told to pick, as a Jewish council, 31 members, who, upon being chosen, were immediately arrested, deported, and eventually eliminated. This process was repeated several times until, without leaders, they became like sheep.

In almost all cases, Jews were unaware of what was about to befall them. They were told they were going to receive Sonderbehandlung (Special Treatment). When the truth was uncovered, the transitional shock was dramatic Many died soon after arrival, not because of conditions, per se, but because of the extreme physical insult.

Stripped of all possessions, German and Polish Jews were forced to work in German arms factories at non-livable wages. Under these conditions it was "every man for himself," except for immediate family. Survival depended upon how successful one was at theft, black market trading, and out-and-out bribery. It was in these circumstances that the work Kombinator (Polish Schemer) was coined.

Stuttgart. Karl and Albert were both filing in at the university on a "when needed" basis. Albert was getting restless. He reminded Karl of his words, "Wait until the war breaks out, you said. See first which way the wind blows. Well, fighting has broken out and the winds of war have blown Hitler's enemies totally out of Europe."

"Odd, isn't it?" Karl reflected. "In the big war I was so proud of our men. I desperately wanted Germany to win.

Now, I'm ashamed to be German. Sure, word of Hitler's military victories is fast to spread. Himmler's radio news blitz sees to that. But news of how my people are faring, no one hears."

Albert was peeved at the bureaucrats in city hall. He complained that he should have gotten his visa to France by now. Karl was secretly happy about the delay, as he wasn't so certain it would be safe to travel to Paris now.

Albert felt he had to take that chance in any event. He couldn't botch up the Calais operation now. He needed to get title to the Calais resort from Claude Rothsmann before the Nazis somehow confiscate it.

While Albert was sweating out his visa, Wally and Sally's romance was budding. Vance was babysitting the plastic raw material flow from Bergen and Sol was sorting through secretly obtained dossiers of Nazi officers to determine the best prospects for Albert to approach.

July. Paris. Albert's visa was finally approved. "What do you think of my driving to Paris?"

Karl grinned, "You mean driving to Paris, or just your driving? Bad and worse!"

After several checkpoint stops, Albert arrived in Paris early-evening. Too late to see Claude at his bank, he sought a hotel room, only to discover Nazi officers took most of the hotel rooms. He finally obtained a shoddy room near the Poor People of Paris.

About ready to seek out the closest decent restaurant, a thought came to him: Find the restaurant Claude chose to host the group that evening after he granted the loan. He might just be there.

Fickle fortune! Claude was there, sitting at a small table with a very attractive lady. At least that was Albert's first observation. Walking up to greet him he suddenly stopped. The young lady just got up to visit the powder room, revealing a German officer seated on the other side of Claude.

Egad, now what? Albert thought. He was about to turn around and ease his way out of the restaurant—then froze in his tracks. The German officer was pointing directly at him. A thousand thoughts raced through his mind as the blood drained from his head. I've been caught! He knows! I'm going to be tossed into a concentration camp!

Reason crept in. Wait a minute. How could this person know anything incriminating about me, especially if he apparently knows Claude?

Claude immediately turned around, saw Albert, stood up, and motioned for him to join them. Albert regained his composure as he strode towards their table, hand extended.

"Albert, I was hoping you would be by this evening," announced Claude. The two shook hands and exchanged greetings. "This is Colonel Richter, Claus Richter."

"Colonel!"

"Herr Steller."

Albert was puzzled but reacted calmly. "You have the advantage, Colonel. Have we met before?"

"I can understand your confusion Herr Steller, but your reputation has preceded you. Claude was right. If there ever were the epitome of German Aryanism, you would be a good candidate. I spotted you the minute you walked in."

Col. Richter looked very much the image of a Nazi officer. His tunic neck was buttoned too small and his face manifested no signs of starvation, making his head appear much larger than it was. Other than some dusting of hair along the sides of his head, he was completely bald. A pencil-thin moustache highlighted his thin lips.

All he needs is a monocle and a cigarette in a holder, thought Albert, and he'll look like a villain who just came right off a movie set.

Claude made the suggestion that the three, soon to be four when the lady returned, address each other on a first name basis. "Claus worked many years as head loan officer for my uncle at our Vienna office before the war. We were reminiscing about some of the unusual loans we both had made over the years. Most were very profitable, but a few, not. Of course I would never reveal the details, but your purchase of the note on the Calais Spa came up as an example of a timely rescue on one of our few bad loans."

The men stood up as the young lady returned. "Albert, this is my wife, Vienna. Vienna, Albert Steller." His kiss on the back of a frau's hand was appropriate.

"An unusual name," declared Albert, "and its attractive owner—a memorable combination!"

"So Albert, what are your plans for the spa?" inquired Claus. "I should say 'would be' spa, or is that a military secret?"

Claus' attempted humor received courteous laughter. The coincidence, obvious only to Albert, struck him off guard, and he let out a guffaw that silenced the entire dining room. Claus was secretly pleased with the outburst, interpreting it as genuine appreciation of a truly clever joke.

Albert apologized profusely for embarrassing his group, and then explained, "No, it's not a military secret, Claus, but with one of the options I'm considering, I'm hoping to interest the military." Albert, sticking his toe in the water for the first time, hoped he hadn't over-done it.

Claus was so intent on his next question that he failed to realize it was coincidence, not cleverness, which made Albert respond so vociferously to his joke. "Can you tell me more about this potential military application?"

Claude came to Albert's rescue. "There you go, Claus, always the deal maker. Once a loan officer, always a loan officer. You know how rumors can help, or kill a deal."

Albert immediately recognized an opportunity. "Herr Colonel, I speak formally because I have a formal request."

"If I may in any way comply, certainly," Claus responded.

"You will do me great honor if you would be an official witness to my signature on the note for the Calais property.

In return for your courtesy, you will be the first to know of my final plans for the Spa.

Claude joined in, "Wonderful idea, Albert, I'll need a notable person to witness the transaction. I can't think of a more appropriate individual."

Claus, who used to worship the ground any Rothsmann trod upon, was, on one hand delighted, but on the other somewhat miffed that Claude didn't afford him the opportunity to respond directly to Albert's request.

"I would be delighted," was his simple response. However, the thought of his being told first of Albert's plans for the spa put a warm smile on his face. They set a time for tomorrow's signing, and then left the restaurant Claus's chauffeured car was still in the parking area as Albert's car pulled away.

"Follow him!" were Claus's terse instructions.

Tie undone, Albert sat in his hotel room's only stuffed chair, brandy glass in hand, reviewing in his mind the evening's events. A knock on the door brought him to his feet, wondering who it could be at this hour.

"A gentleman may ask a lady to come in," said Vienna, after Albert had opened the door.

"Uh, yes do come in," said Albert with a puzzled voice. "Is the colonel about?"

"No, he had to stay for another meeting at the restaurant. Told me to take the limo, he would take a cab home." She finished taking off his tie. "Can a lady get a drink?" she asked while unbuttoning the top of his shirt. "I do hope I'm not making you uncomfortable!"

Gads, what a pretty pickle this is, thought Albert, wondering just how he was going to extricate himself from what was shaping up to be the old Irresistible Force/Immovable Object dilemma. He decided humor would be his best out.

Gently removing her arm from around the back of his neck, Albert replied to her questions, "Certainly you can get a drink, but remember the old saying, "Trink das wasser nicht. (Don't drink the water). And no, you're not making me uncomfortable; you're scaring the hell out of me. Besides, Claus is bigger than I am," he grinned.

"Well, you can't blame a lady for trying," replied Vienna as she ambled out of the room, jacket tossed over one shoulder. "Last chance," she said, turning, eyebrows raised.

"Thank you, Lord!" sighed Albert as he waved "ta ta" and closed the door behind her.

Outside the hotel Col. Richter was waiting in the limousine. "Well?"

"You can trust him," assured Vienna. "He's lily white."

Calais. The signing procedure was completed the next morning; Albert endured the usual farewell formalities and headed north to the spa, no more than a three-hour drive. Claus had written a "to whom it may concern" letter for the local Nazi authorities verifying ownership of the property by Albert's group, vis-à-vis his signature on the document.

Before arriving in Calais, Albert swung by to take a look at the spa. He wasn't surprised to see that the Nazis had taken up residency in the completed but unfurnished three-story portion of the resort.

"May I speak to the officer in charge?" inquired Albert.

"Who wants to know?" was the sarcastic retort of a corporal at the front desk.

"My name is Albert Steller. I own this property, and have a letter of verification to this effect signed by Colonel Claus Richter, head of the SS in Paris. Now wipe that smirk off your face, get your dirty feet off my desk, your stinking tail end out of that chair, and bring me the superior officer of this pig ranch."

Within seconds a lieutenant rushed into the room, buttoning up his tunic and cursing the corporal for "gross incompetence, rudeness, and having an unmilitary manner."

"Thank you for your prompt response, Lieutenant. Here are my papers."

"My thanks to you, Herr Steller," said the still red-faced lieutenant, "for letting us know of your presence. I hope you can understand that these are only temporary quarters. We can find something in town to serve our needs."

Albert milked everything he could out of the situation. "May I use your corporal for a small chore?"

"Certainly, Herr Steller. You have but to ask."

"We own the resort buildings and all land five miles in every direction. I have penciled out a layout for some 'no trespassing' signs. I'd like him to go to town and have about

50 printed up, about four feet square, and placed around the property in an equidistant manner. Incidentally, Lieutenant, what is your name?"

"Kreutz...Adolph...Lieutenant," he stammered.

"Well Lt. Adolph Kreutz, you've been most cooperative, and I'm going to see to it that your immediate superior is going to hear about this. Is he in the vicinity?"

"Why, thank you sir, and yes sir, he is billeted in the rooms above the Pelican Inn at Calais." Gaining some confidence in the situation, he added, "His name is Piotr Siegel, a Captain." Albert couldn't believe what he had just heard. Was this a coincidence? A practical joke? Some kind of scheme Piotr had dreamed up? "I'm sorry, Adolph I was momentarily distracted. You said he was a Captain?"

"Yes, sir. And I was going to add that I wonder about him. He's Polish, and they say he defected to Germany several months before the war started, and was a fierce fighter against his own people. I can't put my finger on it, but I just don't trust him."

Amen to that, Albert thought to himself. He decided to just let Piotr discover on his own that Albert was in the vicinity, but no chance meeting occurred.

Albert stayed in Calais for two days getting a feel of the terrain, and visualizing how the camp could be laid out. He also visited the lower areas of the "unfinished" tower to see what had been done so far on the gas chamber, the crematorium, and the holding area. The ground level area for feeding the prisoners was locked up, and there was no way to see into the lower area.

August. Berlin. Late August in Germany was hot and sticky. But it was home, and Albert was glad he would be there soon. He had just one more stop, Berlin, to see Martin.

His first visit, the boarding house across the street from the Rathskeller. His luck held. One room was available. Next, see if Martin was still at the Volkshausen Hotel. For the third time, Martin found Albert waiting for him in the bar. They were compelled to reenact their little routine:

"You haven't changed a bit, Cousin Martin."

"Took the words right out of my mouth, Cousin Albert. Shall we go out for dinner? I know of a good place."

This said, they adjourned to the same restaurant, same booth. Albert reviewed his trip to Paris, including the escape from Col. Claus Richter's wife, Vienna. Then his quick look-see at Calais. The spa was in exactly the kind of condition needed, an unfinished eyesore. Underneath, the escape facilities were soon to be ready.

Martin had not heard of any of the names mentioned by Albert, like Lt. Kreutz and Col. Richter. Like Albert, Martin was also suspicious of Capt. Siegel and agreed with his assessment that he may be a double agent, as well as a dirty street fighter.

"What do you hear from 'Fat Freddie' Marr and your friendly Maj. Kreuger?" said Albert in a teasing manner."

Head down and smiling, Martin replied, "Ah yes, Maj. Kreuger. Whenever I go to visit Fredrik I always drop by his office to pay my respects, not to mention to stay in his good graces. So far, knock on wood, he hasn't tried to lay a glove on me. Freddie? He's an okay fellow."

"It looks like our tunnel should be ready about a year from now. It's time to start selling our idea to the Nazis. But my immediate problem is how do I give a progress report to Sol and vice versa?"

Stuttgart. Two days later Albert was back home, happy to see Kristine and, incidentally, Karl, who grouched to Albert that a message came from Dover.

"Sarpee yarpou marpid Sarpeptarpembarper." (See you mid-September).

"It's a coded message from Sol," said Albert excitedly. "He left no other instructions, so I have to assume he's driving here."

Albert and Karl had a chance to sit, relax, and converse over the usual cigars and brandy. "Whenever I'm on the road, I get behind on the news," said Albert, looking for a response. "Anything of consequence happen, other than the war?"

Karl answered in a manner only he, though very bitter about the circumstances, could come up with. "Oh, just the usual pogroms: "Hans Frank, that miserable traitor, put a timetable of November for Krakow to be Judenfrei (free of Jews). Two-thirds of the 60,000 Jews there have already been deported. Then he issued orders whereby thousands of Polish leaders and intellectuals are to be killed. The Warsaw and Lodz ghettos were established only three months ago and already both have been sealed. Heinrich Himmler has ordered the establishment of a concentration camp at Auschwitz. The first prisoners, mostly Poles, have already been sent there. Other than that, things have been pretty quiet.

Albert, although sickened about the news, didn't want to get Karl all wound-up. But he was curious about his visions. "How have your dizzy spells been?"

"Ach! It's like back in the 30's," explained Karl. "So much happening at once I cannot tell reality from unreality. All the time I get more tired and less sure of my visions."

"And another piece of bad news: Jews from Alsace and Lorraine, candidates for our escape tunnel, are being deported to southern France. It won't be long before Vichy France will institute "Statut des Julfs." (Rules Regarding Jews).

September. It was the 12th, three days before Sol was to arrive in Stuttgart. Albert remembered he promised Claus that he would reveal the military application of their seaside land in Calais. He sent a wire gram to Claus stating that he was ready to layout his plans, but via a mutual friend who would be in touch shortly to firm up an appointment. Then, to further endear himself to Claus, promised to include him in the group of notables who would be touring the facility when completed.

Late afternoon of the 15th Sol rolled up in his Austin-Healey, and ravenous for some of Kristine's home cooking. Karl was friendlier to Sol than to the others, perhaps because they were of similar faiths and ages. Kristine picked up on this and was particularly mindful of keeping his glass full of brandy that evening. Albert summarized his trips to Paris, Calais, and Berlin but admitted to be shooting in the dark as far as a timetable for him to begin the sales campaign promoting his idea.

"I'm shooting for a date of July 1, ten months from now," declared Albert, "to have a contract with Herr Himmler. Any chance the tunnel will be complete by then?"

"Very slim," said Sol, "we're on a pace for September, and I can't see anything on the horizon to expedite the timetable. I need to get back to Vance and see what I can do to help. Oh, here's one reason I came to Stuttgart," he said reaching into his pocket and handing a small packet to Albert.

"A list of prospects to sell our death camp idea I assume?" Albert verified as he surveyed the list. "Aha! I see our Col. Claus Richter on the list. See you at Calais. I'll be going there in a few weeks."

Both felt it would be an immense help that, rather than taking long trips to report progress and/or get a perception check, some method of communication between London, Calais, Dover, Stuttgart and, for a while, Berlin, be established. Turkey German works nicely, if spoken. But, written down could be deciphered.

"We've got a man in Calais, but it's so hush-hush that only two people in M1-5 know who he is, and I'm not one of them," explained Sol. "All you have to do in order to leave a message for anyone in our group is to telephone this number that I will give you, and leave your message. There's some device that garbles the message so no one else can understand."

Albert told Sol of his promise to Claus, and then he asked a favor of Sol. When he goes back to Paris, would he make an appointment with Claus and lay out the group's plans for a privately owned and run death camp, the whole works. Except, of course, make no mention of the part about the tunnel. It very well may be that Claus might want to help us sell the idea to the upper echelon and give his military career a shot in the arm.

Karl noticed Kristine was breathing heavily, her eyes rolling, her lips beginning to part. Then a voice rang out: ***"Solomon, Solomon, your wisdom will someday give aid to my people."*** Knowing it was the voice of God, everyone in the room was silent. In awe and, knowingly, looked around the room at each other. Sol's whole body shook. He had heard of this phenomenon, but had never been directly involved. What did it mean? When will it manifest?

Sol, now having good reason for soul-searching, did contact Claus, and planted the seed. As Sol left the room,

Claus was already giving thought to which high-ranking officers he knew who were involved in finding a "final solution."

October. Sachsenhausen. Following an afternoon on the town Martin and Fredrick returned to the Sachsenhausen concentration camp. For some time Martin had been "spoon feeding" Freddie to measure his interest in being part of the tunnel project. As far as Martin could tell, Fredrick would do most anything to get away from Sachsenhausen, and Martin had to put his hand over Freddie's mouth on many occasions to quiet his opinion of the Nazis. He also had a coterie of friends who were of the same opinion.

Ideally, when the tunnel was finished and Camp Calais fully operational, Fredrik, his friends, and Martin would be assigned to the new facility. The group had decided earlier that it would be best if Albert were not the Kommandant. It would take away too much of his time for his duties at the facility, leaving little for his main strength, recruiting prisoners from other camps.

They would need someone with experience at being Kommandant He would have to be malleable and not too bright, so he wouldn't be promoted elsewhere In other words, a buffoon. And who better fit than Erik Kreuger— Major Erik Kreuger, Kommandant of Sachsenhausen.

Fredrik was due on the tower in 30 minutes. With no time for a quick game of backgammon, Martin decided to bite the bullet and begin working on Maj. Kreuger.

"Come in, Martin," said the Major in his most inviting voice. His back was to the door as he looked out the window surveying his domain, all the while, hands on hips, nervously thumping his riding crop on his back.

"Thank you sir," replied Martin as he walked in and stood at attention.

"At ease, Sergeant. Please take a seat. What brings you to 'Club Kike'?"

Pretending to chuckle at Kreuger's crude attempt to be clever, Martin replied, "I thought perhaps you might be interested in a bit of information that has come my way. It seems a friend of mine is promoting a military concept that could enhance both of our careers."

Martin then took Kreuger, eyebrows raised and head cocked to one side, through the whole plan: A privately owned, gigantic death camp with the sea as a natural barrier, preventing escape from half of the compound. Human shield concept, no blame attached to Nazis for killing Jews, would free up German guards to do military duty, could serve as a jumping off place for night raids into England, etc. etc.

"This is a revolutionary concept, completely new. In the future, anyone with experience in an operation like this can write his own ticket. His future will be assured. He will be admired and desired." Martin thought he'd best slow down on the rhetoric. Even a buffoon can tell when things start sounding too grandiose.

"So, why are you telling me all of this?" asked the Major.

As we speak I'm hoping to get transferred to Sachsenhausen."

"You would transfer out of the SS, whose membership is limited, to be here, with me?"

"Word is out that you are on a short list of Kommandants chosen to head this new camp. Between my friend and a good word from you, I could be transferred there. What an opportunity!"

Kreuger began to show a trace of excitement as he stroked his chin and searched the ceiling. "I am well acquainted with a number of prison Kommandants who would recommend me," Martin could almost see the wheels turning. A few well placed words here and there..."

1941

The Tunnel

January. Albert contacted Col. Richter. "Will you be going to Berlin soon?"

"Yes, Albert, I plan to be there for two months, starting the fifth."

"Perfect! I want to meet with you to get your thoughts on the two men I plan to use on my attempt to 'climb up the ladder!' Do you want to meet at your office or would you prefer something more, secluded?"

"Normally, it would be proper to meet at my office, but this could raise questions later. Could you suggest some out-of-the-way place?"

Albert knew exactly where he wanted them to meet. "Why yes. I've often stayed at the Volkshausen. There's a very private bar there. Shall we say the seventh, 8 p.m., in the bar?"

Berlin. On the fifth, first thing Albert did when stepping off the train in Berlin was to try to contact Martin. Not in, yet, so Albert took a taxi to the hotel. The clerk at the desk looked familiar, and so must have Albert because he was told his 'cousin' would be sent to the bar as soon as he arrived. He didn't wait long.

"We must stop meeting like this Martin," grinned Albert as they shook hands.

"You may be speaking the truth more than you know," Martin replied. "It seems as though every other man is one kind of informant or another." Then a smile broke out, "But, no problem identifying them, they all wear trench coats."

"Not much progress to report this time, but I did meet with a Col. Claus Richter, an SS officer HQ'd in Paris. He has taken a personal interest in our project. I'll be meeting with him in a few days to get names of some fellow SS men who would be good candidates for me to approach. The names: Capt. Dieter Shultz and Willi Heinrich."

"I've spoken casually to Capt. Shultz," related Martin. "Dieter is well thought of, and would probably be an influence on whichever superior officer he presented you to. Major Heinrich is a real cold fish. Very difficult to read."

Two evenings later Albert was sitting in the same bar, this time with Col. Claus Richter. Albert handed him the dossiers on Shultz and Heinrich indicating his two choices, then stated "other sources" chose these same two. "It won't be by chance we've chosen the best available," he declared.

"I know these two officers," said Richter enthusiastically. "Excellent choices! Both are dedicated Nazis, extremely intelligent and, most important, have open minds to new ideas. Heinrich may seem distant and somewhat difficult to get to know, but if anyone can convince Himmler, it would be him."

Albert hesitated, "But would we want to jump from him all the way to the top, Himmler?"

"In most situations, no." Richter emphasized, "The German army believes very strongly in the chain of command. But Heinrich is Himmler's favorite, for some reason. Perhaps it's because they both share the name, Heinrich. But I'm certain the true reason runs much deeper."

"Then you feel comfortable in introducing me to Capt. Shultz as early as tomorrow, if he is available then?"

"Absolutely! But stay close to your quarters. I'll be contacting you there for the time and place."

"Incidentally, a good word by you to Shultz would be helpful. And here are ten copies of an American friend Sol wanted you to have.

Receiving the envelope handed him by Albert, he hesitated, opening it just enough to see the picture of Benjamin Franklin.

"I'll see what I can do," mumbled Claus.

Early the next afternoon the two met on the front steps of SS headquarters. They chatted informally while tracing the halls to Capt. Shultz's office, where Richter knocked lightly. The Captain was expecting them, so quickly opened the door to invite them in.

Richter conducted the introductions. Shultz first spoke to Steller. "Col. Richter tells me you would like an audience with

Herr Himmler. You were wise to observe our chain of command."

Richter politely interrupted. "I believe this is my cue to exit. You two have private things to discuss which are none of my concern."

"So, Herr Steller, what can I do for you?"

"Ah, Capt. Shultz," beamed Albert, "I believe it is more like 'what can I do for you,' or more broadly, for the Fatherland. The result of my proposal is for a few selected civilians to perform tasks currently done by our soldiers, thereby releasing them to do what they were trained to do, fight."

After this teaser introduction, Albert delved into his overall proposal, covering all of the features of "Camp Calais." Shultz seemed particularly attracted to the concept of the "final solution" on Jews eliminating any involvement by the Nazis per se.

Normally a fountain of questions, Schultz was silent during Albert's entire presentation. "I am in awe," he finally said. "Every time I had a question you would answer it in the next sentence. I did not want to say a word, fearing I would interrupt the information flow. Is all of what you say possible?"

"My group has already purchased the beach property at Calais and most of the construction has been completed for both personnel living quarters and gas chamber/cremation oven complex. Finish work for this as well as the 300-acre barbed wire enclosure can be done within two months of my project approval. We can then house over 100,000 inmates at any given time. We pay for everything. You pay us $5 per head when terminated."

Shultz, excited about all he had heard, asked, "Now, Herr Steller, how can I be of assistance?"

"An appointment with your immediate superior so that I may repeat to him what I have said to you," was Albert's simple reply. "I will be at your Major Heinrich's disposal, and can be reached at the Hotel Volkshausen.

Time slipped by as Albert awaited an appointment with the Major. Then, after a week, he received notice to report to SS Berlin headquarters.

Maj. Heinrich neither shook hands nor smiled when Capt. Shultz introduced Albert, who had a feeling this meeting was not going to go as easily as in the past. Heinrich did ask that Capt. Shultz stay for the meeting so he and Heinrich could compare notes.

"So, you want to help the Fatherland by solving the 'Final Solution' on the Jewish problem? You realize, of course, that your whole cockamamie scheme is totally unfeasible."

Albert was taken aback. No one had come out, guns blasting, abasing his proposal. He sensed that Heinrich would not respect a reply that wasn't equally cynical. "Oh, then by all means give me the benefit of your thinking. What is it that bothers you?"

"You would do well to show more respect!" said Heinrich in a hostile tone.

"I have a great deal of respect for my country, and I hope to show that respect by doing what I can, much as you presently do service to our country in your way," said Albert, equally forcefully. "Neither of us shows disrespect."

Heinrich almost smiled. This man has a mission, he thought. Let's test him a bit more.

"Very well, I will, as you say, tell you what bothers me. To start with why do you choose Calais as the site for your camp while the Eastern regions have so many more Jews and misfits?"

Albert began to change tactics with a hint of flattery. "Good question. It's one that our group initially discussed, but felt that one of the best features of the camp, the human shield factor, would be lost. There was no way the Russians would hold back their fire for fear of hitting a few Jews."

Albert answered each and every question with the facility of an orator. And Capt. Shultz, despite disdainful looks from the Major, chimed in to defend the plan. When it appeared each query had been answered satisfactorily, Albert posed the question, "Would you be comfortable now introducing me to your immediate superior?"

"Not in a thousand years!" answered Heinrich.

Again, Albert was caught off guard. Not in a thousand years, he repeated to himself. I've satisfied him on every question. How can he say this? What is his rationale? Gaining composure he then put Heinrich on the defensive with an apology. "Then my deepest regrets, Major, it is my fault that

I have failed to convince you of the benefits of my proposal. Someone else, then, will gain favors by presenting me."

"Not necessarily." As he toyed with Albert, a smile traced the corners of his mouth.

Albert was again disarmed by Heinrich's comments. Is this man intentionally trying to make me angry? He thought. "You have me Major," Albert admitted. "I am defeated. I cannot understand your objections."

Unknowingly, Albert had said exactly the correct thing. Heinrich now possessed the Alpha Dog status in the conference and could further stretch his ego with the appearance of benevolence. He could bestow on Albert what he had already decided to give—his personal approval of the plan. Smiling broadly now, the Major extended his hand in congratulations. "You are a worthy adversary!"

Albert's thoughts were spinning as he shook Heinrich's hand. He was somehow given victory out of the jaws of defeat. "And you, Major, are a master swordsman. You carved me up like a piece of liverwurst. May we review the fencing?"

"Certainly, and please call me Willi. You posed the wrong question when you asked for an introduction to my immediate superior. Gustav is a nearsighted, unimaginative dolt, a holdover from the last war who still believes the Kaiser will someday return to power. The only thing he could convince Himmler of was his incompetence."

"So," Albert picked up the explanation. "When you said 'not necessarily' on someone else gaining the favor of presenting me, you were saying you, not Gustav, would present me to...?"

"No one."

"Then?"

"Herr Himmler is suspicious of all strangers," explained Willi. "He would have to warm up to you, and this could take months. I will personally review your proposal to him. Then, when he approves..."

"When?" Albert interrupted.

"Yes, when. He will approve it," assured Willi. "Then you will have the opportunity to meet him, but only briefly. You and I will meet shortly before my visit with Himmler to ensure I have all of your facts correct. Please stay in Berlin. This could take anywhere from a week to a month."

February. As he cooled his heels awaiting word from Willi, Albert was able to catch up on the news headlines: "Iron Guard Coup Attempt Fails." "Romanians Riot Against Jews." "Jews in Romania Face Double Punishment for Crimes Committed." "Jewish Council Holds First Meeting in Amsterdam." "Nearly 400 Male Jews Sent, Amsterdam to Buchenwald." "Anti-Nazi Strike Held in Amsterdam." "Bulgaria Joins Tripartite Pact."

The next piece of news was not a headline. The rumor mill was still grinding out news, and it sat Albert upright in his chair: Himmler had ordered the construction of a camp at Birkenau. Rats, thought Albert, might as well call it

"Auschwitz II." Another camp is set up in the east. We could have gotten it to go west. Damn!

London. Sally was a light sleeper. "What is it sweetie?" her eyes still shut.

Wally apologized for awakening her, and then explained he was having trouble sleeping. He had forgotten to discuss with Vance the use of little carts in the tunnel to transport those prisoners too weak to walk. 34 kilometers is a long way to walk, even for the healthy.

Wally couldn't wait until daylight to phone Vance to share his worry, so he woke him up to explain his concern. Had anyone mentioned anything about tunnel transportation? He got Vance's attention.

To quote Karl, "I feel like the little moron who had stoop shoulders and a flat forehead. Ask him a question and he shrugs his shoulders. Tell him the answer, and he hits his forehead with the palm of his hand."

They both agreed they needed to get together and design a simple riding cart. No need for notebooks or slide rules.

The simple design would be made of lengths of 2x2 inch aluminum, a four foot open cube with oversized tires. Facing seats, three wide on each side and two lying prone on the roof would accommodate eight people. Eight car batteries would propel the cart at between 24-28 k.p.h. Steering would be done by a joy stick mounted between the facing seats.

With an eight-foot wide tunnel and four feet allocated to carts, this would leave four feet for walkers. Twenty carts with five round trips each would allow 800 weakened inmates to escape each evening cycle. If needed, more cycles could be added.

Batteries? With all the cars and buses abandoned or lying under concrete and bricks, scrounging batteries could be likened to an Easter egg hunt. Wally was relieved not having to go to Sally, hat in hand, even knowing Winnie always comes through.

March. "I feel like a doofus in this Air Raid Warden's hat," Wally complained to his partner as they walked through the rubble. "You'd think they could come up with something a bit more stylish."

Air raid sirens had not yet begun to blow so they had a chance to look around for abandoned vehicles, marking on a map where they lay. Wally would have a crew go out later and strip them of their batteries. He calculated to be able to outfit the carts with batteries by the end of the week.

Gads, 1941 is really whizzing by, thought Wally. Here it is nearly mid-March, only six months until target date for completion of the tunnel. Then sirens began screaming, jolting Wally out of his thoughts of the escape tunnel and to business at hand. I'd best round up my sheep and get them into the shelter before bombs begin to fall.

Without fail, the sirens had always given a ten-minute window to get out of harm's way. This time, however, the faster, low-flying Stukas preceded the bombers, and bombs began to fall before locals had a chance to make the shelters. The last thing Wally heard was the screaming of an incoming bomb.

With more than 2,000 fires started, confusion reigned. Vance and Sally did not get confirmation of Wally's death for two days. He was among the some twelve hundred Brits killed in the May 10-11, 1941 Blitz, the heaviest of the war.

Vance sent notice of Wally's death to Karl in code. Karl, in turn, notified Albert, still cooling his heels in Berlin. Sol found out from Winnie and immediately called on Sally to express his condolences and his own sense of loss. Many of his students openly wept. Oxford had lost one of its best.

Dover. As usually occurs in times of stress, others' problems are relegated to the sub-conscious, and Vance was no exception. He had problems of his own. Oskar had contacted him with distressing news: Heading for England in the North Sea, the Germans had boarded the freighter carrying his "gray bricks." Oskar had given instructions for the Captain to inform anyone asking that they were construction blocks heading for Denmark, where they now lay docked.

Relating his woes to Sol, Vance felt he had no option but to wait for another shipment, if it was able to run the gauntlet. Vance lamented that if they didn't get the bricks in a timely manner, the tunnel would not make its schedule. Sol slept on the problem, came up with an idea, and motored to Dover for a visit with Vance. He was reminded that Albert was about to seal a deal with the Nazis, and he would be needing some construction supplies to put on finishing touches at the spa, as follows: 200 feet of pipes for showers and about 50 shower heads for faking and gassing of our escapees. Also, for the fake cremation ovens, about 50 pallets of bakery bricks.

"Can you scrounge these up?" asked Sol?

"Not as good as Wally could, but yes, I believe so."

"Good," beamed Sol. "Load them in one of your smaller freighters, and paint over the ship's name. Wait for my message stating the new name to paint on. As soon as you've done this, sail directly for the port at Vlissingen, Belgium. It's the nearest port that can handle freight. The Calais workers will have to truck the load some 50 miles back to Calais."

A half-smile broke out on Vance's face. "Oh intrigue, subtlety, and connivance! Now what do you have up your sleeve?"

"A way to get supplies to Calais, and your plastic out of Denmark and on to Dover with the old 'pea-under-the-walnut' trick," Sol explained. "Timing will be a bit tricky, but when the ship carrying the plastic is over the horizon and parallel to Vlissigen, it is to turn starboard and head for Dover and the tunnel. Meanwhile the Dover ship is in the neighborhood and will calmly take supplies to Vlissigen, bearing the correct name."

"And just how do you propose getting clearance for the Denmark ship to leave harbor?" asked Vance.

"Some influence wielded by a German Colonel." Then he remembered the phenomenon at Karl's home and repeated it under his breath (Solomon, Solomon your wisdom will someday give aid to my people).

Denmark, Havneby. "Sol, Sol. How is my wandering Je...?" Richter checked himself and substituted, "wandering playboy? Where are you calling from, and how on earth did you find a telephone that could get through to Paris?"

Sol caught the faux paus but was not offended. "I'm in Havneby, Denmark, a port city off the North Sea. Ten Deutschmarks got me the harbormaster's telephone. Claus, I need a big favor, or I should say Albert needs it."

Richter chuckled. "For you, not a chance! For Albert, almost anything! What can I do for him?"

"He purchased 50 pallets of bakery bricks from a supplier in Norway," explained Sol. "The ship was commandeered by your navy in the North Sea and brought to Havneby. I need someone of your prestige to get a release.

Richter almost scoffed, "Bakery bricks. You call me for the release of 50 pallets of bakery bricks? How many Jews is he expecting to feed?" Then he suddenly remembered. "Oh yes, bakery bricks. I'm glad you clarified. Put the harbor master on the phone."

After convincing the harbormaster that Col. Claus Richter was who he purported to be, the ship left Havneby, heading south. Sol contacted Vance to paint "Norse 150" on his ship leaving Dover. Like clockwork, both met over the horizon from Vlissengen and the identity exchange was made successfully.

April. Berlin. Albert was notified of this gift of supplies and thought at least some progress was being made in the tunnel project. How much longer did he have to wait before Heinrich was going to get Himmler's approval? Be sure to stay in Berlin, they said. I could have been home with Kristine. I even miss Karl, and his pitiful jokes.

Then, a sudden thought. Why not bring Karl and Kristine here? I'm sure we could go to the museum and the art gallery. Kristine could do some shopping. Karl would have a whole new group of people to insult. He was about to go find a telephone when he heard a rap at the door.

An SS officer stood in the doorway. "Albert Steller?"

"I am Albert Steller," he said with apprehension. Logic told him he was not in trouble, but, what an intimidating sight.

"You are to come with me to SS headquarters."

The car stopped in front of the SS building and as Albert got out, passersby gave him a sympathetic, yet fearful look. It might have been me; their eyes seemed to say.

Willi Heinrich appeared to be in a good mood as he greeted Albert in his office. Standing next to him was a grim looking, bespeckled man in a uniform very similar to, but not the same as, Willi's SS uniform. His eyes darted back and forth and his thin lips were pressed hard together.

"Herr Himmler, Herr Steller," was Albert's simple introduction.

"I am deeply honored," declared Albert, hoping others wouldn't notice his insincerity.

Himmler didn't offer a handshake, and Albert wasn't about to proffer his. Himmler's acceptance of Albert's plan was terse, "You will be given one year to prove your program. We will pay $1 per head when a prisoner is terminated, not $5."

Willi's eyes caught Albert and his head nodded almost imperceptibly. Albert understood. He was not to object in any way to Himmler's dogmatic payment offer. Himmler concluded the meeting with the words, "You will wear an SS uniform with the rank of Captain, and you will be directly accountable to Col. Heinrich. Capt. Piotr Seigel is the officer in charge of anything in that area outside of your activities at...?"

Albert was caught off guard, but responded without thinking, "Camp Calais," as Himmler turned and walked briskly out of the room.

"He is a very decisive man," said Willi, "but do not worry about his counter-offer for payment. You and I will work out something more equitable. Stay on my good side and you will never have to worry about him."

Albert did not respond to Willi's words. His thoughts were drifting back to Himmler's pronouncement that Piotr Seigel will be the area commander. Albert thought to himself, 'Piotr Seigel!' His arch-enemy. Of all Nazis to pick from, why

Siegel? A coincidence? No! He somehow found someone on the inside to put in a few good words. That, plus a bit of pandering. He would deal with Piotr later.

Albert then took the opportunity to follow up on an earlier thought. "Would the Colonel disapprove if I brought my wife and father-in-law to Calais for an extended stay?"

"It would be a good thing. And, thank you for asking permission. You have the makings of a good Nazi. Now, I must place an officer to represent me at your camp. This may not please you. He will have the right to question your moves. You may acquiesce or countermand, but I will be informed in either event."

"I would expect you to do nothing less," Albert agreed. "Have you chosen your man?"

"Yes, Major Erik Kreuger." Albert reacted noticeably. "You know this man?" asked Willi, surprised. Albert was going to say, "Only by reputation," but checked himself in time. "Only indirectly. A childhood friend of mine, Martin Zoner, I think now a Sgt. Major was his aide at SS Berlin a year of so ago. He knows of my program and wants very much to be a part of it.

"I vaguely remember this Zoner," stated Willi, who then leaned back in his chair, thinking of how he would play out his fulfilling generosity, and then exclaimed. "Tell you what! Get Kreuger's approval and I'll reassign Zoner to Camp Calais."

Albert couldn't believe what he was hearing. In what could have taken weeks of undercover activity to accomplish,

Willi has bestowed in a sentence. His first move was to tell Martin of this latest development. He wasn't home yet, so Albert left a note: "Good news: Kreuger being reassigned to our spa. Go butter up so you may follow. Bad news: Siegel assigned Calais as area commander. Good news: Going home to bring family to Calais. Be in touch later. Cousin Albert."

Karl put up a fuss about leaving Stuttgart. Leaving so many memories was difficult. As he readied his and Albert's homes for vacancy of an unknown period of time, he had a feeling that when he returned, things would not be the same. Kristine was ecstatic. She had no problem walking away from Stuttgart to be nearer her seldom seen husband. The voice in her ear was becoming more audible. "Soon you will be very helpful, but at a cost."

Calais. His family all settled in, Albert headed directly to Sachsenhausen for a visit with Maj. Kreuger. Papers in hand, he had no problem finding Kreuger in and waiting.

Both came toward each other, hand extended for the routine shake. Albert, aware of the sizeable ego he was facing, spoke first, "Maj. Kreuger, may I warmly congratulate you for your promotion to camp Calais. I understand that you already possess an understanding of its uniqueness."

Flattered that he was acquiring some small degree of fame, Kreuger was equally as fawning. "Capt. Steller, I've heard of your achievements many times, mostly from your friend Sgt. Major Zoner. He came by to see me only yesterday asking for transfer to my new Camp Calais."

Your Camp Calais! Albert fumed inwardly, but then caught himself. "And have you made any decision on the matter?"

Kreuger was playing his role to the hilt, "I'm considering it."

Albert reacted almost automatically, "I have an idea that would assist both of us. Can you come with me to the new camp for a couple of days and give me your thoughts on camp design?"

Kreuger creased a smile. His chest rose slightly. "Yes, makes sense. I could spend this weekend there."

June. A logistical problem was beginning to develop. There were at least three months remaining before the scheduled completion of the tunnel, with no guarantees of a finish date. For the benefit of onlookers, Albert needed to delay the above-surface preparation or Camp Calais would be a compound full of Jews with no place to go.

Karl was in a snit of excitement when Albert returned to his Calais home, a three bedroom, comfortable house about halfway between town and the camp. "Hitler is going to invade Russia!" he nearly yelled. And soon—in less than a month! It's Operation Barbarossa."

Albert suddenly realized this was significant news. "What are you seeing, Karl?"

"A Kommissarbefehl (Commissar Order) stating political officers in the Soviet army must be singled out and killed, sign of a coming invasion of the Soviet Union. The

Eisatzagruppen (Nazi Jew-killing unit), which follows along behind where the army is traveling. These are the 'Death Commandos' who have killed many Jews."

"We must find a way to use this news to our advantage!" said Albert. "I think this may be our chance to seal Martin's appointment to Camp Calais. As a matter of fact, I think we can get our Major Erik Kreuger to do just about anything we want.

Albert then took two blank sheets of paper from his notebook, wrote Arpoporarpatiarppon Barpbararposarpa (Operation Barbarossa) on each, then put them in his pocket. He then thanked Kreuger for his ideas, all of which he had already planned to use. As a further courtesy he took him to Calais to meet the new area commanding officer, Capt. Piotr Siegel, not Albert's favorite person.

If Karl were there he would have said "Why Piotr?"

When Kreuger arrived at Camp Calais earlier, the first thing he and Albert did was to do a walk around the area to get a feel for how best the existing topography could be used to maximize efficiency. They both agreed on the obvious, use the sea as a barrier to escape.

Existing prisoners could be used to build a twelve-foot double fence around the rest of the 300 acres. The partially built spa should be kept separate from the fenced-in prisoners' area. The area directly above the false "killing areas" could be covered and used for the feeding of inmates, with access to same provided by a fenced-in walkway.

"I need to get back to my duties at Sachsenhausen," said Kreuger as he realized how quickly time had flown.

Albert then reached into his pocket and gave Piotr and Erik each one of them. Of course, neither knew what the cryptic note said, and then asked what it was all about.

"Oh, it's just a little game. See if you can figure it out by tomorrow. If you do, give me a phone call. Then come by and I'll give you 100 Deutschemarks. But, I must warn you strongly: Do not show it to <u>anyone</u>."

No one called Albert the next day, or week, so Albert called Erik to say that the letters spelled "Operation Barbarossa," the code words for Germany's invasion of Russia, as foretold by Karl a month ago. Then Albert added that, while Karl cannot tell anyone their future, he can predict significant events.

"You'll see when Germany invades Russia. Only a handful of officers know of this. Another example would be if Karl predicted that Camp Kommandants were about to be tried for war crimes after the war was over. Things like that."

Kreuger's face turned white as the blood drained from his head. "Surely a war crimes committee would consider whether or not a soldier was simply obeying orders?"

"Yes, that would have a bearing. But in the case of a camp Kommandant, the only way he could be considered innocent would be if his Senior Guard was deemed to have taken the reins of, say, punishment into his own hands unbeknownst to the officer in charge. That soldier would have to be pretty naïve to let the blame fall on him."

June 22. Hitler launched the invasion of the Soviet Union. The next day the Einsatzgruppen began their killings in the USSR, submitting daily reports of their activities. On the 27th, Hungary entered the war on the Axis side.

"My congratulations to your friend on the accuracy of his prediction," beamed Kreuger.

Albert knew this wasn't the sole purpose for his phone call. "Thank you Erik! May I call you by your first name?"

"Yes, I would like that, Albert! Incidentally, I have thought over the request that Martin be transferred to Camp Calais, and I have decided that because I have the utmost confidence in his integrity and obedience, I will not only approve his transfer, but will appoint him Senior Guard as well. Thus, he may choose his own personnel."

Albert replied, "As long as we are using the word 'incidentally,' you should know that if you had been caught with that code word in your possession, you probably would have been shot. But then I did give you ample warning to show it to no one, didn't I?"

To say that Albert just stole the "Alpha Dog" status from Erik would be an understatement. Whatever Albert suggested, Erik agreed to.

Albert was anxious to begin fencing off the inmates' area. He asked Erik when he wanted to send a work crew from camp Sachsenhausen. Kreuger remembered agreeing only that Jewish prisoners should supply the work, not that Camp Sachsenhausen would provide them.

Albert's retort was a classic. "Do you see any Jews around here?"

When work began, Piotr strolled by to watch the progress. Albert came up to him and said simply, "You can watch, but you cannot touch. Your authority ends at this line!"

Piotr was livid, but not nearly as much as when Erik later told him the danger of being caught with that note: "Operation Barbarossa" in his possession. "I could have been killed! That swine hundt!"

A problem arose in the tunnel area. It was unforeseen, as most problems begin. Everything was working as planned until the tunnel came to the fifteen-mile mark with five miles to go. Not only were they running out of the raw plastic, it was increasingly more difficult for the sub to drag all those completed units. It was feared that the metal could tear. They were forced to stop.

"One problem at a time," agreed Vance when Sol reviewed the options. "We've given the units ample covering, inside and out. We even covered the interior wood floor on all sides, a step I believe we can omit. This will leave us with a bare wooden floor, but without compromising a thing, and enough plastic goop to finish the project."

"As for the 8-kilometer gap in the tunnel," offered Sol, "I was hoping we could make the entire 34 kilometers. In case we fell short, however, I've been racking my brain for alternate methods. Every solution came out the same: Start a new tunnel where the original was supposed to end. Do everything exactly the same, except go west, rather than east. The two ends will need to "marry," under water, 8 kilometers from Camp Calais.

"How?" asked Vance.

"We need to work on that."

July, Within a week the guards arrived. Three days later the inmate work crew from Sachsenhausen stumbled into camp. Martin put Barr in charge of overseeing the prisoners. He performed well, warning the Jewish workforce they had only one month to finish the enclosure or face dire consequences. Although he pushed them to the limit, he knew from experience what the limit was and always stayed within it. The project was complete in slightly over the month deadline.

The term "outer perimeter guard" is somewhat misleading. While they do stand guard at the front gate, their main duty is to supervise and/or assist in the pretended murder of Jews in the gas chambers and cremation ovens. They were to be assisted by Jewish prisoners, who would supposedly perform the distasteful task of "handling" the dead bodies. In reality, they would join others in the tunnel to Dover.

While the fencing project was keeping the prisoners busy, Winnie's "on loan" workers were framing-in a sheltered area for inmate meals directly above the two-level killing area basement. Steps led down to the upper basement area. It was here that prisoners, instead of being gassed, would be told they were about to escape. They would be shown a large slide and instructed to slip down to a lower level, equipped with cremation ovens that probably would never be used. It was here the gates to freedom would open up to a hidden holding area in preparation to entering the tunnel.

Meanwhile, Sol and Vance were finally determined to start another tunnel going the other direction and "hooking up" where the currently stalled tunnel ended. The biggest problem was working space. They had to discontinue using the Dover facility, so shared a construction area with workers finishing up the Calais underground area. At night they would bring over unfinished tunnel units, raw plastic and other material, bit-by-bit.

As it turned out, the solution to joining the two ends while underwater was so obvious that it was almost overlooked. As both ends were metal, the ceiling and walls could be bolted together from the *inside*, about two inches from the inner perimeter. They would then cut out the entire center with blowtorches. After all this was done they gave the "marriage," a good "shower" with plastic. All that showed was about a four-inch raised area in the inner circumference.

It took a month to outfit the lower levels with fake equipment, except for two shower heads fitted for use with deadly gas, and two cremation ovens fired by logs and wood chips, just in case an example of their work were demanded.

A wooden imitation of an oven covered with a facade of thinned brick disguised the entrance to the tunnel. Two men could easily swing the whole unit around, leaving a six-foot opening.

Each of the ovens was fitted with a chimney to dispose of the noxious fumes from the cremation process. Emulating the odor of burning human bodies would be the burning of logs and wood chips soaked in an oil and sulfur mix.

A small, five-foot circumference, 300 meters long tunnel angling out and up from the gassing area would take ostensibly poisonous gasses a safe distance away. On the outside, a wire mesh covering the mini-tunnel and a posted warning sign would keep unwanted personnel from nosing around. The group would later find other uses for it in aiding escapees.

August. It was time for inspection of the facility. All currently or formerly involved were invited. Himmler declined the invitation. It seems the architect and builder of the SS nearly passed out when, earlier, he witnessed his first execution, a small one of only 100 political prisoners.

The dignitaries included Col. Claus Richter, Maj. Willi Heinrich, Maj. Erik Kreuger, Capt. Dieter Shultz, and Lt. Adolph Kreutz. Siegel was not on the guest list.

They were given maps of the outer area and, with Kreuger providing dialogue in his finest fawning voice, reviewed the impregnability of the fenced-in area, his 'baby.' "The sea is our friend." He concluded.

Albert was next. He kept it simple. "Gentlemen, in the above ground structure we feed them. In the first-level basement we kill them, then toss their bodies down the chute to the second-level where we burn the evidence."

He also provided maps, of the structure itself, as the tour began. Heinrich, looking at his map, was first to ask a question. "Wouldn't the construction of the structure have been simpler had the function of the basement levels been reversed?"

"If you'll notice that chute to the lower level. We can move five times more going down than up."

"Isn't the gassing room sometimes too large," asked Richter. "There may be occasions for gassing in smaller groups?"

"Ah, perceptive as usual Colonel." Albert was quick to compliment. "Please observe." A partition slowly rolled out of a wall to divide the room in half. Another partition rolled out to cut one of the halves in half. "I can do one more if you wish."

Albert invited them to either use the slide or a small side stairs to get to the bottom level. All declined the slide except Albert.

Schultz was next to question. "How do you get the bones and ashes out of here?"

"First we need to crush the bones. They crumble easily." Albert continued, "Each oven has a trap door leading to a massive pit underneath, almost as large as this room. It will take some 800,000 cremations to fill it. But that won't happen, because we use a vacuum hose to blow the residue out to sea, underwater, on a very limited basis and on the outgoing tide to hide the evidence."

As they walked back up to the top level, Albert answered a yet-to-be asked question. "Why is everything underground? Ease of cover up! Less than one hour with a bulldozer and all signs of the existence of a death camp here is literally covered up. Meanwhile, there are no windows, in the event someone was somehow to get close enough to try and see into the facility. Only seven guards will know of its existence, other than you gentlemen, of course."

Krueger, for fear of displaying ignorance, asked no questions, but tacitly snared some credit for Albert's facility by indicating that he was in on its initial design.

September. Deadline for completion of the tunnel was on the first. Albert had heard nothing from Dover for two weeks and assumed it was on schedule. Karl was visibly and physically upset. Even though Kreuger had convinced Willi Heinrich to close down Sachsenhausen and move all Jews to Camp Calais, they had yet to arrive. But worse were the mass killings that were beginning to happen in Eastern locales.

Wehrmacht forces and Escalon Special, a Romanian unit, erased between 150,000 and 160,000 Jews in Bessarabia. Over 5,000 Vilna Jews were killed, a relatively small number. But disturbing was the fact that local collaborators assisted the Nazis. They established the Bialystock ghetto, and the Drancy transit camp processed 70,000 Jews. The first experimental gassing at Auschwitz was conducted on Soviet prisoners of war. Although the euthanasia program officially ended, between 80,000 and 100,000 people had been killed.

Finally, a message from Dover, "Two days." Albert understood its meaning and excitedly passed it on to Karl.

A much calmer Karl told Albert that he had known since yesterday, and not because of his visions. He then chided his son-in-law for his lack of observation. "Open your eyes and look seaward. What do you see?"

Albert looked over the channel and finally answered, "A ship?"

"Yes, a ship! What is its name?

Albert squinted his eyes. "I can't make it out."

"So, use my telescope!"

Albert was getting peeved. "You said 'open your eyes,' not 'open your eyes and borrow my telescope.' All right, I'm looking," as he peered through the lenses. "N...O...R...S..." then exclaimed, "Norse 150, our supply ship!"

"I hope a submarine doesn't spot it," said a concerned Karl, "although it is getting dark."

Albert assured Karl no harm would come to the ship, as its ID was already registered in Germany and known to all U-Boat commanders as friendly. In the interim, the Brits have been warned to leave it alone.

"I suspect that the ship is waiting for dark to load up excess material, supplies, and equipment, and then take it back to Dover. It must be nice, knowing that neither the Krauts nor Brits are going to bother you," smiled Albert.

Martin and Fredrick were informed of the significance of "Norse 150" and told to keep eyes and ears open. They indicated hearing material handlers loading onto the ship during the past couple of evenings. The next day they heard muffled noises coming from the crematorium, then a rapping sound. A thorough inspection revealed nothing.

More rapping. "The oven entrance," Martin yelled. As the two guards swung open the false oven door, a friendly voice exclaimed, "I expected royalty, not common doormen."

Standing there in a Gestapo officer's uniform was Solomon Rothsmann, who immediately quipped. "Don't shoot! I surrender!" and raised his hands.

Neither man had met Sol, but Martin knew him by reputation and asked, "Sol?"

"Nice deduction, Martin, Albert said you were a bright lad. Well, are you going to invite me in or send me back for a bigger catch?"

Martin was quick to retort, "Well, fee fi fo fum. I smell the blue blood of an Englishman.

After warm greetings with Albert and Karl, Sol sent Fredrik to keep an eye on Kreuger to make sure he didn't drop in on the meeting. Sol's words were what everyone knew in their hearts: The undeniable conclusion that their greatest good will come from proselyting Jews from existing death camps."

Laying out a map, he drew a line starting from the old Polish-German border, southward through the middle of Czechoslovakia, the eastern border of Austria, and the middle of Yugoslavia to the Adriatic Sea. Anything to the east of this line would result in ever diminishing results per man-hour of effort at this time.

The group also agreed that their starting areas should be with the easternmost camps in our chosen area. Then work backwards towards Calais. In all probability the Nazis will deliver prisoners in the westernmost countries to us, but the numbers will be relatively small by comparison.

Intelligence figures for Norway, Denmark, Netherlands, Belgium, France, and Luxembourg total just 209,000, compared to about 330,000 "our area" death camps in Germany Austria, Bohemia/Moravia, west Czechoslovakia and west Yugoslavia.

Karl had to lie down during Sol's presentation with dizziness not related to his visions. "Good Lord," he cried, eyes tearing up, "there were 14 million of us in Europe. How can so many be gone?"

Sol tried to console Karl by clarifying that his count includes only those in peril of death. Many will escape on their own. Many have already left Europe, but unfortunately eastward where 10,000 were killed in Zhitomir near Kiev and over 33,000 murdered at Babi Yar and tossed into an open pit by Einsatzkommando 4a.

"But we must concentrate on the living, not the dead. Our first concerted effort comes soon," Sol continued. "Luxembourg Jews are to be deported to Lodz in mid-October. Poland is further than Calais. If we can't convince the Nazis to divert those prisoners to Calais..." He stopped, the result of failure understood.

Albert had a few words to say. "I've been considering areas of responsibility, as we had earlier. Sol, we can't say enough about your contribution. Keep roving. We have no other way of obtaining this kind of information except British Intelligence, via Sol."

Sol felt humbled as he recalled the words of God, via Kristine several months ago. "Solomon, Solomon, your wisdom will someday give aid to my people." His switch of cargo at Havneby and coming up with a solution for completing the tunnel were problems only a person of wisdom could think through.

Albert announced that, as leader of the unique Camp Calais, his contribution to the cause would be a visit to each and every death camp, and then sell the benefits of sending Jews his way. Further, it's more likely than not that Maj. Kreuger will be assisting in this effort. He did a good job in closing down Sachsenhausen and sending the inmates to Calais. An added benefit is that if he is on the road selling, he won't be here nosing around. He should be perfectly agreeable to allow Martin to operate the concentration camp, and take the blame if anything untoward occurs in his stead.

Karl was indignant. "And what am I, greasy bacon? You have nothing for me to do except stay in Calais and chit chat with your wife?"

"Au contraire," Albert chimed in. "Your job will be most important if secrecy is to be maintained. No inmate within the confines of the fenced-in area must ever know about his impending escape. None will suspect a thing until he or she is standing in the gassing area. It is there they will be told about their escape, to keep quiet, the tunnel, the carts and to slide down the chute to the lower level holding area. One of the guards will review the use of the carts and set the group in motion."

"Keep them quiet?" asked Karl. "How can I plug the mouth of joy?"

"You will think of something," said Sol who then stepped outside and asked one of their guards to relieve Fredrick with instructions to keep Kreuger away from the holding area. Everyone looked at each other and followed Sol to the tunnel entrance where the cart Sol had used to come over was waiting."

It's about an 80-minute drive. Can all of you be gone for, say, three hours?"

No one objected. "All right then, Martin, you and Albert get in the cart, facing backward. Fredrick, crawl up on top. Karl, you and I will sit facing forward where I can operate this little hummer."

Sol had a little dialogue prepared as they slipped silently along. "It's easy to spot the area where the two sections were joined" as they breezed over a noticeable bump. This rig will do about 24 k.p.h. on battery power. Simple string lights were hooked overhead.

"No way to install fans. No way to vent them. But the temperature stays a fairly constant temperature. Look closely boys and you'll see, literally, a light at the end of the tunnel, England. Fifteen minutes for a spot of tea and you should probably head back with the cart. You'll be needing it."

All were seated, ready to return to Calais, when a familiar silhouette appeared at the tunnel entrance. "Albert, aren't you going to say hello?" It was Vance, pleased as punch on the tunnel's completion.

They chatted for a minute before Albert said, "Got to run now. And to quote a famous American actress, 'Why don't you come over and see me sometime?' "

Kreuger, meanwhile, was furious. "Where is everyone? Why have I not been told?"

"Maybe they swam to England," the guard replied.

"Don't talk to your superior officer in that manner," shouted a red-faced Kreuger, or I'll have you shot."

"As I am accountable to Capt. Steller and not you, that would make him, and probably Maj. Heinrich very angry." The guard turned and walked away, leaving Kreuger sputtering in his fury.

The sojourners had returned. Albert looked through the peephole into the crematorium. No one was about. He pushed a button and the fake oven facade swung open. The group was heading up stairs just as Kreuger was coming down.

He calmly said, "Oh, have you been somewhere? I thought I might again look around down here to admire my handiwork."

Albert just rolled his eyes as the two passed on the stairway.

Next day Albert called for a meeting with Kreuger. "Prisoners from the now abandoned Sachsenhausen camp are to arrive in two days. You performed admirably in making this happen," Albert complimented, "and I would like to seek your assistance again."

Kreuger's face turned from grim to grin. "How may I help?"

Albert laid out a map of Europe on the table. Relating the essence, but not the purpose, of Sol's dissertation on the most efficient way of acquiring more inmates, Albert pointed at the location of their target camps. "Germany: Northern portion we have Neuengamme, Ravensbruck, and Bergen-Belsen. Middle section, Mittlebau, Dora, and Buchenwald. Southern part: Flossenburg and Dachau. Eastern: only one, Gross-Rosen will be difficult to move because of its proximity to Poland. In France, Natzweiler, Austria, Mauthausen. In Yugoslavia we may get lucky and get Jasenovak and/or Gospic."

Kreuger studied the map, and offered, "If we go together we have more impact, but it would take longer to cover the list. And, who would watch the camp? If we go separately, the situation is opposite. Personally, I would prefer to go separately. I have my ways."

Exactly what Albert wanted. "Good thinking, although we both might have learned something from each other."

"I would like to start with the three camps in the North," declared Kreuger. "They were close to my old prison, and I know the Kommandants personally."

Albert did the obvious, "Good, I will take the two camps in Southern Germany, plus Gross-Rosen in the East. But first I need to make a quick run to Berlin to assure those some 2,000 Jews in Luxembourg, now rounded up into a ghetto, are coming our way—not Lodz as was originally planned.

Kreuger quickly picked up the receiver of a ringing telephone. "Kreuger here...Jawold mein Colonel...thank you mein Colonel...Jawold, I will tell him. Colonel Heinrich thanks both of us in advance for assisting in Germany's problem, and added that the package from Luxembourg will be coming here instead of Lodz."

Albert just shook his head in disbelief on the timing of Heinrich's phone call. Kreuger agreed that because the camp was soon to be hit with over 22,000 inmates, 20,000 from his old Sachsenhausen camp, the initial processing was Kreuger's responsibility. Albert could afford to be gone for a few days before the sham killings would commence.

October. German troops reached the outskirts of Moscow. Russians continued to retreat, employing an age-old "Scorched-Earth" tactic. Execution of the Jews continued. In Vilna 33,500 are killed. Outside Kovna 9,000 are killed.

Albert's trip to Gross-Rosen camp was a failure, even though Willi Heinrich assured Albert that the SS would approve of any camp relocations. The area Kommander as well as the camp Kommandant would need to approve it first. One did. The other didn't.

As Albert pulled into camp Calais driveway, he could see the mass of humanity shuffling around near the mess hall. Nearly 300 acres in which to move about, yet the inmates were all bunched there like a can of sardines. Albert and Karl shook their heads, already getting goose bumps in anticipation of tomorrow's initiation of the tunnel. Albert thought: Why don't they go to their respective barracks and rest?"

It was simple to spot those who had arrived from Sachsenhausen: Gaunt, ragged, unshaven, and shoeless. From Luxembourg, relatively well clad, but whose eyes reflected the worst kind of fear, the unknown and imagined.

Albert could hardly sleep. Seven years had passed since he and Karl had first posed the question to themselves: What could only two civilians do to help these people? He recalled their first encounter with the voice of God, then reconfirmed their progress to date was more a series of well disguised divine interventions than any abilities he and Karl possessed. They were mere pawns.

Karl was rehearsing tomorrow's instructions. Should he slowly acclimate them to the situation, then hit them with reality? Or, would it be better to yell at them, which would be their expectation, and tell them to get moving.

Kreuger's mind was a whirlpool. He had never, even indirectly, taken anyone's life. He always arranged to be absent when anyone was executed.

Martin had a wisp of a smile on his face as he lay on his back, hands under his head, thinking of how with the help of Albert and his parents, he had finally turned his life around for some good. He wondered what his papa would say now: "I'm proud of you, son. A much better man than I." He went to sleep with that calming reverie.

Fredrik reported to Kreuger at 6 a.m. to inform him that Capt. Steller was now assuming command of the prisoners in order to perform his assigned duties.

Kreuger acknowledged. "Tell Capt. Steller I won't be available for a few days. Going to visit those three camps to the north that he and I discussed earlier."

Fredrik smiled and thought, I don't suppose the idea of being present and accountable for today's executions had anything to do with your leaving, Mein Major? Fredrik told Martin, who informed Albert of Kreuger's departure.

"Best news I've heard for some time!" exclaimed Albert clenching his fists. "I hope this sets a precedent, him gone every time we stage an execution and not around to snoop out the truth. I wonder which emotion was stronger, his fainting at the sight of blood or his not being present at executions so the war crimes committee won't come after him."

Zero hour had arrived. Albert nodded to Fredrik who shouted "Time to eat, Luxembourg Jews only. Others follow later." Having already kept themselves separate from the veterans, the new prisoners were already grouped and heading for the mess hall. Martin and his crew fed them a thick porridge, which they washed down with thin milk, and had them out within 30 minutes.

Karl and Albert could hardly stand the suspense.

Fredrik shouted again, "Time to eat, last names A thru E." This time about 4,500 drew away and shuffled along in the developing line. The hall could accommodate only 2,000, so they ate in groupings. Those done earliest were instructed to walk down the steps along the south side and await further orders. Like robots each man, when done, stood up, drifted to the stairwell and walked down. About 2,400 were milling around when Karl, who had been counting them, appeared about halfway down the stairs, pulling the soundproof door closed behind him. These were all that would escape today.

"Amcha," Karl spoke loudly. It was the only word he could think of to represent the concept of 'Home.' It meant 'Our Nation' in Hebrew. At first no one spoke. All understood the word, but why was it being offered? Almost imperceptible were low-pitched whispers that grew to an audible buzz.

Karl broke in with another 'Amcha,' and all was silent again. "Brothers, please be as silent as possible. The lives of you and other internees are at risk. You are about to escape through a tunnel to England.

Suddenly the audible whispers became louder and took on fretful, ominous tones. One prisoner panicked. "Brothers, I see a dimly lit area ahead, but where does it go?" Others mumbled, "Is this it? Are we about to be killed?"

Several inmates whispered even louder, "Is it to be by gas?" This set off a small panic throughout the whole group. Some started tearing their clothes and began moaning. A small riot seemed inevitable, so Karl yelled, "Trust God, you are being freed! Please listen and follow directions. First, slide down this chute and proceed ahead to the tunnel holding area."

Martin continued with the instructions: "Gentlemen, there are two ways to freedom. You can walk or you can ride, which is easier and faster. So why walk? We have only 30 carts to ride. Each can carry eight people. That's 240 of you for each go-around of 80 minutes there, and 80 minutes back to pick up the next group. You men who are good at math can figure out that at this rate the last group of eight, assuming you don't walk a step, won't get to England for 25 hours.

"On the other hand, at 6 k.p.h., a walker can get there in a bit over five hours. Realistically, you may get there in less than five hours if you can walk faster, or, which is a distinct possibility, we finish with the riders in time to give you a part-way ride. Walkers can start now. Riders go to the farthest carts first, and load up. Select a driver from your group to take you away. You have a 'go' pedal and a steering wheel. Use them wisely and pray for those still at the camp that they may also find freedom."

With the mix of riders and walkers, it took the last man 12 hours to reach England. When he did, a loud roar of accomplishment erupted on the shores of Dover.

Karl was beside himself with joy. "Two thousand four hundred souls saved!" As Prof. Henry Higgins would later sing: "We did it, we did it, we really, really did it!"

"With 19,500 to go, just with our existing inmates," Albert said disappointedly. "It took 12 hours to get 2,400 to safety. At today's rate it will take us over eight 12-hour periods, 96 hours, to get them out. We need to review our plan. I made an idiotic mistake in not calculating the time needed for a return trip to Calais to pick up another batch!"

"Don't flog yourself," consoled Karl. "Like these Jews, just keep going. To start with, we need another 30 carts. This would give us the capacity to handle nearly 500 at a time. Meanwhile, we've got, as you have said, another 19,500 to go. It's 10 p.m. and time to get some sleep. Tomorrow is another day."

Albert decided to radio Vance and have him come to Calais a.s.a.p. to attend a meeting. He felt they needed a fresh look at their system. Meanwhile, Martin and his crew put some sulfur on those oil-soaked logs in the ovens and set fire to them to create a foul smell and some ash residue.

Vance was there by 11:30 and took a quick tour of the underground facilities to get a feel for traffic flow prior to entering the tunnel.

"First off, I wouldn't take the time to feed them in the mess hall. Give them water, then something like a boiled potato or a candy bar as they enter the tunnel. Let those first in line go directly to the gassing area. Count them off until you have the desired number of inmates, then shut the inside door and let Karl give his talk. The rest can be fed, per usual, in the mess hall and await another day for escape. With luck, and planning, we could run another bunch through at the second daily meal."

Karl suggested that they add another 30 carts, so they could do twice as many inmates. Vance reminded them that the batteries had to be scavenged in order to tell Karl, as gently as possible, the inadvisability of more carts. As it was they needed 24 batteries for each cart.

"Twenty-four!" he repeated. "And you probably thought they only needed eight. Those batteries need recharging. Two sets of eight for every round trip, putting the one longest charged to replace the one on the cart, and rotated, etc, etc.

"Next," Vance continued, "rather than giving the choice to walk or ride, everybody starts out walking on the right hand side of the tunnel. The carts are in line on the left hand side and ready to haul. It shouldn't take more than 15 minutes for us to determine who is having difficulty walking. These we load up and head for Dover, where we unload, change batteries, and head back."

"Bedlam," Karl grunts an objection. "Carts going one way, people going another. Bedlam!"

"Until we work out the snags, maybe," Vance admitted. "But with an eight foot wide tunnel, we've got four feet for the walkers and four feet for the carts heading for Dover. Returning carts will just have to dodge about."

"Sounds like a plan," Albert had to chime in before Karl crucified Vance. "And I realize the walkers will have to give ground a bit as carts pass people, but where do they find room to turn around?"

"We thought of this and decided to design the carts to go either forward or backward. No need to turn the cart around. The driver turns around and faces forward. This was Wally's idea."

Karl was determined to uncover a fault in the plan. "Who decides who you pick up on the return trips?"

"The decision is automatic. No need for judgment calls. In most cases those at the rear are having difficulty keeping up with the group, so we pick the last in line first, working our way forward."

Karl wouldn't let go. "So who drives the carts on the return trip? And how about more carts?"

"Some of the men from Dover. They'll be giving up sleep to do it! More carts? I'll see what we can do," Vance assured him. "Just remember those batteries are recovered from derelict cars, busses, whatever, mostly under piles of debris. The work is done on our boys' off time. Now can I go home? It's 1:30 and I'm bushed!"

No need for me to report to Kreuger, Fredrik thought to himself that morning. He won't be back for several days. He went directly to Albert for the day's orders and found him, along with Karl and Martin, discussing Vance's ideas.

Fredrik gave the breakfast orders. The Luxembourg Jews were called first along with the residue of yesterday's "A thru

E" Sachsenhausen group who, when reaching the mess hall door, were instructed to turn right and go down the stairs and wait.

The group decided to try Vance's plan, but use the same number of escapees as yesterday to test its potential. Karl again counted off 2,400 people, closed the door, and delivered his somewhat poignant instructions.

Martin was next with his orders. He could barely stay awake long enough to deliver them. He had been up most of the night boiling potatoes. "Gentlemen, it is 21 miles to Freedom. Some of you will walk the distance in four to five hours. Some of you simply cannot walk that far and will need a ride, which we will provide. Please stay to the right side of the tunnel at all times. We will return with our carts as many times as needed to make sure all reach England. You may take a boiled potato as you begin your walk. Good luck to you and pray for those still in the camp.

"Seven hours," exclaimed an ecstatic Albert. "By golly we cut the previous time almost in half!" He had just gotten word from Vance via short wave. The message simply read: "Sarpevarpen Harpours."

But Karl was still disturbed. "Another 2,400 brothers. Nearly 5,000 so far and only 17,200 to go. Think what we could do with another 30 carts."

"I have a feeling that another 30 carts may be too many for the relatively small space. But, let's wait and hear what Vance has to say. Meanwhile, we need to toss another log, and some sulfur, on the fire."

Vance was there within an hour with more good news. His boys found a way to boost speed on the carts. They could now do a round trip in slightly less than two hours. That's a half hour less than before and a six hour target time for 2,400 people." Albert nearly hugged him.

Karl almost smiled. "What do you think? Do two runs a day or more bodies in one session? And, what do you think about more carts?"

"Maybe some additional carts—say 10. More than this and we're liable to get things jammed up. I'm for two runs a day, 2,500 people each, and an hour break in between. This way we start at 7 a.m. and quit at 8 p.m. Things are looking a bunch better than they were yesterday at this time."

"For you maybe," said a bitter Karl. "Two ghettos have just been established. In Lvov and at Theresienstadt. I know, I know. East is out of our hands, but I can't help but mourn for their souls. Odd, though, I'm feeling a sense of impending disaster, explosions, whistles, lots of water. Yet for many it is an occasion for celebration.

Albert treated himself to a rarity—lunch at home. A chance to eat something other than a sandwich, and some companionship other than "the boys."

Both had the same thing on their minds; Karl was not acting his usual jovial self. No words of consolation comforted him; he agreed with no one's ideas. Nothing pleased him.

Albert's diagnosis: Karl is severely depressed about the Jews we weren't saving, rather than being grateful that we were saving some. Even Karl agrees that this bothers him.

Kristine's analysis went deeper. Karl's actions were symptomatic of something more complex. He is still angry with God, and has even accused him, via the Nazis, of trying to wipe out the Jewish nation. He wants to get rid of his anger, and to reconcile things with God.

If this reconciliation were to suddenly happen, he would be the happiest man in the world. His anger comes from dreading the process itself. Of saying he is sorry. Of admitting he has been wrong.

Albert noticed Kristine's eyes slowly close, as she grew quiet. Am I about to hear the voice of God? he asked himself. A deep voice sounded as Kristine spoke the words, ***"Kristine, tell your father his father awaits."*** Awaits for what? Which father? Albert asked himself.

A wire from Kreuger came to Albert. "Ravensbruck is ours, 18,000 pigs. Coming home for now, will try others later."

Wait a minute, Albert thought to himself. We're not ready for another 18,000. I just hope delivery won't be for another two weeks yet."

Kreuger acted like the cat that ate the canary when he returned from the north Germany camps. Martin gave guarded congratulations, more out of habit than of truth. Albert's plaudits were more sincere; 18,000 Jews heading for freedom was no small feat.

Kreuger didn't have a clue that what he had done was a direct benefit to the enemy. "Well, old ma...er, Karl. Now what do you think?" He had always felt Karl looked down his nose at him.

"I could have told you before you left that Ravensbruck would choose to close and send the inmates here, just like I could have told you that the Kommandant has a rose tattooed on his left chub and ghettos are about to be established at Lvov and Theresienstadt. Moreover, on your next trip north you will fail at Neuengamme but succeed at Bergen-Belsen. Of course you already know this because you have a commitment from his pencil-thin schnurbarted aide, who, in fact, really runs the camp."

Martin and Fredrik barely contained their laughter, while Albert was looking daggers at his father-in-law. They needed this oaf to stay at Camp Calais. He might be replaced with an efficient, by the book Nazi officer.

Red-faced, Kreuger stormed out of the room saying what sounded like, "someday I'm going to get even with all of you morons," while Albert, trying to sooth his ruffled feathers, hustled out right behind him saying, "Major, we need to talk."

Albert followed Kreuger into his office, closing the door behind him. "Please forgive Karl. He is very outspoken without meaning to injure. Sometimes he gets imagination mixed with reality. Plus right now he is carrying a very heavy personal burden. I can't reveal it."

Kreuger, of course, knew every bit of it was true.

"I would very much like to hear what you think was the key to your success," declared a sincere Albert.

"If you're asking me my opinion."

"I am."

"Then I'll tell you what I think," Kreuger was now calming down, "fear—plain, old fashioned, unadulterated fear."

"Of what? A prison break!"

"No, nothing that mundane. Fear of being tried for war crimes. Humorous, though, none had considered this possibility until I planted the seed, and then watered it with a rumor that a War Crimes Commission was being formed by our enemies." By now Kreuger was back to his old obnoxious self. "And then I told them about Karl."

"Karl! Our Karl?"

"Yes, what other Karl do we both know? I've heard his predictions. They've all come to pass. You should use this too; it's a powerful weapon."

Albert began to wonder if he had gotten too close to the problem to remember that he too had used Karl as an attention-getter. "You're right, Erik. I think I'll make a quick trip to Gross-Rosen, and plant a seed." A question popped into Albert's head. "Why then are you not also fearful of being punished by this same War Crimes Commission?"

"Simple," said a smiling Kreuger. "This is supposed to be a civilian camp. I would be tried in a civil court. All I need is a good attorney, like everyone in America seems to have.

Gross-Rosen, Germany. After informing the group that he would be gone for a few days, and to keep the escape rolling,

Albert got the 15-minute interview he wanted with the still dubious Kommandant at Gross-Rosen, and got right to the point.

"At a time in the near future, Herr Kommandant, those who have had the responsibility of operating concentration camps will be subject to a war crimes trial. This information comes to me from a seer. If you doubt his abilities then I will tell you of an event soon to happen and you can judge for yourself. He sees much water, one small explosion, then many, many large ones and the American flag. For certain, the U.S.A. will enter our war, soon. I will verify these events for you, as they happen."

Albert thanked the Kommandant for his time, got up and walked out.

November. Calais. German submarine sank U.S. destroyer Ruben James off Iceland. Albert sent this news via a wire to the Gross-Rosen Kommandant and added a P.S.: Much water, one small explosion, U.S. flag.

December 7: Japanese bomb U.S. base at Pearl Harbor, Hawaii. Albert repeated with another wire and a P.S.: Much water, many, many large explosions, U.S. flag. U.S. will enter our war in four days."

Albert received a wire from Gross-Rosen the next day: Please come to my camp. Would like to talk more.

Albert was in no hurry, but out of courtesy returned the wire with a reservation for a meeting in two weeks. Meanwhile, the 17,000 remaining inmates from Luxembourg and Sachsenhausen, plus 10,000 of Camp Ravensbruck's 18,000 prisoners had been processed.

"That's 32,000 saved to date," said a gleeful Karl.

"As expected," continued Martin, "we received 15,000 from the Bergen-Belsen camp via good old Kreuger. And from the western countryside, the Nazis have sent us 29,700. Our total prison population is now 52,700. Shouldn't we be thinking of moving to our two shifts per day schedule?"

"Absolutely," said Albert emphatically. "Particularly, as I'm hoping for another 100,000 by next month." Compared to last month, the mood in camp has taken a definite upbeat.

Albert's attention was directed to today's second shift of inmates to be processed, being herded toward the mess hall. Martin was walking toward him accompanied by Piotr Siegel.

Before Albert could say anything, Piotr spoke. "Martin was kind enough to invite me to 'cross the line' this small distance so that I might deliver some news. It comes to me from Poland, via Berlin. Have you heard it?"

"When you phrase it that way, probably not. However, I have a feeling I'm going to find out...like it or not."

"I'll be brief," assured Piotr. "The first transport of Jews arrived yesterday at the Chelmno, Poland death camp. They are now being called death camps instead of concentration camps, although those who are political prisoners and misfits are sometimes spared extermination. My friend you now have some real competition!"

"Not really," smiled Albert. "Ours is run by civilians, much more efficiently. The others by Nazis who, when you come down to it, haven't the stomach for it.

Seigel's face darkened to a scowl. "Pompous words, spoken in ignorance!"

"Really," Albert snapped back, "then where do you suppose our inmates are coming from?"

Piotr wheeled around, plotting Albert's death as he stomped off the yard. As Albert turned the corner, he was blocked from sight by the main building, where some Nazis had offices. He realized that he hadn't checked to see if there had been any changes inside, and decided to pay them a visit.

As he entered the small reception area he heard a "Sir! May I help you, Sir?" It was a different voice. The surly corporal had been tossed.

"What is your name, soldier?"

"Marr, sir. Corporal Wilhelm Marr."

Albert wasn't certain he heard correctly. It could just be a coincidence. "From Stuttgart? You have a brother, Fredrik? You once tried to terrorize Martin Zoner?"

Wilhelm did not appear to be flustered. His answers were precise. "Yes, sir. Yes, sir. I don't remember that incident, sir."

"Just checking." Albert thought he'd string Wilhelm along a bit. "Is Lt. Kreutz in?"

"Yes sir," wondering what the hell was that all about as he got Kreutz on the intercom. Albert asked if he could meet him in his office. "Yes sir, go right on back."

"Captain Steller. What a pleasure. What can I do for you?"

"I would like to ask you a few questions, if I may," and without pausing asked, "What do you know about our operation?"

"Well, sir..."

Albert broke in. "Please, Adolph call me Albert. I am, in reality, a civilian." In seeing the puzzled look on Adolph's face, Albert added, "I'll explain later."

"I know Camp Calais is a concentration camp, maybe executing some prisoners. Whether they are Jews, political prisoners or what, I certainly couldn't tell from here." He asked Albert to come and look out the window. All that could be seen was a panoramic view of the fenced-in area and, beyond, the sea. His sidewall blocked a view of the mess hall.

"I was authorized by Himmler himself to operate this camp. Other than a few German soldiers as guards, it is operated by civilians. Himmler insisted that I wear a uniform and carry the rank of Captain. For show, I suspect. Anything else you can tell me?"

Adolph was hesitant, sucked on his lower lip, and finally confessed. "You must be killing a lot of inmates, because I can smell that foul smoke most of the day. This is about all I know."

"Thank you, Adolph. I can see myself out." Wilhelm gave a smart salute as Albert walked by, getting a good look at Wilhelm's view of the camp as he passed.

Not much view there either, Albert mulled.

Fredrik was counting inmates at the chow hall when Albert walked in. He waited until the count was finished and motioned for him to come outside. "What's up, Albert?"

"Sergeant, I want you to get into the habit of calling me "sir." I don't like it any better than you, but such a slip at the wrong time, and we're history. What I came to tell you was to report to Lt. Kreutz' office on your next break. Do you know where his office is?"

"Um...I'm not sure. Is it that little hole in the wall on the north end of the spa?"

Albert could hardly contain himself in anticipation. "Yes, that's it."

He gave Martin a review of the situation, and they did a quickstep to catch up with Fredrik just as he was entering the reception area where Wilhelm was seated. Both did a double-take, shouted out the other's name, strode toward each other, and embraced.

Older brother Fredrik was first to speak. "How long have you been here? The last I knew you were in Stuttgart."

"I got here about a month ago, and the last I heard from you was Sachsenhausen!"

Martin just had to muscle in on the conversation to take a verbal poke at Wilhelm. "And the last time we had an encounter was when you came shouting at me from around the corner. Scared the wits out of me."

Albert was next. "And the last time I remember seeing you, Wilhelm, you were flagging your tail down the road as fast as your chubby little legs would carry you."

"What have we here, old home week?" Kreutz had caught the whole scene. Albert did an abbreviated review on how and where the four had first met, but omitted the part where he had tossed Fredrik on his butt.

By now, shuttling the prisoners to freedom was such a routine that Karl and a guard could almost handle it alone. Albert asked him if he and the rest of Martin's guard could finish up these last three hours so the reunion could adjourn to the nearest tavern.

The closest tavern was about halfway between Camp Calais and the town of Calais, near Albert's home. He had taken off his uniform, only wearing it when on duty. The tiny tavern could hold only about twenty patrons. Fifteen, mostly soldiers, were there when the celebrants arrived.

Within an hour, some of the other soldiers had gotten rowdy. One of them jostled Albert, spilling part of his beer then grumbled, "Watch where you're going, civilian."

Albert chose not to confront the soldier. "Sorry, soldier. I'll be more careful next time." He dared not hit a man in uniform.

Martin could see a fight in the making and knew Albert, an experienced boxer, could handle this drunk with a couple of swift blows. He stepped between them, confident his earlier training by Albert and some experience of his own could dispense with the troublemaker.

"Corporal," Martin said in a soft tone, "if you're having a problem with my friend here, you'll have to deal with me. He's only a civilian, and didn't we join the army to protect them? So, why don't you be a good little corporal and leave us alone?"

Three of the corporal's buddies stood up and assumed a threatening pose. Fredrik and Wilhelm followed suit just in time to see Martin strike the corporal square in the nose, dropping him to his knees. He blocked a punch by another and struck him also on the nose. He ducked a third soldier's roundhouse swing and hit him so hard in the stomach he belched and threw up his beer.

"Just like you taught me!" exclaimed Martin, seeing Albert's look of amazement.

By now the brothers entered the fray. Wilhelm blindsided the fourth soldier with a sucker punch sending him to the floor He picked the soldier up, grabbed him by his collar and the seat of his pants, and tossed him out the door. Martin and Fredrik likewise booted out the other three, and as quickly as the confrontation had started, it was over.

Albert had noticed Wilhelm's sucker punch on one of the soldiers, but still thanked him for helping Martin. Fredrik also saw the cheap shot, but said nothing.

Next morning a wire gram from Berlin awaited Albert. It was an invitation for him to attend the Wannsee Conference one month from now, January 20, 1942. The confab had evidently been scheduled months ago, because its purported agenda was to decide "Endlosung" (the Final Solution of the Jewish Problem), i.e., how best to get rid of them. But the concept of mass murder had already been implemented. All that had to be made official was the most efficient method, gassing, and then cremation.

1942

The Gathering

January. Wannsee, Germany. Albert was not one of the official speakers at the conference, but at the cocktail hour he was the center of attraction. Two camp Kommandants cornered him, both questioning the moving of prisoners to Calais. Their facilities were being converted to death camps, not to their liking.

One was from Gross-Rosen to whom Albert had spoken earlier. "I have an opportunity to be General Rommel's aide. I must know today if you are willing to take my inmates."

"I was willing to take them a month ago," Albert reminded him. "Nothing has changed. How many are there and when will you be sending them?"

"There are approximately 17,000, and they will be arriving by rail within a month."

The other Kommandant from Dachau had another lame excuse for ridding himself of prisoners. "I am eligible for reassignment. You will receive about 20,000 in two weeks." Albert thanked them for their confidence in Camp Calais. That totaled 98,000 incoming prisoners and 41,000 had traversed the tunnel, Albert mentally calculated. We now have 57,000 in house and room for another 43,000. This is too good to be true.

It was!

Albert retraced the day's events and conversations in the quiet of his room the evening before heading back to Calais. He awoke suddenly when he remembered a portion of a conversation whose significance completely slipped by him at the time:

The Gross-Rosen Kommandant said he was sending his inmates by *rail*. Is there a rail spur near Calais we aren't aware of? Must talk with the group about this.

Calais. The first thing Albert did upon his return to Calais was to contact Kreuger and tell him he was anxious to report on the Wannsee conference, but needed to delay their meeting for a few minutes. He needed to hold a quick meeting with his group. Very important.

When he got the group together, he expressed his surprise that there may be a rail spur nearby. It's important to know if, in fact, there is. Albert gave orders to fan out and search, on foot, all directions. If one is found, a meeting will be called to deal with it.

A beaming Kreuger greeted Albert. "I just got word from Neuegamme. Remember, the only camp in Northern Germany to turn us down earlier? They want to send us their entire prisoner population. About 16,000. They finally saw the light. Or heard my impromptu cocktail hour dissertation, thought Albert.

"Nice going, Erik!" But he was worried. The camp could now hold only another 27,000, plus the some 4,500 escaping daily. One more inmate transfer and Camp Calais could be at capacity. How can we move any faster? thought Albert.

Kreuger bubbled on, "Only three camps, Mittlebau Dora, Flossenburg, and Buchenwald remain, and we will have moved every camp in Germany to Calais. That is our goal!"

Here's a chance to build better relations with Kreuger. Albert pondered. "Well Erik, this calls for a celebration. Shall we transfer to my office and pop the cork?"

Kreuger was ebullient. "Very good idea, Albert."

As Albert poured the champagne, Kreuger noticed a cablegram on Albert's desk, calling his attention to it. "First, Erik, we toast your successes." And both gulped down the libation. The message read: "Immediate, see Capt. Siegel for decoded information."

Reluctant to have to deal with Siegel, but curious as to the message's contents, Albert hurried to Piotr's office. As he read, his smile slowly evolved into a stricken look. "Oh Mein Gott, this couldn't happen at a worse time!"

"What is it?" asked Piotr, wondering what was afoot.

Albert read aloud. "Per your implied approval, we will be using your facility to warehouse guns and ammunition and maintain a fleet of seaplanes. Material is on its way. Will be using your prisoners for labor. Also, spa will be converted into hospital. Good luck always, Maj. Willi Heinrich."

"Well, a hospital in the area," stated Piotr. "That's always good news."

Martin and group took only about three hours to find the beginning and end of the spur. It started about five miles north of Calais, where it appeared to be at least occasionally used to approximately two miles beyond Camp Calais' north and east prison fence.

"The Gross-Rosen Kommandant must be planning to deliver the prisoner railcars there," commented Albert. "Willi Heinrich undoubtedly plans to dump their supplies and ammunition there also."

"It might be a good idea to check the area after the big guns and the new prisoners have been delivered," said Martin. "We will need to check in the new prisoners. Also, I have a feeling that Staff will be interested in the disposition of the big guns."

March. The building supplies and prisoners from Gross-Rosen arrived the same day via rail, as anticipated. The ammunition supply sheds were to be built inside the fenced area amongst the prisoners' barracks.

When Albert saw Gross-Rosen prisoners spewing out of the boxcars he was aghast. It wasn't the condition of the woebegone that disturbed Albert. He had seen this many times before and was able to bear the sight knowing they would be free someday. This delivery was almost 100% women and children. Men now represented 90% of the prison population. He couldn't mix women and children in the same barracks. Now he had to totally rearrange everything!

Workers were everywhere. Guards had to be particularly watchful, lest some venturesome Jew try to sneak out. Gone were the days of relative peace and tranquility. And, bad news for Karl. The "Struma," a ship loaded with Jewish refugees, was refused entry to Palestine and sank off the Turkish coast. All 769 passengers drown, except one.

"These may have been some we saved earlier," moaned Karl. "And it bothers me I had no feel for this occurrence. Am I losing it?" No sooner had he said this than he felt a strong twinge. "In Poland. Killings are beginning. Belzek? Not certain. Auschwitz? Many Jews sent there from Slovakia. I'm not as clear. Sobibor! Yes Sobibor is beginning to build a death camp.

Albert headed home, dog-tired from trying to keep three balls in the air at the same time: Checking out the escapees; helping locate best places to build weapons storage sheds; reassigning barracks occupancy. He didn't need to even think about what needed to be done next.

But Kristine had something on her mind. "Zucker!"

"Please Kristine. Later. And what is with this 'Zucker'? (Sugar) You've never called me that."

"I was trying to be pleasant because I've decided to do something which you may not approve of." No reply. Albert was either dozing on the couch or just didn't wish to answer. She continued. "I've decided to work part time at the new hospital starting tomorrow; they need nurses."

To Kristine's surprise, Albert answered, "I think you have a good idea there." Maybe it will help her come out of that shell she's been hiding in these past few years, he thought. "Try to arrange your hours so you can ride home with me. Incidentally, what made you want to work at the hospital?"

"Mama thought it would be good for me."

Albert sat up, wondering if he had heard correctly. "Mama? You mean Papa!"

"No, Albert, I mean Mama. She talks to me almost every day now. She has helped me feel better about myself. She wants me to do things."

Albert didn't know whether Kristine was joking or not. A sudden thought came to him. Had Kristine developed the same powers her father has, or were they limited to just a bridge between her and her mother? Then Albert recalled Kristine echoing the "Voice of God" a year or so ago. But she can only transmit His voice. Also, unlike Karl, she cannot "feel" the future. They had entirely different abilities.

"I haven't told you or Papa about this because I was afraid you wouldn't believe me."

Karl knew something was amiss the minute he walked through the door. "What is it, Kristine?"

"Papa I was so afraid, but I'm not anymore. I thought the voice would punish me if I told, but now I know she won't. I didn't recognize her voice because I had never heard it."

"Her voice?" Karl pondered a moment, afraid to ask. "Is it your mother?"

"Yes, Papa, I'm almost sure!"

Karl knowingly nodded his head. "I remember my Mama talking with her Mama. I thought she was 'Meshuga.' I myself have heard Amy, but just recently, only twice. And then just a few words. How long have you been hearing her?"

"Over three years. Only occasionally at first, but now almost daily."

Karl was becoming a little teary-eyed. "What sorts of things has she said?"

"Mostly to take care of your Papa. The last time she said something about my being of great help to many people."

Karl was choked with emotion and excused himself from the room.

May. Albert thought he would stop by Kreuger's office to say hello. He was looking out the window, shoulders heaving, obviously weeping. Startled to see Albert standing there as he turned around he quickly said, "Blasted cold. Having a deuce of a time getting rid of it."

Albert didn't buy it. "Are we friends, Erik?"

"Certainly," as a slight smile surfaced.

"Then tell me what's bothering you. I'm a great listener."

None of Kreuger's friends had consoled him in such a manner. He almost started crying again. There was a minute of agonizing silence. Erik finally gathered his composure. "I have seen, sometimes ordered, men beaten, but never have I seen a man die, let alone in the manner you have."

Albert was getting a bad feeling. Is Erik going to say what I think he's about to say? Albert tried to be flippant. "Why, did you want to take a peek at our operations?"

"Absolutely not!" Kreuger was vehement. "I have been ordered by Heinrich to observe an execution."

Albert's gut was churning. "Did Willi tell you how many deaths you need to witness?" Kreuger shook his head.

"Erik, you have no choice but to comply. You don't want to end up in prison. Let's plan this. Make it as simple, and palatable as possible. First of all, you don't need to participate. This is the worst part of the whole procedure. All you need to do is just observe. Next, Willi says 'an execution.' Not two, five, or twenty. Just once. Also, it needs a little window dressing. It should be at least two people so you can report 'deaths.' I would suggest four to six (knowing Kreuger couldn't handle six) so you can give Willi the feeling you're talking about multiple deaths."

Kreuger was beginning to feel somewhat better. "Thanks Albert, I feel better now. I think I can go through with it. Another favor. Please keep our discussion under your hat."

"Goes without saying! By the way, did Willi say when he wanted this done?"

"No. Do you suppose if we put it off long enough he will forget?" he said, half hoping.

Albert knew he had to give a stern answer, also wishing the execution could be put off. "No Erik. As a matter of fact we should do this fairly soon. Willi will be judging you by your response time."

Karl didn't react one way or the other when Albert told him of their predicament, simply saying, "God will provide."

Albert looked at his watch and exclaimed, "Oh boy, am I in trouble! I was supposed to pick up Kristine an hour ago. Forgot all about her working at the hospital."

He drove up in a cloud of dust only to see what appeared to be the same old hole in the wall. Only the back half of the hospital was complete. There was almost no patient load.

"Yes sir," said Wilhelm, "your wife already left for home. There wasn't much to do. She said you weren't to be by for another two hours so she decided to walk home, only 4 to 6 kilometers."

Albert was peeved. Damn her, that's still a long hike. Her feet must be killing her. He sped off toward home.

It was about an hour earlier that Kristine had unlocked and entered her front door. Watching the house, as Capt. Piotr Siegel had recently suggested, was that troublesome corporal that Albert and his crew bumped into a few months back. He immediately went to the tavern to tell his buddies that Capt. Siegel was right. The civilian lived almost directly across the street from the tavern, and his wife was home alone.

"Why don't we stroll over and have some fun?" said the excited corporal. "Ach! We've already been in enough trouble," complained a cautious companion. "She's a civilian, moron. Ever see a civilian complaint hold up in court around here?"

Three shots rang out in quick succession, piercing the left rear door of Albert's sedan. His reflex was automatic as he piled out of the car to hug the ground. He worked his way belly-crawling to the other side of the car, all the time hearing nothing, seeing nothing. Only about 70 meters from home, Albert made a zig-zag dash and into his home

That little delay ought to have given the boys enough time to finish their business, thought Piotr.

Albert, unaware of what had happened there an hour earlier, was still a bit miffed when he ran into the house "Kristine!" he said in a loud voice. He heard something in the bedroom and rushed in to see Kristine groping at the covers and trying her best to cry, or scream, but could only muster a throaty sob. Most of her dress and slip were torn off.

Albert could scarcely believe what he was seeing. It took a few seconds for the truth to register. "Kristine" he shouted and fairly dove to her side. Embracing her he spit out, "Who? Are you all right?" He picked her up oh so gently and placed her in the car, and floor-boarded it back to the hospital. To further complicate the scenario, three more bullets smashed through the front windshield at an angle so as not to hit anyone. But it startled Albert almost off the road

"What is it sir?" a concerned Wilhelm questioned tentatively as Albert whisked Kristine to the functional portion of the hospital. A doctor was in and a bed available.

"Was that Kristine?" Wilhelm asked anyone who would listen. Without asking permission to leave, he ran to find Karl, Martin, and Fredrik.

"I'm not certain." Wilhelm answered the battery of questions issued by Martin and Fredrik as the trio ran back to the hospital. Karl was struggling unsuccessfully to keep up.

By this time Albert had regained most of his composure. Seeing his friends at the door of the room, he got up out of his bedside chair and quietly whispered, "Kristine was raped, by several men. She has been sedated. The doctor says she incurred several bruises but no internal bleeding. Seems all right. She needs rest. That's all I know for now."

Then with an echoing voice, Kristine whispered, "***Those who sinned were led by another. He won't be easily found!***"

"A message from God," said Karl. "Finding the rapists should be no problem. But their ringleader may be difficult to locate."

A low buzzing sound came from the hallway as the foursome slowly walked, chattering quietly, toward the outside door. Karl was too worried to be angry. The brothers were fuming. Martin was seething, plotting death to the yet unknown assailants.

While Karl went home, the boys had blood in their eyes. They needed revenge, and decided to drive to their favorite tavern and maybe pick up a lead to the culprits. The place was quiet, save for six soldiers in the back corner laughing and talking loudly. "Shh!" whispered Wilhelm as he put a finger to his lips and gestured toward the six boisterous celebrants. "I think we've found them!"

The loudest of the group slurred, "Ach, I would give a week's pay to have seen the expression on that civilian's face when he got home."

The boys listened intently, pretending to be having a conversation of their own.

"And you, you little worry wart." Martin spotted the loud mouth. It was that corporal troublemaker. "You thought we would be caught and sent to a firing squad!"

The boys heard more incriminating boasting. Convinced they were the rapists, a plot was hatched.

"We can't just saunter over and say, 'come with us fellows,' then take them outside and shoot their butts," said Wilhelm. "We could mosey over and kick butt, maybe, but what good would that do? How about we just go get the police?"

"You've just given me an idea," exclaimed Martin. "If we try to involve the police at this point, those rats will just lie, and it's our word against theirs. We can't get the police to take them out to the hospital for Kristine to I.D. because she's too sedated. If we wait until she's clear-headed our suspects might just have gotten away."

"We understand the problem, Martin," Fredrik said impatiently. "Got any ideas how to solve the dilemma?"

"Yes, Fredrik be patient. If we get into a fight with those goons in the corner, you know, really smash up the place, the police will come and toss all of us into jail. In the morning

Karl comes to the station to bail us out, explains the situation, then they take the bad guys out to the hospital for Kristine to identify."

Martin's idea was enthusiastically adopted, although no one spoke. "Now, go to Karl's, tell him our plan, and then get your patootie back here as fast as you can. It may take all three of us to handle them. Oh, and have Karl call the police about five minutes after you leave. Tell them there's a fracas at the tavern."

When Fredrik returned, the three avengers walked over to where the six soldiers were seated and stood in a small semi-circle behind them. Martin came directly to the point, "If any of you brave troopers had nothing to do the rape of my friend's wife earlier this evening, I would suggest you get up and leave now while you can."

One of the soldiers rose slowly from his chair, back to the wall, and scurried out the door. Another one got up and was about to repeat the other's exit when the apparent ringleader of the soldiers involved in the rape shouted to him, "Sit down you whimpering dog. We can whip these three pansies."

No sooner had the challenge been issued than Wilhelm unleashed his favorite weapon, the "sucker-punch" on one of the seated soldiers, now out of the battle before it had hardly begun. Picking up his fallen foe's chair, he hurled it across the table at a second adversary.

Waiting for their opponents to turn and get to their feet, Martin and Fredrik lit into the rapists with a vengeance.

Martin, again, struck the nose, then dealt a hard punch to the stomach, blocked an incoming fist and repeated the process on the next man. The two lay on the floor in agony.

Fredrik and his opponent were grappling on the floor, rolling over and over, smashing chairs, and breaking table legs. Fredrik finally applied a chokehold and soon had his man unconscious.

The fifth soldier was getting the best of Wilhelm when police arrived to stop the melee. Police took the lot of them and put them in jail.

Karl arrived at the police station mid-morning to bail out the boys, explained the situation to the chief and asked if he would bring the five soldiers to the new spa hospital late afternoon for Kristine to identify. She needed time to clear her head.

Police brought an extra nine soldiers, fourteen total, from which Kristine was to pick the four guilty ones. Without hesitation she picked the correct four, omitting, of course, the fifth and sixth soldiers in the fracas who did not participate in the raping. She then called the boys to her bedside and thanked them profusely for their ingenuity, courage, and friendship.

Police were about to take the four guilty men back to jail for holding until a military tribunal would decide their fate. Meanwhile the corporal was smiling as he consoled the worrywart. "We're as good as free," he bragged.

About this time Albert walked in wearing his SS Captain's uniform. The guilty parties whispered, almost in unison, "the civilian!" Every chin dropped except for the corporal, who slowly slid down the wall to the floor.

"Could you fellows hold it a minute?" Karl asked police. "Albert, I told you God would provide."

"We can't just..." was as far as Albert got.

"In your birthday suit, who's to say you're not the emperor," Karl opined.

Albert walked over to the police chief, "Both parties, injurer and injured, are affiliated with the military. Let's just consider our unit a military tribunal. Give them to us."

Up to this point Albert had been too concerned about Kristine's condition to think about the perpetrators. As he began to think about what they did, his anger began to swell. He felt like pulling his Luger side arm out and emptying a clip of shells into each man. Martin recognized the look in his eyes and grabbed his arm.

"Our revenge will be sweeter," Martin assured him. "I'll go alert Kreuger that an execution is being prepared for him to witness. Come to think of it, I'll see if Siegel wants to be a witness also. It might satisfy him enough to keep from nosing around, and that men really are being executed here."

"Good, tell them it will be in 45 minutes. Karl, go pick out four inmates to dispose of the bodies. You'll have to give them a short course on what is happening, what to do, and that freedom will be their reward." Within 30 minutes his task was done and all was in readiness. Piotr was standing in the middle of the policemen, trying to find out what they were doing in his bailiwick. When he got the gist of all the activity, he began to ease his way from the area, but Karl finally spotted him and passed on Albert's invitation to witness an execution.

Piotr was about to be caught in his own web. If he refused to be a witness, this would place him under suspicion with Albert's crew. If he did become a witness, one of the guilty soldiers might point the finger at him as the mastermind.

First, he tried the "legality" approach, asking where the alleged crime took place. Finding out it was away from Camp Calais, he began to question the legality of Albert being the prosecutor. But when discovering in was in Albert's home, he recanted. Then he asked for permission to talk to the prisoners. Albert saw nothing wrong with the request.

As the convicted soldiers huddled around Siegel, it appeared, by the look on their faces that they were being consoled. In reality, Piotr was lying to them, knowing they wouldn't be alive to rat on him. "Just as your shower begins, run through a sliding door that I will have opened. Between the time allowed for a shower, usually five minutes, and your running, you'll have time to make it to a five-foot wide air vent and on to safety. Capt. Steller will just have to blame themselves for not being familiar with the buttons and handles which control their new devices."

The process began: Fredrik, gun in hand, took the four condemned men to a ten-foot square gassing area, and told them to disrobe. They could see the showerheads, so complied without complaint or question.

Kreuger walked to the mess hall on wobbly legs, and as he stepped in, Albert and Piotr could see him struggling. He attempted to express his condolences to Albert, but his effort fell far short of perfection. "Straighten up, your Fuhrer is watching!" said Siegel sternly. Amazingly, Kreuger came to attention, strode to the killing area, and remained composed for the balance of the procedure.

"We have no windows, so you'll have to crack the door and peek in to verify the number of victims."

"Four," Kreuger stated.

"Right. Now we close the door, throw the left switch, wait 30 seconds, and then throw the right switch. Then, in one minute, we turn off both switches. What we have done here is to turn on the gas, then a fan to circulate the fumes. When both are turned off, the prisoners will have been exposed for two minutes. Ample time to kill them."

Little was heard from the rapists inside. No screaming or yelling—just gurgling sounds. "The slightest inhale of gas 'freezes' their vocal chords. They want to shriek, but can't," said Albert.

Albert turned on the fans for another minute to be certain all of the gas was gone, and then opened the gas room door. Both could see four twisted bodies with contortioned faces massed into one corner, as if trying to find that open door before a quick, but agonizing death. On signal the four inmate recruits crept into the room, carried the four bodies to the chute, and slid them one by one to the cremation room below. Kreuger made the comment: "Those dead men looked reasonably healthy." Albert's short retort was, "Yes, these just came in. Now, there's no sense in waiting around until the bodies are cremated, so why don't we go to my office for a snifter to forget what we saw. I don't like this any better than you."

A half hour later, they returned to the crematorium. All three walked over to the two authentic ovens where the ashes and bones of the assailants lay. Just hours ago they were, unknowingly, about to go to their doom. In the pull of a lever the remains dropped into the cavern below. Siegel breathed a deep breath. He had gotten out of a real dilemma with assistance from fraulein luck and craftiness.

"When you're ready, Erik, compose your report for Heinrich," advised Albert. "I will verify and co-sign." From this event, Albert and Erik maintained a mutual, but guarded respect for one another. Albert had absolutely no respect for Plotr.

"Odd isn't it?" Albert later commented to Karl, "Those four, while deserving to die, did not die in vain. In so doing they saved the lives of four innocent Jews! *In making a straight line, God sometimes uses a crooked stick!*"

July. Work on the ammunition dumps, both inside and outside of the prison confinement area, was nearing completion. Bedlam had been reduced to organized chaos, and nerves had become raw. Albert had successfully separated women and children from the men's barracks. Prison population had slowly dwindled to around 38,000.

Then the biggest influx to date brought the number up to 110,000, 10,000 over capacity. No one had warned Albert of this activity.

As they filed into the compound, Karl noticed something different. All were now wearing the yellow Star of David, a recent edict issued by the Nazis. "Where are we going to put them all," moaned Karl. "Where did they all come from?"

"On your first question, I'm not certain yet," answered a bedraggled Albert. "On the second one, inquiries to the prisoners indicate Netherlands, Belgium, and France. Now we must postpone going after those three remaining camps in Germany. There is some encouraging news, however. Many of them, mostly French or from the Drancy Camp had been destined for Auschwitz."

"I just wish the news from Poland was encouraging," Karl complained. "Construction of the extermination center at Treblinka has started. Worse, some 300,000 Warsaw Jews have been deported there, and there are still 60,000 left in that ghetto."

"Karl, what was our agreement?"

"Not to belabor events East. We can do nothing to help our brothers there. Don't punish ourselves by thinking about it."

"So, what did we decide was a way to take our minds off events in Eastern Europe?" prompted Albert.

"Think of something amusing. Maybe even tell a joke. Come to think of it, I haven't told you a joke for quite a spell."

"Please, tell me a joke," pleaded Albert in feigned sincerity.

"A German lad walks into a tavern and orders three beers. He drinks some out of first glass, some out of second, and some from third. He repeats the process until all three beers have been downed. He leaves, comes back one month later, and asks for three beers. Bartender says, no need to order three at a time, they get a bit stale. I can bring them one at a time.

"No, you don't understand," said the lad. "My two brothers left Germany. One went to Australia, the other to America. We agreed to go to a tavern once a month, like we did when all were here, and, in remembrance of our kinship, have a round of drinks."

"One day the lad walks in and orders two beers. The bartender, being a sensitive fellow, said he was sorry for the loss of a brother and asked how he died. The lad replied, 'No one died. I just quit drinking.' "

Two hours later Karl was sour-faced again. He walked up to Albert, handed him a slip of paper and glumly said, "How can I pretend nonchalance when I read this? I am dying inside!"

"What is it?"

"Read it."

"We were ten brothers
Our business was the wine trade
One brother died
So we remained nine.

Yidl, with your fiddle.

Moyshe, with your bass.

Play me a little song

While they lead us to the gas chamber.

Now I am the only brother left

With whom can I share my tears?

The others have all been murdered

Don't forget their names!

Yidl, with your fiddle.

Moyshe, with your bass.

Hear my last little song

They're taking me, too, to the gas.

We were ten brothers

We never hurt anyone."

"Where did you get this?" asked Albert, now becoming concerned about leakage of events behind the fence.

"From an inmate in the upper basement, waiting to be set free. He must have misunderstood my Amcha talk, thinking he was about to be gassed. He came up to me with this slip of paper, asked that I keep it for posterity, and disappeared into the crowd."

A mist formed over Albert's eyes. He stood there for a minute, gazing into space. Suddenly, realizing something, he jumped to his feet. "Now we have a real concern."

Albert reflected for a moment then uttered, Judas priest! How could this happen? We've been so careful."

"I have a feeling sooner or later you're going to tell me how could 'what' happen, but I'm holding out for sooner," said Karl, sarcastically.

Albert was about as angry as Karl had ever seen. "Think, man, think. You said he must have thought he was about to be gassed. This may mean who knows how many inmates believe Camp Calais is an extermination center, exactly what we don't want them to think! We want them to have *some* hope."

"Hey, I'm your father-in-law here. No need to talk to me that way."

Albert snapped out of his fit of anger. "Karl, I had no call to use you as my whipping post. Please accept my apologies."

"Well, I was available. Apology accepted. Incidentally, I had a small shiver last week, and its 'epicenter' was close, in Dieppe. The English Commandos tried a raid on this newly acquired German port. It was a disaster for the English. Just wanted you to know I've still 'got it.' "

Albert wasn't quite ready to give up. "Could one of our boys inadvertently let the cat out of the bag?" He was mumbling to himself as he walked to the hospital to pick up Kristine, who was another concern to him. "She really shouldn't have gone back to work so soon."

He heard Kristine in the back lobby conversing with someone. "Probably Lt. Kreutz," he thought. But the lieutenant had already gone home and all the other doors were closed.

"Was the aggressor's assault on me an atonement for my earlier ill feelings toward Albert for his frequent absences?" Kristine asked the voice.

"Of course not," came the whispery reply. "God doesn't punish in that manner. You were being blessed with the opportunity to save lives of the innocent.

"Oh Mama, do you really think so?"

Albert heard only her last question, but none of the comments by Amy, i.e., 'Mama', i.e., 'the Voice.' "Talking with Mama's ghost again?"

"Don't make fun of me, Albert. You know Mama and I talk from time to time. Besides, she gave me a message for you: 'A captain awaits a captain in the Pelican's belly.'"

Albert had to scratch his head on this one. "I give up. Can you tell me its meaning?"

"Well, you're a captain and Calais has a Pelican Inn. Let's go there and see what we can find."

Arriving at the Inn they saw nothing until going around back to the restaurant portion. It was empty except for one man with a freighter captain's jacket on in the corner.

"I think we found the answer." They walked over to his table and Albert asked, "Have we met before?"

"If you are Albert Steller, we have. Remember the ship 'Norse 150'? I was her Captain then and brought you a load of supplies from Dover, kind of secret like."

"Yes, Yes I do remember. But I'm afraid I wouldn't have recognized you."

The Captain motioned for them to sit down, and began. "I have sad news to deliver. A good friend of mine and business associate of yours is dead, killed by the Nazis." Before Albert could ask questions the Captain continued in a hushed voice. "Oskar Dvergsdahl, shot in the back."

Albert was shocked. He hadn't even thought of Oskar for months. Now he was dead. "How did this happen?"

The Captain looked around, leaned over, and related the story. "The Nazis found out about his plastics formula. They tried their best to get him to reveal it. He refused all attempts.

"A few of his crew who were with him while being interrogated told me of the beatings he endured and the pain he suffered. Finally he cracked and told the Heinies the formula was kept in a shed near the raw material site. The second he got out of their car he started to run, or should I say 'lumber.' He wasn't a very graceful man. Anyway, hands cuffed behind him he didn't move very fast. Then it happened. A trigger-happy guard opened up with his machine gun.

"The guard was just reacting to a man trying to escape. He didn't think that when the escaping man died, the formula died with him. Oskar was hoping for this exact scenario. He knew he couldn't hold out much longer and planned his own death...a swift one...to maintain secrecy."

"Did his crew give him a proper burial?" Kristine asked.

"At first glance, no. But, as for something Oskar would have wanted, a resounding yes! You see the Nazis, venting their anger at Oscar, tossed his corpse into the gray muck. Took six days for the body to sink below surface. Oskar was home in the muck and goo that was his life."

Tears came to Albert's eyes. He didn't know why. Oskar wasn't a person he considered to be a close friend. "I think Oskar considered us to be his friends," Albert reasoned. "In protecting his formula he was protecting us." He reflected further, shook his head and eulogized, "Greater love hath no man—"

"—than to lay down his life for a friend," Kristine finished the verse.

The Captain bid his goodbyes. Albert and Kristine remained. No one spoke for what seemed an eternity. "Let's go home," Kristine finally suggested.

September. Karl was concerned, and relieved. Concerned that his abilities may be slipping; relieved that the burdens of this ability may finally vanish. The Nazis had begun their attack on Stalingrad two weeks ago, and he hadn't seen or felt a thing.

"I can tell you something right now, however, the Russkies are going to stop them cold, literally and within six months force them to retreat. This will be Hitler's furthest penetration. This is the beginning of his end!"

"Can you get off of your soapbox long enough to pass the Kohl"? Albert pleaded. Kristine fixes it so delicately. I hear my stomach begging for it.

"Do you want me to bake something special for next week?"

"And next week is...?" asked Albert.

"The anniversary of the tunnel's completion," exclaimed Kristine excitedly. "And the first group of Jews escaped to freedom."

At an average of 4,500 escapees per day it didn't take long to work off Camp Calais' excess population. As of mid-September the inmate population, men, women, and children numbered 53,000. With the construction upheaval also completed, a calm settled over the camp. It wasn't to last long.

Jewish inmates from the Gurs Camp in France, destined for Auschwitz and Sobibor, were sidetracked to Calais. Only 18,500. Then came the three remaining camps in Germany: Mittlelbau-Dora, Flossenburg and, finally, Buchenwald—a grand total of 54,000. Within three weeks total population grew to 125,500, which was over capacity by 25,000. Their goal to transfer every camp in Germany had been reached.

Kreuger was unusually quiet. Looking out of his window at the scene below took up most of the day. Harbored seaplanes for spotting submarines; prisoners' barracks mingled among ammunition warehouses; prisoners either working around the warehouses or shuffling aimlessly around the fenced compound. And, the horizon. Always watching the horizon, as if he were waiting, or wishing, for an Allied invasion.

"Fine with me," declared Karl as he and Albert had been discussing Erik's placid behavior. "Now I don't have to worry about his snooping around the killing area."

"No need to worry about that," assured Albert. "Leopards can't change their spots, and Kreuger can't stand the sight of blood. You would do well to try and be amicable.

He's the perfect Kommandant for our purposes. And you know, I almost like him."

Martin interrupted the dialogue. "A couple of SS officers are heading this way. They came out of nowhere!"

Albert snapped to and Karl disappeared. "They look very official," he thought as he spotted them walking briskly toward his office. I hope they're not replacing Kreuger." A closer look and he took a deep breath, relieved at the sight of Sol and Vance.

Warm handshakes followed. "I wish you folks would give me a warning, instead of a myocardial infarction, when you plan a visit."

"Blimey, what fancy words," joked Sol. "What does it mean?"

"Heart attack. Got it from Kristine. She's working as a nurse now in our newly built hospital. What brings you here?"

Vance spoke first. "Our naval department says those seaplanes are creating havoc with our subs. We want to destroy them, discourage harboring them in the future. What say you?"

"Well, using torpedoes is a bit dangerous," warned Martin. "One miss and an ammo shed could go up and with it the rest of the camp. Bomb? Even more risky. The tunnel is pretty obvious. Easy beach access from the mess hall. Plant a few bombs and get out quick."

"Kind of what we thought," agreed Vance. "We accomplish both goals. Destroying existing planes and discouraging use of the camp as a future harbor because of its obvious vulnerability to commando raids, which they'll have to think it was. We wanted to check with you first, though, in case you knew something we didn't.

"Also," Sol warned, "we've had reports from the French underground about Jews running around the countryside trying to find this magic escape hatch."

Albert was furious. "Another leak! All of the sudden people, both inside and outside the camp, seem to know what we're up to. We've got to find that Cantor."

"Cantor?"

"Jewish singer...squealer...big mouth."

"What makes you think it's a Jew?"

"Has to be, otherwise by now we'd be toasted," Albert reasoned. "Anyway, this is my problem, and I'll have to deal with it. Oh, by the way Sol, how do I get in touch with the underground? I need to find those Jews looking for Jacob 's ladder before they lead the foxes to our little nest."

"Be at the screened gas vent terminal at 10 p.m. tonight," instructed Sol. "Several members of the French fighters will be there to exchange notes and try to find hiding places for the Jews they've rounded up. Meanwhile, Vance and I should be introduced to your Maj. Erik Kreuger. We saw him looking out of his window, and he surely saw us. We may be making regular trips to see you, and we need to belay any potential suspicions."

"Major Kreuger," Albert began, "this is Major Sondheim Rickmann (Sol) and Captain Franz Wunder (Vance). This is my good friend, Erik Kreuger. Erik, these gentlemen are on a routine inspection tour from Berlin and want to ask you a few questions."

Albert was grinning broadly. Sol and Vance had no prepared questions and were taken by total surprise. All right Albert, thought Sol. I can handle this. He then asked a battery of nonsensical questions that had Kreuger sweating. For certain he would avoid any contact with these two inspectors on any future visits.

Albert was still grinning, this time in admiration of Sol who was handed a bag full of lemons and made instant lemonade.

Immediately after Sol and Vance disappeared into the tunnel, Albert called a meeting with his staff. He related his suspicions regarding both inside and outside leaks.

Fredrick responded first. "I don't see why you're concerned if the inmates believe this may be an extermination center. Don't we want them to believe they may die here?"

"We want them to believe there is no way to escape and resign themselves to this fact. Certain death, no! They need an element of hope. Desperate men do desperate things."

"You mean like riot, revolt, try to escape?"

"Exactly!"

"I've got an idea on how we might ferret out the potential informant," offered Wilhelm. "We use another informant. Someone who would sell out his own mother to better his situation."

"Yes, good idea," exclaimed Martin. "A 'Kombinator'—a schemer who knows his way around. Makes a point of gathering information."

"Sounds like an untrustworthy individual to me," warned Albert. "Wouldn't he sell you out at the drop of a hat?"

"Not really," explained Wilhelm. "He protects his sources. It is his livelihood. Once he abuses his employer, he's out of a job unless, of course, he finds an employer offering more."

"So, now piquing Albert's interest, "What does a fellow like this cost?"

"Privileges, extra rations, easier duties, cigarettes," explained Wilhelm. "But don't offer him freedom right away or you'll lose a good informant. Keep the possibility of freedom as a carrot."

Karl finally spoke up. "I know the next question: How do we find this informant? Get me some old prisoners' clothes, and I'll find us a good Judenrater (Jewish informer)."

"Martin, I'll be backing you up this evening when you go to meet this fellow from the French Resistance. I'll stay behind 8-10 yards," cautioned Albert "and out of sight. I was never one to trust these Frogs."

As planned, Martin and a Frenchman met that evening. No handshake, just a nod as they sized each other up. There was something familiar about this Frenchy, Martin thought. His moustache looked fake, he wore an eye-patch; his beret was so skewed that it covered one side of his face, and a cigarette dangled constantly from his lips. Martin decided to question him. "I'm curious why you chose this spot as a meeting place. We release our deadly gases at the end of that vent and you seem unconcerned about the warning signs!"

The Frenchman ran his fingertips over his lips, indicating he was unable to speak, and motioned a woman over. Martin repeated the question.

"Sol assured us there was no danger," she told Martin. I took him at his word, with some trepidation. He did tell you about Jews nosing around the coastline, trying to find an escape route. We are constantly running into small groups of from 6-12."

"Sol has told you about our operation?"

"Not very much, only that you have a way to smuggle Jews out of Europe."

Martin saw an opening "Would you like to help those 'Wandering Jews' get out of France?"

"And out of our hair. Mon Dieu! Oui!"

"Let's make this simple," concluded Martin. "Bring however many you have rounded up to this spot after sundown each Friday. We'll wait around for two hours, no later. A password: You say 'Amcha'. We reply 'Our nation.'

November. Karl had been donning his costume for almost one month with no success in locating a good informant. He was limited in time because of his duties giving the Amcha talk, and he was too well fed to be mistaken for a true inmate.

Finally, a ragged diminutive prisoner with a pronounced nose approached Karl. "Got a cigarette?" Karl almost choked trying to keep from laughing as he thought, measured by his stature, his nose should be the size of Napolean's, but it looks more like Goliath's. If he had a nose full of shekels, he would be a very rich man."

Curbing his chuckle, Karl answered, "I only smoke a pipe, and I'm not about to share, but if you're who I'm looking for, I can arrange a pack now and then."

"Arrange and come back, then we talk!"

"Talk, then I arrange."

After a two-minute standoff the little Jew blinked. "You want to know who has been asking a lot of questions and passing answers on to the civilian?"

Karl was startled by the accuracy of the statement, as well as mention of a civilian's involvement. "You seem to know your trade. I'll go get some cigarettes."

"And don't forget matches!"

"What do I call you?" asked Karl as he handed the little Jew a pack of Lucky Strike Greens.

"Call me Ishmael."

"You're kidding, of course?"

"Ishmael is my name. Information is my game."

Karl was beginning to like Ishmael. The little Jew has a sense of humor, he thought, despite misery everywhere you look.

Ishmael began gathering information. "What concerns you that you turn to me for help?"

Karl related offhand statements made that indicated some person, or persons had at least limited knowledge of Camp Calais' internal operations.

"You want me to find out who is trying to find out what, about the goings on somewhere in the camp? Those are pretty vague instructions. But I find out. I think I know where to begin probing."

Karl was becoming more and more dependent on current events from Sol or Vance and less on his ESP. He generally passed the news on to Kristine. She enjoyed being kept current, but not Karl's commentary.

"Listen to this." Karl was in his usual snit. " 'On October 8, Gerhart Riegner called Rabbi Stephen S. Wise in New York and Sidney Silverman in London from Geneva about Nazi plans for the extermination of European Jewry.' This is news? Under whose bed have they been hiding? Oh, it gets better. 'The United States Department of State held up delivery of the message to Wise, who received it from Silverman on August 28.' What kind of panky hanky is this?"

"It's hanky panky, Papa. So why did the United States not deliver his message?" asked Kristine. "Isn't it the home of the free?"

"Home of the brave, Kristine. And the land of the free! Let me finish. And then Rabbi Wise releases to the press the news contained in the Riegner cable. Good for you, Rabbi!

"I read on, 'The Polish Government-in-exile asks the Allies to retaliate for the Nazi killing of civilians, especially Jews.' So what do they do? Nothing! That's what they don't do. Nothing! 'An Allied declaration is made condemning the Nazis' bestial policy of cold-blooded extermination.' Well, Oy Gevalt!

"Ah, some good news for a change. 'Himmler just announced Germany was 'Judenfrei' one year ahead of schedule.' Thanks to the efficiency of Camp Calais' should be added. What Herr Himmler doesn't know is all those Jews came here and escaped! So, go eat an uncooked slab of Schinken (ham)!"

But Karl didn't remain in a jovial mood long, and he complained to Kristine. "The majority of Croation Jews have been deported to Auschwitz, and the deportation of Jews from the Bialystok district to Treblinka has begun. This I didn't get from Dover. This I feel."

December. A prisoner Karl had not noticed before walked up to him and handed him an empty, crushed pack of Lucky Strike Greens. "Great Caesar's ghost," Karl shook his head. "A prisoner, and Ismael has his own lackey."

"Follow me," were his terse instructions.

"Wait just a moment. I need to get something first." Karl jogged to Albert's office for another pack of cigarettes. The two met behind ammo shed no 3. "What have you found, Ishmael?"

"You have some inmates guessing whether certain prisoners are being set free or are being shipped elsewhere to be executed. Neither sounds plausible, but they feel something is amiss."

"What? Who?"

"It was a small thing, but sharp eyes picked up on the fact that every now and then after a load of inmates disappeared, like all others, no smelly smoke came out of the chimneys."

Karl winced, thought to himself the boys are forgetting to toss a log and some sulfur in one of the ovens. He held up the cigarette pack. "Ishmael, these inmates are playing the guessing game; how many are there?"

Ishmael expected Karl to react more visibly. "I'd say about a dozen, all university professors. They stick together fairly closely. Not likely any of them have talked to the riff raff about this."

Karl had an idea. "When could I meet with these gentlemen?"

"It's your whip. Anytime you want."

Karl corrected himself. "I meant to say how long will it take you to assemble them in the back corner of the mess hall. How soon could you do it?"

"In 12 days, or 30 minutes if you have two packs of cigarettes."

"One now, the other when they arrive."

The professors arrived, dirty, unshaven, ragged clothes, in groups of two and three.

Ishmael got his other cigarette pack and was motioned to leave. These were university professors, Karl thought sadly. They could have been my associates. There by the grace of God—he didn't finish his thought.

"Karl! Karl Cohen! How did you escape this hell on earth?" came a question from a reasonably well-dressed inmate. He could see Karl didn't recognize him. "Walter Boenke. Berlin. 1909. Taught calculus. By the way, danke for the warning letter."

"Sorry, Walter, I taught elsewhere. I really pity this Karl fellow if he resembles me."

"You certainly look like him. Of course it was over 30 years ago. He did have a rounder face and a very full schnurbart under his nose."

"Gentlemen," Karl began, "I am led to believe you have noticed an erratic flow of smoke from our chimneys. I believe I can explain this phenomenon. Please follow me." The group was hesitant. Were they, at this very minute, being led to their execution?

Too late to run. An armed guard appeared. "Fredrick, would you escort these gentlemen to the great white way." With the guard behind them, they had no choice but to go forward. Suddenly an oven door swung open, revealing a huge chamber and a few inmates milling around. Karl appeared and gave them a quick review of where they were.

"Usually, knowing too much can get you into trouble," Karl warned. "In your case it brought you an earlier freedom. And Walter, you always were jealous of my moustache."

The prisoners were given a few minutes for a fast lesson on using the tunnel. Not much time for Karl and Walter to catch up on three decades of living. A few tears were shed.

Karl then grabbed Fredrik by the sleeve and told him what happened. "Boys, you've got to be more attentive. Had someone from outside noticed the same thing, we'd be given a terrible spanking."

Walter butted in on Karl's words to Fredrik. "You're not going to believe this but I remember this young man. He was a guard at Sachsenhausen, but very kind to me when I was entering the compound. I had fallen and he helped me, very gently, to get up."

Fredrik was all smiles. Each gave the other a warm hug goodbye.

Karl turned and immediately sought Ishmael. The little Jew hadn't given him anything further about this someone who was passing information on to "the civilian." He was nowhere to be found.

As if choreographed, Karl spotted a civilian talking to an inmate. At the same instant Ishmael pointed a bony finger and cried, "There he is! The civilian!" Neither was hale enough to do more than jog toward their prey, who, seeing two men hurrying his way melted into the crowd.

Jews from the French countryside streamed toward the coast, still not knowing where the rumored escape route was, but feeling it truly existed. Too many of their friends had left the relative safety of hideaways to find it. Some captured, some left to wander.

As the Resistance ran across a group of fleeing Jews, the French would herd them to a place of relative safety and take the accumulation of rag-tag escapees to the appointed spot every Friday after sundown. Most made it into the compound, but the numbers were less than Martin had expected. Was there a "Judenrat" selling some of his brothers to the Nazis...small enough numbers not to be noticed, but enough to make it worth the risk?

Watchful of being followed by the French, Martin's group would take a circuitous route back to the vents. One of the spa group would help an escapee enter the downward sloping vent and told to follow the person ahead.

Watching the fugitives as they entered the tube one by one was a study in facial expressions. Apprehension...brow raised, eyes wide open; fear...brow furrowed, mouth corners turned down; determination...steely eyes, lips pressed together; gladness...brow even, big smile; suspicion...one eye squinted, mouth partly open and jaw extended.

Each Jew was immediately led to the tunnel's gathering area, given a boiled potato, instructed on procedure, and integrated with the ongoing shuffle of inmates heading for freedom.

By this time Martin's group was running on fumes, getting 4-6 hours of sleep average per night. But there was a light at the end of the tunnel. They were down to a prison population of only 41,000—roughly three week's work, if no others were transferred in. By rough count, and it had finally come down to this method, approximately 210,000 inmates, transferees, walk-ons, however one wanted to designate them, had been saved from the firing squad, carbon monoxide, gassing or other ways of killing.

1943

The Intruder

January. Karl was almost dancing around Albert's office. "I knew it, I knew it. Hitler has reached the apex of his conquests. The Russians have raised the siege of Leningrad. The Nazis are pulling back."

Albert had a good night's sleep and was feeling frisky. "Do you know this because of your acquaintances in high places?"

"No, because of my acquaintances in Dover."

"And why is it that Sol and Vance keep you abreast of current events and not me? I do outrank you, don't you know!"

"Maybe if you were a bit more patient you would catch the news too. They're coming over this afternoon to discuss something with you."

"No need to alert Kreuger. He'll see them coming from out his window and beat a hasty retreat."

As in their last outing, Sol and Vance strutted through the outer camp to Albert's office. He could sense that this was no ordinary meeting coming up. Still in good humor from breakfast he decided to toss a bomb, and try to shake them up. They had just sat down when Albert asked innocently, "Well fellows, when is the invasion?"

Vance, whose heart skipped a couple of beats, instinctively rose to go and close the door. It was already closed.

Sol was instantly on to Albert's game. "Well, old boy, we rather thought tonight would be as good a time as any."

Vance, a step behind from the outset, now caught up. "Unless, of course, you have a bridge date. The allied Command can make it another time, they and some 800,000 men."

"So, gentlemen," Albert asked. "What's up?"

"Invasion!" quipped Sol. "Sometime next year if all goes well."

"Holy jumped up Jehoshephat, fellows." Albert whistled. "I was joking."

"We hope to invade France in one year, but no later than June '44. Our big question is where?"

"Certainly not here!" Albert said emphatically, "for all the reasons we gave the Nazis."

Vance was equally emphatic. "Which is exactly why this would be the perfect spot. We've come to see you now to give you time to think it through. We think you'll come to the same conclusion. Your job is to find a way, or develop a system, whereby one day there are 100,000 inmates here and the next day zero!"

Albert just shook his head. "I understand what you're trying to accomplish, and why. But I'm not sure it can be done. We may have to reduce that number down to 50,000. We could give the look of 100,000 bodies with a combination of dummies and people."

"Well, give it some thought," offered Vance. "We'll be checking with you in a few weeks to see what you've come up with."

No more than a week after Karl was joyous over Hitler's failure to take Leningrad, he was dejected over sensations of disaster in Poland.

Kristine tried to console him. "Papa, you agreed we can do nothing to help inmates in the East."

"That doesn't mean I can't grieve for my brothers. Do you feel the disturbance?"

"Yes, Papa, but it's difficult to make out. There is a rebellion. I think in Warsaw. Also, many Jews are deported from Warsaw, and are killed. But there is some good news: In Treblinka they are offering armed resistance!"

March. Martin had to fill in for Albert at the gas vent, now affectionately called "the Tube." Albert had the flu. It was Friday after sundown, so Karl couldn't help. Martin had only guided once, but did accompany the escapees on an earlier trip. Just to get a feel for it.

This particular group of Jews was late in arriving. Their Resistance guides had been delayed when a German scouting mission kept them pinned down. It seemed to Martin that there were more than the usual numbers of fugitives. Accounting for the increase was a family of twelve. The youngest, a boy of twelve, was carrying a small dog.

Martin gave the lead person instructions on how best to wend his way through the vent. He was tentative at first, but soon drew the courage to step into the very small, dark hole. The dog began to bark at something off in the distance.

"Dog! Be quiet," the boy said in a hushed voice. But it was to no avail. The dog continued to yap. A woman, obviously a "painted lady," sidled over to the boy to pet the dog, and see if she could calm it down. But there was no shutting him up.

Martin decided there must be someone continuing to come their way, or the dog probably would have quit barking. He belly crawled away to see what the dog could be hearing. Then he saw that same scouting party, 200 meters away and coming straight at them!

It was a "Judenjagd" (a patrol that tracks down and kills Jews in hiding). There wasn't time for more than a few more people to get into the tube. Worse, he didn't want those soldiers to find the vent. He was about to yell. "Everyone, scatter and run for it!"

In the same instant one of the Resistance members grabbed the dog and quickly slit its throat while the lady, not seeing the killing, grabbed her floi-floi, then got up and ran in a direction away from the group.

The boy was mortified. He had never seen anything killed before, let alone his pet dog. To the Frenchman, slitting throats was a common event. He tried to console the boy, but the lad was too stunned to respond, or to see the heroic lady get up and run, drawing the soldiers away.

Miraculously the lady got away. It was too dark for the soldiers to get a good sighting on their guns, so the bevy of bullets spinning by her couldn't find the target, and she was able to outrun the heavy-booted soldiers.

Within 20 minutes the patrol was out of sight, still chasing the fleet-footed floozie with a floi-floi. The group could now take a deep breath and continue, each with a flashlight, entering the vent. Martin was shaken. He had come within a short breath of exposing their position. He wondered where the "mystery" Resistance leader was.

May. Karl had been in a bad mood for the past two months. Evil doings had occurred, but he was unable to sense any specifics. And it was more difficult to get information from Kristine. So far, knock on wood, she was getting much of her news from the hospital staff.

"It's all-eastward, Papa; you mustn't let it trouble you," Kristine consoled. "Only two occurrences have involved our people. More transports from Salonika and Auschwitz and a small uprising in the Warsaw ghetto."

"Which is going to get worse," Karl added. "And the others?"

"In Poland, mass graves have been discovered at Katyn, but they were Polish officers massacred by the Soviets. And finally they are getting around to persecuting the Gypsies. A special section is made for them at Auschwitz called 'Gypsy Camp.' "

Karl spat on the floor. "Zigeuner" (Gypsies), the scourge of the earth. I'm not sure which clan is worse, the Roma or the Sinti. They all beg or steal for a living. Contribute nothing to mankind."

"Papa, take some time off. Go to Dover. Talk with someone other than us."

For once Karl listened to someone else's advice and took a cart to Dover. He found Sol organizing construction of more barracks for incoming Jews. "Welcome to New Bethlehem," he yelled as Karl approached. "This is the holding tank for our Jewish brothers en route to parts unknown. We can house about 100,000 and it's now at capacity."

"What about the other 130,000 we've sent you?"

"Ah, yes, I forget you haven't been kept abreast of our work here. At first we were met with quite a bit of opposition, but once the Americas and South Africa were convinced that our efforts to save human lives were sincere and ongoing, the barriers quickly came down. So, to answer your question, about half went to the U.S. Midwest and the rest divided between Canada and South Africa."

Karl's load was lightened. "Progress is a beautiful thing."

Albert was waiting for Karl as he emerged from the tunnel. "Got some news this morning which may give us an opening for access to a new area. But we have to act fast."

Karl perked up. "Wonderful," he cried. "There are on. 21,000 here. The Tube brings in but a pittance. We'll soon be out of business, unless--?"

"No Karl, it's useless to try and snooker away any inmates from Auschwitz—yet. Let me tell you, in a nutshell, what's evolving. The Russian Front is soaking up all of the Nazis' reserves, supplies, everything including boxcars."

"So, boxcars are something special?"

Albert just shook his head. "How are Jews transported from place to place?"

"Boxcars!"

"Right, Boxcars. Now listen, Karl, and try not to interrupt until I've explained it all."

"If I wait until you've explained it all, I wouldn't be interrupting would I? All right, I'll keep quiet."

Albert continued. "Germany is starting to lose to the Russians. Also to the Allies in North Africa. It's only a matter of time before they invade Europe, probably in Sicily. Nazi Kommandants are sweating bullets. If Jews are found in their prison, it's a wartime tribunal for them. If they kill the Jews first, and this comes to light, it's a wartime tribunal for them. It's a 'lose-lose' proposition!"

Karl's eyes brightened. "Oh, I understand now. The Baltic States have no way to send prisoners to Poland and the Russians are coming. Why not put them into ships and send them to Camp Calais? As a finishing touch, we can wave our magic wand and guarantee no ship will be sunk en route, but no guarantees going back."

Albert added that the same situation exists in the Adriatic Sea with the American soldiers coming.

"Finland, Estonia, Latvia, Lithuania, Norway, Yugoslavia, Italy, and Greece," Karl rattled off the countries involved.

Albert was impressed with the geography lesson. "A bit less than 350,000 altogether."

"I suppose this means we won't be seeing you for awhile?"

"Yes, Karl, I'll be on the road for several weeks, and I should be leaving soon. Can you watch the farm while Kristine and I hit the big town of Calais tonight for a farewell dinner with champagne?"

"You have to ask? When you do leave, which way will you go first?"

"North. Lithuania has almost half of all those countries combined."

Two days later, Albert hooked a ride on one of the seaplanes still docked at Camp Calais. He wondered why Vance's crew hadn't blown up those seaplanes yet. For now, he was glad they hadn't.

Estonia. The two largest camps were in Estonia: Klooga, near the town of Tallinn, and Viavara, near Narva. Albert's plane landed at Tallinn, where he got transportation to Klooga. The Kommandant, Maj. Gerhardt Volken, who had overheard his conversations earlier at the Wannsee Conference, warmly received him.

"Yes, Captain Steller, I am familiar with the concept of your camp and it appears to be working superbly."

"Let me get directly to the point, Maj. Volken. I am reimbursed for every Jew liquidated. My population is dwindling, and I would like more inmates. As you may know, Col. Willi Heinrick has pre-authorized any transfer from other camps, whose Kommandant may accept or decline. The Soviets are advancing and, judging by your population, your methods may be a bit slow. Do not be concerned about a lack of railcars. I plan to take them by cargo ship."

"Well, Captain, you certainly don't mince words, nor shall I. Cornering you at the conference was like trapping a Jew in the forest. I wanted to discuss this very issue with you for the reasons you have outlined. I understand my position here is tenuous at best. I am more than happy to rid myself of this liability. When can you take the inmates?"

"Our ship, Norse 150, trails me by two days. You may load your prisoners immediately upon its arrival."

Albert was dumbfounded at how rapidly the major acquiesced and judged morale here to be quite different than it was some three years ago when the Nazis came goose-stepping through the streets of Tallinn.

If Albert thought Klooga was a snap, he was in for a surprise at Viavara. Maj. Volken called the Kommandant there while Albert was en route and informed him of the agreement made. He was ready to sign the necessary papers when Albert walked into his office.

Albert discovered these two camps in Estonia housed internees from Latvia and Lithuania as well. Together they had a population of over 210,000, almost as many as Camp Calais had already freed to date.

Not much sense in heading south to the Adriatic area yet, he reasoned. It'll take four months to process this new group as it is. Good thing we can control the flow by using our own ship, good old Norse 150.

Calais. Kristine was surprised to see her husband home so soon. "I'm sorry your trip was not so successful. Why were the Kommandants reluctant to accept your idea?"

"Why Kristine, you cut me to the quick. What makes you think the trip was a washout?"

"Well, I assumed..."

Albert just smiled.

When Albert informed Kreuger of his successful trip, the Major was delighted. Unlike the two Kommandants in Estonia, the enemy was not heading his way. Russia was on the other side of the world and the battle for North Africa was a mere joust.

The only thing bothering Erik at present was the insistent rumor that Jews were escaping to England. He wondered where do these Jews come from? How are they getting away, if, in fact they are getting away?

"I'm proud we run a tight camp here, Albert. We know who comes and goes, and how many, at all times. I owe it all to my experience at Sachsenhausen," said the pumped-up

Kreuger. "And I might add, Martin's work here has been exemplary. I trained him, you know!"

That night a deafening blast shattered the quiet of the camp. The long-awaited attack on the seaplanes was finally pulled off. No one was injured or killed and all commandos got in and out without a hitch.

Kreuger ran outside in his skivvies, too numb to understand at first what had happened. As he finally realized the truth, his earlier conversation with Albert came to mind. All he could think to say was "Kreuger, you idiot!"

The Nazis combed the area, looking for clues. From whence did the Commandos strike? No suspicion was cast on the mess hall area. Martin had seen to it that any telltale footprints were erased, and then replaced them as if coming in from the sea. Luckily, footprints in the ocean are hard to track.

"Raid from the English Channel" was the conclusion of the Geheime Staats Polizei (Gestapo).

July. Karl was visiting in Dover with Vance when Sol walked up. "Hear the news about Sobibor?"

"You're going to tell me? I must be losing my Roh-Eh Hanoled?"

"Don't worry Karl," said Vance "It's just tunnel fever. Happens to all of us." Calais and Dover both were aware that Karl's abilities were fading while Kristine's were increasing.

"So, tell me the news!"

Sol was brief "Himmler has ordered that Sobibor, an extermination camp, be made a concentration camp. Also, there was a fairly serious uprising at Treblinka. Both of these camps are in old Poland. See anything significant here?"

"The uprisings I can understand. The change at Sobibor is probably the first step in a new policy designed to 'hide the evidence,' you know, bury the bodies under the new barracks. It is not a war crime to have a concentration camp, assuming the inmates are treated decently."

As Karl emerged from the mess hall, the "lackey" handed him an empty, crushed pack of cigarettes. "News from Ishmael?"

"Please get some cigarettes and follow me!

"Egads man! You've improved your vocabulary. Last time you could only grunt 'follow me.' Wait here while I go get some cigarettes."

Ishmael was his usual bubbly self, smiling through two new missing teeth. "I have a two-pack piece of information."

"Give it up Ishmael. You know the routine. One now, one at delivery."

"This is delivery," Ishmael objected. And, totally confident, he replied, "Judge for yourself. Yesterday afternoon I finally see the civilian, walking around, talking with the new inmates. Then I see him walk to the side of an ammo shed and out comes a German officer."

"German officer?"

"Difficult to mistake them for a Jew," he quipped. "Anyway, they keep moving. Walk over to hospital building, talk some more, then leave, each in different direction. I couldn't get close enough to see their faces clearly, but I'm sure it was same civilian."

"Anything else?"

"Yes—my two packs!"

"Two packs?" Grinning from ear-to-ear, Karl tossed both Lucky Strike packs with matches. "Now get out of here before I change my mind."

Karl hurried to tell what Ishmael had said, but Albert spoke first. "Have you heard the news?"

"No, have you heard mine?" Karl quickly retorted. "But, go ahead. What's your news?"

"The Allies have made an amphibious landing on Sicily. Still quite a distance from the death camps on the Adriatic, but we're getting there! I'll wager this news is better than your news."

"No bet," Karl shook his head. "My news could be very bad."

Karl related what Ishmael had told him, taking the wind out of Albert's sails. "This could be very serious trouble, the worst yet."

Karl's next question was expected by Albert. He also wondered how the civilian and the new player are going to be found. He was tight lipped in thought: Step up contacts with Ishmael. Offer him a carton of smokes, if necessary. Advise the men we meet tonight at 8 p.m., Albert's office.

Albert called to ask Kristine if she could catch a ride home tonight with Wilhelm. He was going to be late. "Yes,

I'm sure I can. But don't you be too late, I'm feeling antsy with some premonitions, like Papa used to get." she said stoically.

"Can you tell me about them?"

"Very soon that Italian dictator, 'Pipolini?' is going to be assassinated in a very cruel way. Soon after that, the Italians will surrender. And after that, this seems so strange; Italy will declare war on Germany. Can you believe that?"

"Not an unbelievable scenario," Albert smiled at her pronunciation of the dictator's name." I don't want to wish anyone dead, but Mussolini may be an exception."

Albert laid out to the group what Karl had been told. The first question from Fredrik was predictable: "Can this Ishmael be trusted?"

Martin picked up the question by emphasizing whether or not he could be trusted, what harm could be done in pursuing it. That they dare not, not.

"I'll press Ishmael to work full-time on his watch," Karl assured the others. What else can we do? We'd be spotted in a minute if we put on our grubbies and tried to infiltrate."

Martin came up with a thought: "But we have the ability to infiltrate without being seen. Set up a telescope in the attic of the mess hall. Get Ishmael and a couple of his buddies to stay put in the general vicinity of where the civilian was spotted earlier. A signal from the attic will send the spotter to get a closer look before they get away."

Albert saw some flaws in the plan. "Who is going to man the telescope? It would be difficult for us to alternate watches. Who knows what any of us may be doing at any given time. Also, say we do succeed in giving Ishmael a closer look. It's not likely he would recognize any of the mystery men. For that matter we may not either."

The group discussed other alternatives, but could come up with nothing workable. Finally, they agreed to offer more cigarettes to Ishmael if he and his boys would tighten up their watch. If this didn't work they agreed to talk some more.

August. Bedlam again. Inmates from Estonia began off-loading at Vlissingen, Belgium, the closest port to Camp Calais. No land transportation was available, so the prisoners had to walk the some 10 kilometers remaining. This required more guards, albeit temporary. The input was from the Klooga Camp only, about 91,000 inmates. With the existing population, Calais was 22,000 over capacity

Karl was always counting noses; then calculated when today's arrivals are gone, they will have freed 352,000—not as many as Moses, but then they didn't have a sack full of epidemics to toss around.

Sol strode into the compound, as usual, as if he were part of the staff. Kreuger found it necessary to make a run to the town of Calais and quickly departed via the back way. Albert watched the exit and mentally verified what he thought earlier was beginning to be a pattern, Sol and/or Vance walk in, and Kreuger walks out.

"Good to see you, Sol. Is this a social visit, or business?"

"All business, I'm afraid. Staff wants you to do a test run on that 100,000 exodus. They feel now would be a good time, what with your influx of inmates. No one, including probably you, is going to be able to keep track of their numbers for a while yet. When can you do it?"

Albert pondered the enormity of what Sol was asking, and asked for one day to examine his options and another day to set up. He couldn't see how the numbers could be more than 25,000.

Sol grimaced. He had a figure closer to 100,000 in mind, explaining that the Jerries would never expect an invasion the next day with such a large amount of prisoners in jeopardy and impossible to process that many Jews overnight. An invasion at Calais would be a shoe-in.

"I totally understand and agree," Albert lamented. "But if it truly can't be done, wouldn't it be foolish to risk men's lives just because you want it to work? However, let's give it a go and see what happens. With 25,000 I can tell if 50,000 will work or not."

"Good show!" Sol beamed. "I'll be expecting to see some inmates, en masse, in three days."

Albert immediately called a meeting with his group and explained his discussion with Sol.

Martin was first with a suggestion. "Obviously we're going to know when 'D-Day' is, so we'll want only the healthiest prisoners making the test run. Therefore we should first process only women, children, and invalids prior to this time, and begin immediately."

"Good thought, Martin, declared Fredrik, "and taking it a step further, we should develop a workout regimen to get the healthiest inmates in even better shape. Kreuger will just think its punishment."

"Also a good idea." Mimicked Karl. "But a word of caution. This will take extra rations for these men to sustain a good physical condition. We must be very careful how this is done."

"Gentlemen," Albert interrupted. "Those are genuinely great ideas. But we need to back up and consider the immediate task at hand."

"Then we do the same," explained Martin, "but leave out the workout sessions. We four go into the compound about 8 a.m. and each hand-pick, as best we can, 3,125 healthy looking inmates. This totals 12,500. As we pick them they go to the mess hall, get extra rations proceed to the holding area, get instructions and begin to head out, all walking. No carts until the escapees become more spread out."

"And this whole process," asked Albert, "from picking the men through the mess hall on to the starting gate, and to halfway through the tunnel takes, what, about four hours?"

"I'd plan for six, just to be conservative." Martin confidently replied. "Then we wait a couple of hours so things don't get jammed at the mess hall, and for time to feed the other inmates. We repeat the whole process and Voila! Zee 25,000 prisoners go poof!"

"So, if I understand your calculations," Karl asked cautiously "in six, plus a two hour wait, plus six hours for group two—fourteen hours total—all 25,000 should be in England.

"Maybe not all," Martin clarified, "but all will at least be hidden, and most of the way through the tunnel."

"What about Kreuger?" Fredrik fretted. "Won't he get suspicious? Or maybe he'll just think we're changing our method of choosing prisoners for elimination," he remarked as an afterthought.

This time it was Vance who showed up in his Nazi officer's uniform. Albert glanced up at Kreuger's office and could almost hear him say, "I'm out of here."

The reason for Vance's visit was because he wanted to see how things go from the "sending" rather than the "receiving" end.

Albert smiled, happy for his "Dover Boys" to get a peek at the white cliffs across the sea for a change of scenery.

As fortune would have it, everything went smoothly and in slightly less time than the fourteen hours predicted. If the prisoners got into better physical condition, as planned, maybe they could do 50,000 in 24 hours. For certain all 50,000 would at least be hidden in the tunnel.

"Just as we had hoped" Vance was all smiles. "I think we might be able to fool the Germans with as little as 50,000, a good compromise between Albert and staff."

Karl felt badly that he hadn't picked Ishmael as a member of the test run. He was small, but in reasonably good shape. Ishmael, on the other hand, felt relieved. As far as the inmates were concerned, those who went to the mess hall and failed to return were history. Their philosophy was to do whatever it took to stay alive. Rat on your inmates, be as helpful as possible to the guards, and accumulate as many cigarettes as you can.

September. When Karl came home from the spa, it was obvious that Kristine had been weeping. "What is it, child?" he asked with obvious concern.

"Oh Papa I hate these feelings, and they seem to be coming more often. There is trouble in Bialystok again. The remaining Jews there, about 30,000, have been ordered by the Nazis to appear for evacuation. There was an uprising, but it was soon put down. All were taken to Auschwitz.

"I'm so sorry Kristinalein," Karl said consolingly. "But remember what you yourself told me earlier, not to worry about that over which you have absolutely no control."

"And I had another sensation," bemoaned Kristine. "Again books are being publicly burned throughout Germany. Also, an uprising was attempted in the Vilna Ghetto. It was aborted but the rebels escaped to the partisans. Soon after, the ghetto was liquidated and the remaining 7,000 Jews were sent to Sobibor."

Karl assured his daughter, "When this war is over, those fretful voices will vanish."

The month was a non-event. No word from Ishmael. No word from Sol or Vance.

October. Albert had a sudden inspiration, fathered by a constant nagging about the civilian and his occasional visits to the compound.

His investment in cigarettes proved as fruitful an information gatherer as had Karl. He went into the compound, collared the nearest prisoner, handed him a pack and said he wanted to see Ishmael. The communication system was working as efficiently as ever. Ishmael appeared at Albert's office the next morning, in his hand an empty, crushed cigarette pack.

"I'd offer you a cigarette, sir, but I seem to be fresh out."

Albert couldn't help but smile at his audacity. "That's all right, Ishmael, I don't smoke anyway. I would, however, like to avail myself of your services."

"Like some information?"

"Like some information. Very important information."

Ishmael became cautious, "What do you want me to find out?"

"Nothing. I want just your recollections about the civilian. Specifically, what times of the day did he usually come into the compound?"

Ishmael stroked his gnarly beard and looked up into the sky as if God were providing the answer. After a few mumbles he finally said, "Well, he always came in the afternoon. It was sometimes early or, sometimes mid-afternoon. Always well before dark. But, when that officer showed up, it was at the latest, about one, two hours before dark."

"Any other observations?"

Again Ishmael was pensive. "I may have seen the civilian somewhere before, but I can't be sure. Oh, the officer was smoking a cigarette. Funny what made me remember that!"

"Ah, yes. Your cigarettes. That information was two-pack stuff."

Ishmael caught the two packs, tossing them in the air as he went whistling (as best as an almost toothless man can) out into the compound. A meeting was called and Albert reviewed the information he had gotten from Ishmael. Martin, as usual, was first to see the possibilities. "No need to man the telescope around the clock. Just from, say, noon until 7 p.m., seven hours."

All agreed that each person could take a one-hour shift each day. But with everyone in the group, plus Fredrik's two men made only six. They needed one more watchdog.

"I have the perfect man for seventh spot!" declared Albert. "A little drum-roll, please."

Fredrik took two pencils and tapped them rapidly on top of the table. "Kreuger!" exclaimed Albert, donning a victorious demeanor.

"Oh, that's amusing," chuckled Karl. "For a second there I thought you said 'Kreuger'."

Martin, somber-faced, said: "He did, but you are joking. Right, Albert?"

Albert was miffed his stroke of genius was unappreciated. "Martin, pretend you're me. Try to come up with reasons why Kreuger would be a good candidate."

"Other than the fact he's a buffoon?" snorted Martin. "Come to think of it, that would make him gullible. Believe most anything you tell him. So, what would we tell him?"

Fredrik, trying to think of something horrific enough to frighten Kreuger, chimed in. "How about telling him exactly what we saw! We suspect spies are snooping around."

"Snooping around. Snooping around seeking the best spot for the Allies to invade! Shouted Albert. "Give that man a Kewpie doll."

Kreuger would love it. All agreed it would provide Erik with a chance to be one of the boys, be a hero. Someone suggested to give him the twelve to one shift, "I'll wager he'll still be peeking into his telescope every chance he gets." Said Martin "I just hope he doesn't spot something and go running down before we have a chance to get some questions answered for ourselves."

Albert saw Kreuger the next day and filled him in on the details. "We could really use your help. Erik. Not wishing to break up your business day, we'd be happy to give you the twelve to one shift. We've got a good place from which to watch, but yours is perfect and you could certainly get a great look."

Erik, as usual, feigned hard to get—for about 45 seconds, and indicated he felt it would be his duty to help catch the spy, and that Nazis should work together. "We begin today at noon."

Albert did a big eye roll. A quick peek over the shoulder as he left the room showed Kreuger's right eye glued to the telescope.

Another unexpected influx of prisoners, although modest in number, was the result of German police rounding Danish Jews up for deportation by ship. The Danish population began a rescue program that ultimately saved 7,299 Jews. Small revolts were beginning throughout Europe.

November, Three weeks of telescope duty had been fruitless.

No civilian. No Nazi officer. But, the calm was about to end.

Darkness was creeping in. Fredrik had the last shift and was about to put his telescope away. The same for Kreuger, who was becoming bored with the procedure.

Movement!! Fredrik swung his telescope back. Kreuger refocused as a figure ran into the compound from around a corner. The mystery civilian turned, put his arms forward, and waved his hands rapidly as if trying to stop something.

Fredrik yelled, "Wilhelm!" just as two shots rang out. Kreuger mumbled to himself, Corporal Marr? The figure struggled to stay upright, but crumpled into the compound mud in a grotesque heap.

Lt. Kreutz heard the shots and turned around just in time to see out the window that his aide had fallen. He quickly ran outside, picked Wilhelm off the soaking wet ground, and cradled him in his arms, shouting for help.

"I told them nothing. I told them nothing" were the last words Wilhelm could muster. His body went limp and his spirit began its journey to Valhalla.

A doctor soon appeared, did a quick exam, and shook his head. Kristine pushed her way through a developing crowd of inmates to confirm it was Fredrik's brother who had been killed. She was too shaken to weep.

By this time Albert's entire group reached the scene. Fredrik gently picked his brother up, took him inside, and laid him on a hospital bed. Following traditional German upbringing he showed no emotion, but was fighting to hold back tears. "You little turd, why couldn't you ever play it straight?" were the last words to his brother.

Erik arrived at the bedside, only then finding that Wilhelm had died. "It is obvious who had been the civilian. Wilhelm was still wearing a non-military jacket. Evidently he had simply taken off his tunic and put on a civilian shirt. No one paid attention to his pants, so, from a distance he did not look like a soldier. I am very sorry for you all, especially Sgt. Marr."

Albert wanted to diffuse any attempt by Kreuger to look into the run of events. "Herr Kommandant, I personally will thoroughly investigate the matter and give you a full report within the week."

Suddenly the door swung open. It was Capt. Siegel. Looking around at each person, he gave the obligatory condolences for their loss, turned around and walked out.

"My, doesn't word travel fast," said Martin cynically.

"No judgments should be made until all the facts are in," said Karl, sternly. "All of us, except Fredrik, need to conduct an investigation to identify the murderer. Fredrik, you should go through Wilhelm's things to see what clues you can find."

Kristine wept while driving home with Karl and Albert. "I should have said something, but I was too afraid to look."

"At what, dear?" asked Albert.

"At his face. I didn't want to know who he was." Then she quickly explained. "I had a dream last week. A young man was dying. I held him in my arms but wouldn't look at his face. Then, a German officer walked into the room and took him away from me. The boy said he told them nothing."

"Them?"

"I don't know."

The group met three days later to see what clues were found, and what they may indicate. Fredrik started with his search of Wilhelm's personal effects. He had torn the place apart looking through all of his desk drawers at the office. Nothing of significance except a shoe box full of American money hidden under a pile of dirty clothes."

"Albert and I checked out the scene of the crime," reported Martin, "and questioned many of the adjacent inmates as well as hospital employees. Nothing of importance, except from Lt. Kreutz. He said he heard

Wilhelm's last words, 'I told them nothing, I told them nothing.' Everyone saw Wilhelm's actions after turning around to face someone, undoubtedly his killer. The way he extended his arms and frantically waved his hands was tantamount to pleading for his life."

"Boys," Karl addressed the others in a grandfatherly way. "I still have a little insight left. Let me tell you what I think happened. Then you can tear it apart: He felt he was doing his duty to the Fatherland by gathering information about the operation of Camp Calais. Wilhelm appeared to be a loyal soldier to the Reich. For this he would receive no hush money. But I believe he was stringing along this German officer by stalling for time."

For what purpose?" asked Martin.

"To continue milking the cow. He knew something the German officer didn't want revealed. Enter the box full of money. I don't know what hold Wilhelm had over him, but it must have been incriminating. The fact the money was in U.S. dollars, I can't explain."

"And he must not have given the officer any useful information." Albert picked up, "As evidenced by his dying words, 'I told them nothing,' the exact words Kristine heard from the dying youth in her dream."

"Couldn't have said it better myself," growled Karl, "but I wish you'd at least have let me finish, it was my story."

Fredrik was still wary, "That officer is going to give us fits before we finish here. He was too persistent for my liking.

And another thing: Why didn't he kill Wilhelm sooner...or later?"

Martin was quick to respond. "I suspect he wasn't killed any sooner because the officer felt he couldn't afford to lose a good source of information. Somehow he discovered the data was bogus, and then killed your brother to shut him up."

"We haven't any clues to the identity of the mystery officer yet, but we did accomplish one good thing," Karl concluded, "Wilhelm has been vindicated!"

Albert added a P.S., "More than that, he has also alerted us to a heretofore unknown source of danger, the mysterious officer."

December. Camp Calais processing priorities continued to be women and children. Kreuger wasn't yet aware that the camp's population was shifting heavily to men. All he could see was men walking and jogging around the compound, "being punished," which pleased him to no end. What didn't please him was Albert's insistence on cleanliness, always changing straw in the barracks once a week.

Albert had an inspiration. "Karl, rather than toss away that old straw, why not use it to make dummies, you know, scarecrows!"

"Scarecrows!" objected Karl. "Why not broomsticks for the inmates to fly out on?"

Albert, trying to be patient, put his hand over his forehead for a moment, and then explained to him that if

Camp Calais wanted to fool the Nazis with an Allied landing here, we have to show a full complement of inmates. Part of this full house is going to have to be dummies set outside to look like prisoners...at least at a distance.

"We'll issue clean uniforms and tell our inmates to use the old ones to stuff with the old straw. Then jam a long stake down the back, and push into the ground to keep it upright. Between the motionless dummies and prisoners shuffling around, things will appear normal. Obviously, we won't do this until a few days before D Day."

Activity at the Tube had slowed to a crawl, literally, for the past month. Martin enjoyed the respite. Stooped over for 300 meters, stumbling about with just a flashlight to show the way was dog tiring. He theorized that either the Resistance had gone out of business or most of the Jews in the area had already been evacuated.

Then, almost overnight, Martin was flooded with women and children trying to run from backbreaking work. Throughout the Netherlands, the Nazis had drafted the families of Jewish men for forced labor and sent them to Westerbork, one of the few remaining non-extermination camps remaining.

The French Resistance was an amalgamation of Nazi hating freedom fighters, and before the war, would never have had occasion to mingle socially—doctors, railroad workers, grocers, and farmers. Now they were a brotherhood. Few were fond of Jews, but willingly they would round them up by twos and fours to bring them, weekly, to the Tube.

Martin enjoyed studying their contrasting faces. One night, his eyes locked on one Frenchman in particular. Beret, face darkened, eye patch, the omnipresent cigarette hanging from a corner of his mouth, and always keeping his distance. This one had a familiar look. But don't these Frenchmen all look alike, he mused to himself.

After a few weeks the influx of escapees abated. Each week the same French guides, including the one with an eye patch. Martin put a quizzical look on his face and said to Karl, "I could have sworn his eye patch was on the other eye the last time I saw him? And, whatever happened to the fleet-footed floozie with the floi floi?"

1944

The Deliverance

January. After a "pin drop" quiet holiday period, the group struggled to get back into their routine. The momentum had disappeared. Even Kreuger seemed sluggish.

"This is the worst vacation hangover I've had for years," complained Albert. "I just can't seem to get motivated. I wish things were back to normal."

"Normal," snapped Karl. "You call what we do normal? No dear, I haven't the time for another cup of coffee. Must run to the extermination center and pretend I've turned on the cremation ovens, then, after we've led a couple of thousand Jews to freedom, toss some oil soaked logs and sulfur onto the coals so everything will smell real nice. Mein Gott, do I love my work!"

For Kristine, her thoughts were never wholly her own. Her visions were not as precise as were her fathers', and, to date, she had not endured physical discomfort. On New Year's Eve she had visualized another uprising, this time at Sobibor. And, in Northern Italy over 1,000 Jews were being deported to Auschwitz.

When Albert heard that Jews in northern Italy were being deported—and to Auschwitz, he realized it was time to make another trip to "sweet talk" the Kommandant the death camp. This time it would be to those Adriatic countries he had considered earlier, and again transported by ship.

Adriatic Sea. All the captured Jews from Yugoslavia, Albania, and Greece had been rounded up and divided between camps in Jasenovak, near Belgrade; Gospic; by the Adriatic Sea; and Sajmiste, near Albania—all 125,000 in Yugoslavia. This is less than the 214,000 in the Baltic Sea area, and considerably further.

Snatching prisoners in the Baltic area from the walls of death was considerably easier than Albert would ever have imagined. But, the sea route from Mediterranean to Atlantic is another story. Getting near the Strait of Gibraltar, laden with British guns, is something Nazi ships, other than U-boats, are hesitant to attempt.

This was the first objection of the Kommandant at Gospic. "Why should I entrust my inmates to you in an unknown freighter trying to run the gauntlet at Gibraltar?"

"Pardon me, Herr Kommandant, if I appear puzzled at your comment. The risk is all mine. You have been entrusted with these inmates to work them to death and/or eliminate them. If the British blast the ship out of the water, your work will have been done for you. On the other hand, I would lose a very valuable cargo. Further, you would be absolved of responsibility by any world court. I am assuming this risk for you. Why keep them here and take that chance? Remember your neighbor across the waters, Italy? They are now on the side of the Allies, and just itching to get even."

"I assume you will be approaching Jasenovac and Sajmiste while you are in the neighborhood?"

"Yes, Herr Kommandant," Albert said with authority. "And I assume you want to wait until I see them before you give me your decision?" But before the Kommandant could open his mouth to answer, Albert added, "I have too many other places to visit, and I only make one call. Do we have a deal or not?"

Hesitating for a moment, he finally acquiesced. "We have a deal!"

Kommandants in both Jasenovak and Sajmiste followed suit, just as easily as had Viavara in Estonia. Albert decided to skip Italy this time around. The camp was just too close to the fighting. Anyway, the Allies should free them soon.

On his trip over and back from the Adriatic area Albert scrounged rides wherever he could: Bus, cargo plane, train, car. Even though the selling job went fairly fast, it took him three weeks, round trip. A cargo ship would have gone much faster, but Albert felt that shipping in alien waters was not his preference as a Mediterranean ocean cruise. He did try to keep Vance advised of Norse 150's comings and goings so it wouldn't, in fact, be 'blown out of the water.'

March. The first load of 15,000 prisoners from Gospic arrived, and immediately women and children were filtered out of the mix and, although mentally unready, were prepped enough to make the next trip to Dover. Less healthy males were also sectioned off, destined for the exit following theirs. Healthy males got a day's rest, and were then put on extra rations and a mild workout program with existing inmates.

Karl began counting again. "You say there are about 125,000 coming in from the Adriatic area? That will make almost 500,000 brothers we have helped escape. Look out Moses, we're catching up!"

Albert just smiled. With Martin double-checking his figures, their calculations were closer to 700,000 without further arrivals.

Sol and Vance made their quarterly appearance wearing, as usual, their German officers' uniforms. Sol was now a Colonel.

Albert chuckled, both at Sol's promotion and in seeing Kreuger beat a hasty retreat. "Sol, as long as you were giving yourself a higher pay grade, why didn't you go for General?"

"Next time, old boy—next time. I know you're wondering, but I can't give you any more data on D Day except that it will occur within six months. Calais is still a distinct possibility, but we're also looking at Normandy."

Albert was surprised because of the skimpy beaches there and the fact that the Allies will be looking straight up into the barrels of the Jerries. Hang the element of surprise. It would be no different at Camp Calais and the going considerably easier.

"Would you be insinuating that the Allies may be making a serious mistake by invading Normandy?" Sol said with a hint of a smile.

"Oh, just a small innuendo."

Karl was compelled to interrupt at this point. "Innuendo, such a fancy word for an Italian suppository." Everybody groaned in unison.

"We could hypothesize all day, Albert, but in the final analysis, Staff will make the decision. Meanwhile, can we eat here? In town, I mean."

They lunched at the Pelican Inn. Martin, who had been invited, spotted Piotr Siegel alone in a corner booth. "That fellow looks familiar," he said, knowing full well who he was.

Albert turned, saw Siegel and motioned for him to come join them, hoping they could put an end to their feud. Piotr motioned back a "no thank you," and got up and left.

Martin's face was grimaced as if trying to remember something. "Albert, I have a sinking feeling. He reminds me of that French Resistance member I saw at the Tube. He had on an eye patch. Each time, it seemed, it covered a different eye. He wore a false schnurbart and beard, had a darkened face, and his beret pulled over to cover one side of his face. He always had a cigarette dangling from his mouth. Oh yes, and when we had our first 'conversation' he motioned that he was unable to speak."

"Eye patch, dangling cigarette. Sounds sinister." Albert paused, the description still bounding around in his head.

Then, as the evidence led to a single conclusion, he jumped up. "It's him!"

"Who is 'him'?" asked Sol.

Albert lowered his voice, barely audible. "Piotr may be the mystery officer who killed Wilhelm. Just listen to this: Wearing an eye patch over a different eye tells me both of them are good. He's trying to hide his identity. Always smoking a cigarette. Remember the spotter who saw the officer figure smoking a cigarette?"

"You can't toss a man into jail for wearing an eye patch or for smoking," joked Vance.

"No, but wouldn't it be damaging if he were at the scene of the crime?"

"Can you prove this?" asked Martin.

"Circumstantially, yes. Just listen: Remember when Siegel came through the side door and into the room to offer his condolences? How did he know Wilhelm had been shot? And, no one knew for certain he had died until he was taken inside. There was no one outside to tell him except some inmates, and none of them would have known his name. There was a rumor a few years ago that Siegel might be a double agent, but what would this have to do with Wilhelm and Siegel.

"And why was Wilhelm paid off in U.S. dollars?" Sol asked, and then answered his own question. "Because the money came from Piotr, who was taking it from our account, which was 100% U.S. dollars."

"One more thing," added Albert. "I seem to recall my first meeting with Lt. Kreutz at the Spa. He told me at the time he didn't trust Siegel. Why would he say this to a stranger? Maybe Kreutz is the double agent and was trying to warn us.

"So, do we do something, or just wait until he blows the whistle on us?" Vance said impatiently.

Martin answered with questions of his own. "Why hasn't he informed on us by now if he knows for certain of our operation? And even if he does know, is there a reason he doesn't want to tell?"

"I agree with Martin's thinking," said Sol. "He may have a fatted goose of his own and doesn't wish to kill it. Let's just wait, keep an eye on him, and go ahead with business as usual, for now."

The men agreed, then headed back to the spa, where they saw a Nazi officer's car parked out in front. No one knew for certain who the owner was. They hoped it was Siegel's and not some other Nazi who might recognize Sol.

They stood outside momentarily, wondering whether to boldly walk into the building or just send Albert in first to scout out the situation. Sol, always up for a challenge, settled the issue by opening the front door and motioning for the rest to walk on in.

The foursome breathed a collective sigh of relief to see the car did, indeed, belong to Siegel. He was facing a desk, rocking side to side in what had been Wilhelm's swivel chair. A burst of adrenalin pulsed through Albert's chest as Siegel turned to face the group, a sub-machine gun in his lap. He raised it with no doubt of his intentions.

"Gentlemen, it seems the cat is out of the bag," he said calmly. "The expression on Martin's face back at the restaurant was, if you'll pardon the expression, a 'dead giveaway.' Now, as your great and wonderful Oz once said, 'you've forced me to make a cataclysmic decision!' "

Albert was trying to quick think a diversion. "So, it was you who killed Wilhelm!"

"Of course. He knew too much, was feeding me worthless information, and his silence was beginning to drain my pocketbook."

Albert tried feeding his ego, "Well you really fooled us, but for now why don't you just put that weapon back on your lap? Your trigger finger is beginning to twitch. Makes me very nervous."

Siegel was like a cat toying with an injured mouse. "Very well, I'll lower it, temporarily. Now let me tell you something to make you even more nervous. Your account at the Calais bank is $30,000 leaner; Wilhelm has $5,000 of it, and the remainder, $90,000, I intend to get. That's U.S. dollars now—not the soon-to-be worthless Deutsch-marks. Evidently you have not yet expended the funds lent to you by Rothsmann."

"How did you...?" and before Albert could finish. "My little secret. Thanks to an enterprising young teller, we can take from your account at will. Now that I'm comfortable with this arrangement, this is exactly what I intend to do, after I not so quietly dispose of you. And I have the inside track to be your successor if I so elect."

Sol tried more stalling. "And all along we thought you were the double agent."

"An acting roll I played with great pleasure," he smiled. "Got me into places I would not have been able to, like the Tube. The French Resistance was not difficult to penetrate, as my mother was French. Just ask Martin about the floozie with the floi-floi.

"This made me realize you were not executing prisoners and were somehow smuggling them out of the compound, I suspect by your 'Norse 150' cargo ship. No matter. Once you have been cremated, along with Freddie, I will have the freedom to roam the compound. The method of your little disappearing act will be discovered.

"Meanwhile, I will continue to earn a small stipend as a reward paid by my German friends for turning in an occasional Jew during my 'French Resistance' activities. Wilhelm earned his 'hush money' by keeping quiet on my 'entrepreneurial' sideline."

All the while Piotr was facing the group, he could see some movement in a large mirror placed so that Kreutz's aide could see his office.

"Kreutz, komenze hier mach schnell, or I'll shoot these men immediately." He had no choice but to come out from his office, hands up, standing together with the others.

Before any of the group could stall more, Siegel announced, "Gentlemen, it is time," taking a few backward steps for a better angle at the men. "And Albert, in case you were wondering, this time I won't miss."

As he started to raise his weapon, the bullets spewing from his gun began spraying the floor, then a sidewall. Siegel, with only seconds to live, dropped to his knees, a quizzical look on his face. His gun was still pumping out bullets, as he finally twisted and fell over apparently dead, face up.

As Vance was saying "What...the...devil," Kristine stepped from around the corner her gun still smoking.

"Silencer" Kreutz answered the unasked question. "She must have used a silencer. You didn't hear the shots.

Karl, out of breath from running, dashed to the scene of the crime and saw that Kristine was all right. She told him about her frequent disturbing visions of Piotr, and that she could thwart Siegel's plans with no danger to herself. Wilhelm's jacket and gun belt was still hanging in the hospital closet. She had cautiously taken his gun and waited for everyone to show up. When she thought the time was right, she stuck her head around the corner, aimed the gun at Siegel, and pulled the trigger until the gun no longer recoiled.

"There's no point in my hanging around now," said Kreutz. "The Gestapo are very thorough in their investigations, and will find me out more sooner than later. So permit me to introduce my other half. My English name is Butch Bruce—Scottish Guard. My German half you already know."

Sol mustered a weak smile and, just shaking his head, declared "You are the double agent. Not Siegel! Nice job, you had everyone fooled."

Albert was still tongue tied, so Butch was first to gather his wits. "First, we need to remove our nosy friend and destroy all evidence—cremate him!" Martin shook his hand warmly. "No one but us knows your identity. Are you sure you can't stay here?"

"No. I would be too ineffective now. Besides, in my disappearance you have a scapegoat for Piotr's death. Thank Winnie, who sent me here to make sure nothing happened to you. My work here is finished. So, ta ta for now. I'll be heading back to jolly old England via your tunnel."

Sol suggested that one of Fredrik's guards haul Piotr to the crematorium, and clean his blood off the floor.

"The way I see it," Albert started, "we're no better or worse off than we were before our altercation with Piotr. Still, no one else knows about our operation."

Martin felt comfortable, "I agree. We do know that Piotr, first, discovered our prisoners were not being eliminated; second, had not yet found the tunnel; and, third, has probably told no one because that would put an end to his cash cow."

"So you're saying no one is the wiser?" asked Vance.

"Not unless there's a partner in crime who has not, as yet, been revealed." Martin surmised. "It appears, however, the sword of Damocles still hangs over our respective heads."

Sol, this time the voice of reason, concluded, "Boys, we just have to keep doing what we've always done. When the next emergency arises, we deal with it then, not now."

"There is one small task I want to do right now," observed Albert. "Go to the bank, uncover Piotr's 'enterprising young teller,' and recover that $30,000 he undoubtedly has put away in the same bank. Make sure our bank balance, $120,000, is intact before you close out the account. Stuff it in a sack, bring it all back, and put it in our office safe. It would be a shame if the Nazis were to steal back that same $1.2 million that we've been paid so far."

It wasn't difficult to prove to the bank manager that $30,000 was missing from Camp Calais' account, and who the culprit was that systematically absconded with the funds. As Martin stuffed the money into a canvas sack, he and Fredrik fantasized what each could do with all that money. Fredrik felt he would get a good education, then go to Berlin and work in the financial sector. Martin simply wanted to travel the world.

April. London. Albert and Karl were invited to attend a meeting of Staff in London. U.S. General Dwight D. "Ike" Eisenhower had been named Supreme Commander of Allied Forces, much to the chagrin of British General Bernard "Monte" Montgomery, his chief adversary. Both leaned forward in anticipation of what was going to be said.

There was only one item on the agenda: The invasion of France—"Operation Overlord."

Staff had already narrowed the invasion to two locales: Normandy and Calais. The Nazis had originally been planting their strongest defenses at Calais because it was the shortest route across the channel and the most obvious point of attack.

But, there were other reasons. The British had constructed hundreds of dummy tanks, artillery, and planes near Dover to simulate a buildup of forces preparing to cross the channel there. However, the theory that the Allies would not attack Calais because of the concentration of prisoners there was now suspect. The Allies, now bombing Germany day and night, were killing many innocent civilians. Why would they spare prisoners?

The Allies have always leaned toward Normandy because of the Nazi's predilection toward Calais. But, the presence of Camp Calais has now tossed everything into a cocked hat.

Winston Churchill was first to speak. "Albert, it's good to finally meet you. Your input will be most helpful in the outcome of this most important event."

Montgomery, not to be upstaged, dove in first to voice a key question: "How many prisoners can you get out of harm's way in a 24-hour period?"

"This depends upon which assumptions we use," cautioned Albert.

Monte's retort contained a pinch of sarcasm. "Well then, Mr. Steller, why don't you enlighten us?"

"Bottom line number of bodies we can get out of harm's way, i.e., somewhere into the tunnel would be 50,000 maximum. If all prisoners are to have reached Dover, 25,000 to 30,000."

"Somewhere I heard the figure of 100,000 being bandied about," Monte said with a slight smirk forming on the corners of his mouth.

"The appearance of 100,000 can be accomplished, with some luck."

"Luck?"

"Yes, sir. Albert gritted his teeth at the way questions were being drilled. "It would be a simple enough task to have the prisoners make dummies. We already have the means to do this. If, say, 50,000 dummies were made, stuck upright into the ground and moved about from time to time. The luck part depends upon the Nazis buying the illusion."

"Do you think they will?"

"The only person we really have to deceive is the Kommandant," Albert assured. "I can almost guarantee he will leave the premises if our boys, Sol Rothsmann and Vance Worthington, show up in their SS uniforms. This is easily arranged."

There were a few other questions of lesser importance discussed. Winnie thanked Karl and Albert for their time and explained Staff would hopefully come to some decision on the invasion site after the two had gone.

"Gentlemen," praised Ike, "this small group may be carrying out the greatest exodus in modern history."

"Never have so few done so much for so many!"

Monte Montgomery was first in the group to stand and applaud their audacious coup. "They had the naivety to think it could be done, and the courage to try."

Calais. Sol had told Albert that D Day was scheduled for June 1, weather permitting, and advised the compound should begin shedding some pounds in readiness. This was simple enough to do, even with sporadic additions from the Tube. It was the possibility of an appearance of truckloads full of prisoners showing up unannounced that worried him.

Another thing worried Albert. Just how was he going to instruct the inmates to begin making the dummies? Assuming three weeks of old straw needed, they should begin making their "scarecrows" by May 13.

May. Albert asked Karl to locate Ishmael. He needed someone to disburse a certain piece of information to the inmates without making a big public announcement. Management is going to give the inmates a fun project, after they are given their clean uniforms. They are to save their old straw for the next few weeks, stuff it into their old uniform to make a scarecrow. Judging will be done May 30. The ten most realistic looking will get a carton of cigarettes each.

Karl, after being told the reason for this odd request, got a pack of cigarettes and gave them to an inmate with instructions for them to be delivered to Ishmael. Next morning he came up, crushed empty pack in hand, to see what Karl wanted and, of course, received his pack for services to be rendered.

After hearing about the scarecrow contest, Ishmael told Karl, "This will require two helpers. We'll have to go to the barracks, one by one, to give instructions, and, you know, answer questions and all. A pretty tough assignment."

"Grave robber!" Karl scolded Ishmael, and then promptly gave him two more packs.

Freddie's mind was wandering as he happened to look towards Calais. He rubbed his eyes to be certain they weren't playing tricks on him. Dreading having to tell him he motioned for Albert to look north.

There were miles of dust rising from the road. It could be only one thing, truckloads of prisoners. As the trucks became visible in the distance, the trail of dust continued to rise. The size of the convoy seemed enormous. Finally, the lead truck came solidly into view, preceded by three Nazi officer autos.

Albert gasped. The trucks weren't full of prisoners. They were loaded with equipment and soldiers. It was a construction battalion. The line of trucks seemed endless as they formed a semi circle in a huge field about 3 kilometers behind Camp Calais.

About an hour later a German officer, appearing to be a Major, got out of his limo to enter the spa offices. "I wish to speak with Herr Steller!" he said curtly.

"I am Capt. Steller."

"If you wish to be a captain, then so be it," said the Major. "But for now I am the commanding officer of this entire area, including Camp Calais. Where is the current area commander Piotr Siegel?"

Without hesitating, Albert replied, "He's dead, sir. We found him dead in our office. Also the adjutant, Lt. Kreutz, is missing. We gave him a burial with full military honors."

"We'll look into this more thoroughly later," said the Major. Meanwhile, he thought to himself, I'm glad the traitor is dead.

"Who do I have the pleasure of addressing?" inquired Albert.

"Major Dieter Shultz, SS."

Something about the Major seemed familiar to Albert. "I was briefly acquainted with a Capt. Schultz in the office of Willi Heinrich. If you are he, then congratulations on your promotion.

Dieter broke into a smile. "Thank you, Albert. It's good to see you again. Sorry about the abruptness of our reacquaintance, but I had to put on a show for the men. Let me be quick to clarify your position is not in jeopardy. I am here to prepare for the invasion."

"Then you believe it will be at Calais?" Albert used the word 'it' (Allied Invasion) as a foregone conclusion.

"It has to be. Too many problems elsewhere." Dieter continued. "Even though your facility will make an Allied landing difficult, we felt it necessary to add to our defenses here. My job is to oversee construction until a field officer can be permanently assigned."

This could be valuable information, Albert thought. "Any idea who it will be?" He asked.

"Haven't the foggiest idea."

Albert assured himself, you will, soon enough. He began to probe. "What do your engineers have in mind?"

"First, we need to move those ammunition sheds from the compound further back to the tree line where the men's barracks will also be placed. In back of them will go our heavier artillery. These are our Big Berthas. As you know, they are made by Adolph Krupp, the world's premier armorer. From there our shells can reach far enough to blast any Allied ships out of the water. In front of these guns and all the way into the compound we will scatter machine gun nests, faced with concrete."

"When do you plan to place these big guns?"

"Ah!" said Dieter, as proud as a new papa. "The beauty of your choice of property for your camp is that it contains a little known railroad spur. This allows us to keep the guns in a central location. With six hours notice we can have those guns here, atop our flatcars, beefing up the defenses."

"Looks as though you've planned things very well, Dieter," complimented Albert.

"The Allies will pay a dear price if they intend to land here."

After exchanging a few pleasantries the two went their separate ways. Albert hurried to his office, made notes on the Nazi's planned defenses, contacted Martin, and told him to get this information to Staff right away.

Two hours later Staff met in an emergency meeting to consider these new developments. It was too good of an opportunity to pass up, but required the use of the tunnel for some 10 hours. This would be long enough to get 25,000 commandos to Camp Calais, timed to arrive ashore during darkness.

Upon exiting the tunnel at around 10 p.m. Commandos, still underground, are to access the outdoors via the existing Tube, which will have been enlarged to easily accommodate a much larger group. The work on this should begin immediately.

Half the men are to work their way to the trees in back of the enemy barracks. The other half will remain in the swale where the Tube terminates. Both groups are to be in place and ready to attack at 7 a.m. Two hours later the last prisoner will have departed Calais via the tunnel. During this two-hour wait, Commandos will attach high explosives to Jerry's big guns timed to go off at 7:20 a.m.

The rear assault and the flanking move is a deadly combination, but it will be the element of surprise that should allow the commandos to take and hold the Calais position.

Timing would have to be precise. If the prisoners begin their trek through the tunnel at 3 a.m., the last inmate should be setting out by at least 5 a.m.

"What day is this to take place?" Albert said in a disgusted tone. "How in great Caesar's ghost are we supposed to plan our timing?"

"They said to just be ready." Martin declared. "One thing I can tell you for certain, the main attack will be at Normandy. They had no plans for a diversionary move, but the new developments at Calais almost demand it. There will be no air support or naval bombardment. The commandos will have to blow enough munitions to make it look like an all-out invasion."

Albert was visibly peeved. "I don't care what Staff says about maintaining the appearance of having a 100,000 population. I'm going to reduce the number of inmates to 20,000 by June 1. By the time Kreuger figures it out, and has the gumption to report it, our war will be over."

Kreuger was feeling about as useful as a bib on a Billy goat. An interim commander was taking over and a permanent one on the way. What was he supposed to do to justify his existence? All he ever wanted was a little respect! Then he remembered an earlier conversation he had with Piotr, who said he strongly suspected the inmates weren't being exterminated and were somehow escaping.

Poppycock! He thought to himself. I'll just meander down to the gas chamber and check it out for myself. Besides, where could they have all gone?

He strode into the mess hall, down one flight to the gas chamber and down again to the cremation parlor. The inmates saw nothing unusual about his being there, and

Fredrik was too busy herding prisoners into the gathering area to notice him. Who would have expected him to be there?

When he saw the tunnel opening and inmates filing through, he sunk to his knees in shock. How could this be? Regaining his composure, he slowly stood up and made his way out of the area, into the compound and back to his office.

What was he to do? On one hand he must report this immediately to Schultz. On the other, he might be considered an accomplice, albeit unknowing, to the deception. Not only would his career be destroyed, but his very life as well. Totally incapacitated by indecision, he defaults to saying nothing.

May 29. The ammunition sheds have been moved to the rear, heavy artillery has arrived, machine gun nests have been faced with concrete, and the troop's barracks built. All is in readiness. Into the office of Camp Kommandant Erik Kreuger walked Gen. Maximilian Von Schlugenhaugen, the new area commanding officer.

Kreuger, looking out the window as always, turned around abruptly and started to severely scold the intruder for not asking permission to enter. "You oaf—Herr General!" he quickly corrected himself, then stuttered, "My apologies I thought you were some other oaf—I mean—"

"Be quiet, fool," the general shouted. "Get Steller up here." Kreuger was on the phone in an instant, and in five minutes, Albert was standing at attention before the general. "At ease Captain, I am happy to finally meet you. I missed your informal talk at the Wannsee Conference. You are rendering an outstanding service."

"Thank you Herr General, but I couldn't have done it without the help of Maj. Kreuger."

Kreuger was dumbfounded, but delighted, by Albert's comments. He wouldn't soon forget this kindness.

Most of the prisoners had been working diligently on their scarecrows. It was a day early, but many couldn't wait to show off their creation and were carrying them around the compound.

Albert hadn't noticed this yet, but Von Schlugenhaugen spotted the activity. "What are those inmates doing with the dummies?" Kreuger could see Albert was caught off guard and struggling for an answer and came up with a brilliant explanation. "Oh, those are dummies we plan to scatter around the compound to make the Allies think there are many more prisoners here than there really are. It should give them pause for thought before they attack. A little idea I came up with a few days ago."

"Good thinking, Kreuger!" said Von schlugenhaugen. "I can almost see now why you are a camp Kommandant."

Albert nodded approval, then grinned, knowingly. Kreuger is up to his old tricks, taking all the credit. But who cares? He just saved my bacon.

May 30. Ishmael and two cohorts went around the compound to judge best of show scarecrows. It didn't take too long for them to make the pre-arranged awards. Ishmael was given, in appreciation, two packs out of each carton distributed. Such a windfall, Ishmael gloated.

What a wasted effort, thought Albert.

May 31. Albert had been processing inmates almost double-time to reach his goal of down to 20,000 by June 1. Karl had become worried over the calmness of Kristine. Her world was about to be turned upside down, and she went about her business at the hospital as if she had taken up permanent residency.

"The world is finally going to find out the truth about all the atrocities which have been committed by the Nazis," she told her father. "Two men, I can't recall their names (Alfred Wetzler and Rudolph Vrba), escaped from Auschwitz and went to Slovakia where they gave detailed information about the killing of Jews in Auschwitz. Their report will reach the Allies tomorrow and will be named, I believe, the 'Auschwitz Protocols.' The problem is, the Nazis will keep killing our people all the way to the end of the war, another year yet."

"Kristine, you must be preparing yourself mentally for what's ahead of us these next few days," declared Karl. "How we're going to get through the tunnel without the Nazi's knowledge is beyond me,"

"Everything will be fine, Papa." Kristine then spoke as if in a trance "***All will reach their destination***." She spoke in a strangely familiar voice.

"The voice of God." Karl marveled.

June 1. Official word arrived from Dover: Commandos are to begin fighting at 7:30 a.m. Their mission: Destroy the big guns first, the machine gun nests second, kill as many Nazis as possible, and make it look like an all-out invasion. Retreat to the tunnel at your own discretion.

June 2. Albert called a quick meeting with his group to plan how they should exit. After much hassle and protest, they decided to take care of themselves first, but help as many escapees as possible along the way. Karl and Kristine would lead the pack. Fredrik and his three guards scatter about halfway down the line, Martin near the end with Albert bringing up the rear.

Everyone was enveloped in personal thought. Would the plan work? Would they survive the ordeal? The tension in the air was insufferable. Martin was considering what was now becoming a plot, still weighing the possibilities of world travel and that $120,000. He had to force himself to put this obsession out of his mind. It was wrong!

Karl thought it was time for a little levity. "Funny thing happened on the way to the synagogue last Saturday," as Karl mimicked a stand-up comedian. Everyone groaned, but negative thoughts eroded.

"Oh Fredrik!" called Karl. "Why don't you come over to my house tonight for some cigars and brandy? No one is going to be able to sleep anyway."

"No thanks, Karl. I'm going to be deep in thought. Lots of personal recollections to mull over. I won't be sleeping much."

Everyone went to bed to at least try to sleep.

Karl began a violent shiver. Heavy boots, Nazi symbols, much running, and stomping. A familiar but unknown figure was thrashing about in the water drowning. Someone in a teasing voice yelled, "Ollie ollie outs in free." Karl was frozen with fear.

There will be no sleep this evening.

June 3. By 2:30 a.m. the group began herding the inmates, as silently as possible, to the tunnel holding area. Karl had arranged for Ishmael, convinced his number had finally come up, to lead off. It was 3 a.m. The last Tommie had come through, going inland, exactly three minutes earlier. Karl and Kristine took their positions at the front.

By 5 a.m. Albert, not wearing his uniform, was ready to get the "tail end" prisoners moving, nudging an inmate in front of him.

Suddenly he felt a sharp pain in the back of his left shoulder. He quickly turned and to his amazement saw Piotr, who immediately struck Albert with his favorite—the sucker punch, sending him to the ground.

As Piotr stood over Albert, knife in hand, he gloated, "Never send a boy for a man's job. In case you are wondering, I faked being dead, and let fat Freddie's underling carry me over his shoulder to the crematorium. I overpowered the poor lad. I dispensed of him with my trusty dagger. I placed his body in the oven where he still lies. I have been biding my time until this moment."

Albert struck back with a sudden upward kick which sent Piotr's dagger flying. Taken by surprise, Piotr now faced Albert. After a few minutes of sparring, Albert unleashed a hard strike to Piotr's nose, followed by a punch to the mid-section, and then a smash to the jaw—putting Piotr out cold.

What to do now about Piotr was an easy decision for Albert. Piotr was also wearing his civilian clothes. The Nazis would soon find the tunnel, spot a civilian lying face down, and then dispense of him in short order.

At 7 a.m. Von Schlugenhaugen was standing on Kreuger's balcony, surveying the quiet compound that stretched below him. The sea and its inevitable morning fog interrupted the view. He had had a rare good night's sleep and was feeling in fine fettle.

"How are these Jews normally awakened in the morning?" asked the General.

Kreuger, standing beside him, stated that Albert, too soft on the men, would merely announce it was time to get up.

"Well, then, we mustn't disturb them too much," mused Von Schlugenhaugen. He put the loudspeaker to his mouth,

"Come out, come out, wherever you are," not really expecting much of a response.

"Oh, this one should do the trick." The general was still in a playful mood and yelled into the loudspeaker. "Ollie, ollie outs in free." Fear would have gripped Karl had he heard these words. This time Von Schlugenhaugen was expecting some type of response. None came.

"Kommen sie Hier! Mach Schnell!" (Come here immediately!) Still no response. By now the red faced general was furious and issued the type of expletive which can only be taken as an order to "break down those barracks doors and haul their lazy rear ends up."

One by one the complying soldiers yelled, "Mein General, no one is here!" The general turned to Kreuger, "What is the meaning of this? Where are the prisoners?"

The quick thinking Kreuger answered, "They must be in their feeding place." Von Schlugenhaugen whirled around, motioned for his aides to lead the way, and headed for the complex, oblivious to the fact that there was no way all the inmates could be in the food dispensary area at the same time.

Kreuger was hard on the general's heels, every step of the way trying not to think of his inevitable, upcoming confession. But all avenues were blocked. "Herr General, please follow me." When they reached the holding area, then the tunnel, he said, "I think they went this way, to England, about an hour ago."

The general's first thoughts: I'll deal with Kreuger later. No time to waste. He ran back to the spa, blowing his whistle all the way, grabbed the loudspeaker, and ordered his men to come immediately.

All he could think of was the fact he had over 70,000 men at his disposal. He was going to catch and eliminate those Jews. "Go through the tunnel, catch those Jews," he said over and over as he waved his arms, motioning toward the mess hall.

His men had no idea what was going on and ran blindly in the direction the general was pointing. They couldn't know there was little hope of catching the escapees, or that 25,000 Commandos had them in their sights to be caught in a deadly crossfire.

But the Commando leader was having problems of his own, at a loss on how to proceed from here. It was 6:45 a.m., thirty minutes before time to attack, and all the German soldiers were running out of the barracks, heading toward the spa. Have they already seen us? Should we attack now while the Jerries are so exposed? Wait until 7:15, as per our orders? What?

By now the compound was full of soldiers, and about 3,000 had already entered the tunnel in a futile attempt to catch up to the Jews.

It was slightly after 7:15 a.m. The Commandos were ordered to hold their fire. The leader was trying to determine the activity of the Germans. Whatever it was, knock on wood, they weren't coming back right away, and their numbers seemed to be diminishing.

"Oh, my God!" the Commando leader agonized loudly. "They're going into the tunnel. There goes our avenue of escape. Worse, what if they catch up with the Jews?

By now 10,000 Nazis had streamed into the tunnel. The British leader made a decision. In just a few minutes, the big guns were set to be destroyed. The machine guns were all permanently pointing seaward toward the open compound and tunnel entrance area. He motioned for his men to occupy those nests and be ready to open fire when the big guns explode.

A German soldier decided the issue when he spotted activity at the machine gun nests and alerted the others. They immediately began running inland toward the British, firing their weapons. Other above-ground Germans followed suit, but those underground or in the tunnel could not hear, and stayed in hot pursuit of the escapees.

By now 25,000 soldiers had jammed the tunnel. Jews last to leave were about seven miles ahead. Unknown to these "undersea" Germans, what followed was a massacre.

The explosives planted on the cannons went off with an ear-shattering roar, forcing the oncoming Germans to hit the ground. As they got to their feet the unexpected crossfire and machine guns took no prisoners. With another 15,000 soldiers in the tunnel, the general finally saw the gravity of the situation and halted any further entry

Out of 70,000 men, the general now had 40,000 in the tunnel. Of the original 30,000 above ground, 25,000 embattled Nazis remained to face a like number of Commandos. It was a turkey shoot. The British were heavily protected and the surrounded Germans had little cover. Soon their numbers were down to 20,000...then 15,000...to 10,000. In a little over one hour the Germans suffered 20,000 casualties. Surrender was Von Schlugenhaugen's only option.

From the relative safety of his balcony, Kreuger could see the entire disaster unfold. Thousands of his countrymen had been killed, and he was as least partially to blame. He stripped away the trappings from his tunic, sat down, put his luger pistol on his desk, looked at it for a few moments, put the barrel up to his head, and pulled the trigger.

Here was a man who had only recently witnessed a public execution and a rigged one at that. He had never killed a man, nor even shot at one. This time he didn't fail.

The Commando leader pondered: How were they and their 10,000 prisoners going to return to England? No way of knowing how long Nazis would still be in the tunnel, between them and Dover. How long could they hold this position, particularly with prisoners? They solved the problem by pushing 5,000 of the Germans through the only door into the mess hall. The other 5,000 were directed, via the Tube, into the gassing area. They were told to stay put or the valve gets turned on.

June 4. Word spread quickly throughout the Third Reich. "The Allies have invaded at Calais."

"I knew it! I knew it!" screamed Hitler. "Take half of the forces from Normandy and move them to Calais. Who was the fool I let talk me into putting men at Normandy? And our Panzers, move them all out of Paris to Calais."

"But, Mein Fuhrer."

"Do it, now!"

As tanks and truckloads of German soldiers began moving toward Calais, the Commandos began preparing to hold their position per staff's new orders. Machine guns, anchored in concrete, were now pointed the wrong way and needed to be chiseled out and turned around. They had not blown any ammo sheds during the earlier fighting, so ammunition shortage would not be a problem. And over 1,000 men were now stationed at the tunnel's Calais entrance in case any Nazis inside decided to turn around.

Meanwhile, Dover mustered some 20,000 men to deal with the pursuing Nazis when they reach the English shore.

June 5. Weather in the channel for the past week had been stormy. Today was no exception. Intelligence on activity at Normandy was difficult to come by, so the movement of German soldiers and tanks away from the area went unnoticed. Eisenhower and Staff decided to start the invasion on the sixth, weather-be-damned. For the rest of the day and into the night, Allied forces loaded onto an armada of ships.

Pockets of German soldiers positioned themselves around the perimeter of Camp Calais, waiting for troops from Normandy to arrive before launching a counter offensive. Some help came, but not from Normandy. The Commandos were also anticipating reinforcements coming via the tunnel. None came. Each side had barely enough to maintain the stalemate.

If conditions were hectic above ground, in the tunnel they were totally frenetic. The inmates had not had as thorough an indoctrination on the method of escape as other groups did. Some weren't even aware that they were, in fact, escaping. It didn't take long for the carts to become almost useless in aiding the more infirmed.

Karl did his best to control those in the front, either by putting his arms out while rapidly walking straight ahead, or by walking backward while facing the crowd. Without his constant reassurance it would have been like a fire in a theater, with everyone trying to get out at once. He and God began an ongoing, one-sided conversation.

"God, I know you're there because I can feel your breath, so don't try to duck out on me now. I've done everything you've asked of me. Help me to get the last of my people—okay, yours too—to safety. Yes, I know Moses got there first, and with many more folks, but 700,000 isn't exactly chopped liver. If we all get to Dover safely, I promise to go to the Synagogue every week. In any event, I have returned to the faith."

Recalling Job 14 he began to wax philosophical. "Man who is born of woman is of few days and full of trouble. He comes forth like a flower and fades away. He flees like a shadow and does not continue."

He thought of Kristine's mother, Amy, the love of his life. There was a game they would play, over and over again.

'Where are you?" he would ask.

"I'm hiding!" she would answer.

"Where are you?"

"I'm hiding!"

"Where are you? I want to give you a big smoochie kiss!"

I'm hiding—in the closet!"

At 10 a.m. on the fourth, Karl, Kristine, and the leadoff escapees reached the shores of Dover. The journey took seven hours, an hour more than planned. Kristine and Karl hugged. Karl said openly. "Dear God, let Albert get through safely. He is like a son." Then an agonizing thought crossed his mind, "I never told him I loved him."

Sol and Vance were at the tunnel to welcome, congratulate and assist Karl and Kristine out of the path of the horde of escapees pouring out.

About the time leadoff inmates were streaming out of the tunnel, Fredrik and his group were well over halfway through, but still behind schedule and trying desperately to keep the panicky escapees from falling all over one another. He thought of his brother, Wilhelm. So much to offer the world but he took the low road, bemoaned Fredrik. He remembered the melee where he, his brother, and Martin took on those six soldiers at the bar in Calais and landed in jail. It was a great fight, he smiled.

Martin was about 30 minutes behind Fredrik. His thoughts were intermittently on his future back in Germany, or maybe England...Spain...America. He could now have the ability to pick and choose. It boggled his mind.

Two hours ago he was concentrating on reaching his group's common goal of freeing as many Jews as was possible. He felt good about his achievement. Then he began to fantasize about world travel. The means to do this was in his grasp. He fought the temptation, but it kept coming back.

Martin strongly suspected that Albert had forgotten that canvas bag containing the $120,000. He had told Martin earlier to put it in the office safe, and then became too distracted to remember it. Martin hadn't forgotten it.

Albert was overseeing the escape process when a spine tingling thought came to him. He hadn't remembered to take the money out of the safe, and it was too late to go back. Then, a relieving recollection: He was fairly sure he saw Martin with the canvas bag in hand. Good old reliable Martin!

June 6. D Day. The Nazi commanding officer at Normandy spotted the seemingly limitless number of Allied ships advancing over the western horizon and immediately phoned Berlin. "This is it, the invasion, here at Normandy." The phone was silent for a moment. Then a voice came on, "But,

Calais, I thought..." "I don't care what you thought; I know what I'm seeing!"

No one wanted to phone Hitler. He was still in bed. The commanding officer made a grave error in calling back those forces heading for Calais. They had almost reached the halfway point and could not now get back to Normandy before the Allies were well inland.

Between the soldiers and escaping inmates there were, early on, slightly over 65,000 people in the tunnel. It didn't take long for the air to get heavy, affecting both groups alike.

Finally, a breath of air. Albert felt the beginning of a zephyr and knew that Karl and Kristine must now be out of the tunnel. But right now he was concentrating on what he didn't know and couldn't calculate: How far behind were the soldiers, how many were there, and could he stay ahead of his pursuers?

Albert was becoming weaker by the minute. He had lost a significant amount of blood since Piotr's knife had struck deeply into his back shoulder.

Fredrik and other mid-point escapees finally reached Dover, walked another half-mile to get out of the way, and fell to the ground, exhausted.

At 2 p.m. Martin exited the tunnel. Kristine had been surveying each individual who came out. When she spotted Martin she cried out his name and waved her jacket as she saw him give a canvas bag to Fredrik. When Karl arrived, Fredrik gave it to him.

Martin was nowhere to be seen. Karl asked where he was. "It's difficult to explain." Fredrik struggled for the right words. "He had been considering taking the money in Camp Calais' bank account. I guess for quite some time. I doubt if he returns. He's on his way to London to offer his services to the Allies. After the war he says he can be found back in Stuttgart. He said to do what you will with the money, as long as some was used for Kristine's medical schooling. He felt that she would be a great doctor some day.

"To tell the truth, I was tempted to take the money, but when Martin told me about Kristine's education, I'd gladly give it to her for what she has given us."

At first Kristine sobbed quietly, as if touched by their generosity. Then she began to weep uncontrollably. "Albert! Albert! Don't you give up on me now," she cried, almost admonishingly.

"What are you seeing?" exhorted Karl, now shaking Kristine by her shoulders. "Albert should be through the tunnel by now!"

Kristine wailed, "He is leaving us. I can feel his presence fading. Oh, my dear husband! Where are they taking you?"

Karl stiffened as a recent vision reappeared: Water pouring into a well. Someone was inside, being whirled around. A swimmer, now almost recognizable, was gasping for air. He drifted upward out of what was now a coffin, into a vast expanse of water 20 fathoms deep. Heavy boots stomped into the tunnel.

Albert could now see, literally, a light at the end of the tunnel, and calculated the tail-enders were no more than two miles from Dover. The entire compliment of 40,000 German soldiers was now well into the tunnel; and the faint sound of boots clomping on the tunnel floor became audible. The lead soldiers were approaching and closing fast.

In desperation the Nazis began firing their weapons in the direction of Dover, putting the escapees in full flight. Bullets ricocheted off every surface, striking several inmates. The bullets were nearly spent, so did little more than knock escapees to the ground. Albert stopped to help a fallen inmate. A bullet grazed his head. He slumped to the floor in a semi-conscious state and struggled to get up. Then, he temporarily collapsed, less than two miles from safety, alive but senseless.

Sol finally connected with Karl and Kristine. Vance was up on the office deck with his telescope, looking for familiar faces.

Karl asked Sol for his bullhorn, and tried to catch Vance's attention. "Vance, down here!" He scanned the shore then acknowledged with a hand wave. Karl yelled instructions, "Turn out the tunnel lights."

Both Sol and Vance ran to the plant and turned out the tunnel lights. The Nazis were now enclosed in total black. The advancing Germans frozen with fear stopped in their tracks. The escapees, now seeing daylight, sped up.

Karl admonished God for again exposing him to that persistent vision of the watery well. Karl was then brought to his knees with the feeling that this apparition would never appear again. The reason came like a flash of lightning.

The sound of a muffled explosion directed all eyes to a foamy swelling of the waters near the Calais shore.

No one could have foretold the collapse of the tunnel. The 700,000 inmates who escaped earlier had some bearing on its failure. But the abuse of 40,000 heavy-footed Nazis, 25,000 hard running Commandos, and 20,000 stumbling escapees, all in a short time frame, took its toll at the weakest point: the merger of the two ends of the tunnel five miles off the Calais coast.

Fifty fathoms of pressure pushed water into the tunnel's gaping wound with an explosive force that snapped its brittle plastic construction. This sent a violent whip-like action across its entire length, and an accompanying shattering snap at the Dover terminal. Five foot wide cracks opened up all along the way. The tunnel filled so rapidly, no one inside could escape.

Within a few minutes 40,000 brave but unsuspecting German soldiers had drown. The muffled yelling and screaming and floundering, turned to dead silence **as Pharaoh's army must have done**. Most bodies were floating aimlessly within the tunnel, now a massive crowded tomb. A few had gotten through the gaping holes, but had expelled their air well before reaching the surface.

They were the lucky ones. The Nazis at Camp Calais, who were being held prisoner in the gassing area, were below sea level. They were trapped by the rising waters gushing in from the tunnel. There was no way out, except for the enlarged air vent in an upper corner.

Many fought, clawed, and pulled others under to get to the air vent. Soon they were up to their necks, then treading water, still fighting for air. Some, with time to consider what it was going to be like to drown, simply gave up, and slipped under the water.

Albert was being tumbled about, but at least not in the dark, and with not that much force. But, he too was soon caught by the rising waters and gasping for air.

He stroked upward and out of the tunnel, gashing his face, arms, and legs on the tunnel's ragged edges. He was 20 fathoms from the surface and pulling desperately. He fought to keep from inhaling but could no longer hold. Utter panic enveloped his entire being as water rushed into his exploding, agonizingly painful lungs.

A sudden calmness came over him as he drifted up toward a beckoning light.

ABOUT THE AUTHOR

My dad owned a weekly newspaper, so I grew up in the business.

I graduated from the University of Oregon journalism school in 1954 and wrote news articles for nine years.

After a two-year stint in the navy, I changed professions to "investments." I eventually started my own investment management firm from which I retired about ten years ago.

I have considered writing a book for years but with no inspiration. Then this story literally popped into my head compelling me to put it on paper.

Albert O. Martin